PRAISE FOR
MARY KITTREDGE

KILL OR CURE
"Fast-moving, high tension . . . A gripping good time."
—*Kirkus Reviews*

"Well-plotted and absorbing."
—*Deadly Pleasures*

"An artful plot that has heartbreak, violence, terror,
tenderness, and a marvelous treatment of
intergenerational family love."
—*Mystery News*

"Lively . . . Kittredge comments acutely on family life,
motherhood and victims' rights and neatly ties up the
threads of a messy crime."
—*Publishers Weekly*

FATAL DIAGNOSIS
"Distinctive . . . the novel is rich in technical
medical detail."
—*Star-Tribune*, Minneapolis

"A good read! An inside look at hospitals that you aren't
going to see on soap operas."
—Hillary Waugh, author of *Last Seen Wearing*

BANTAM BOOKS BY MARY KITTREDGE

Fatal Diagnosis
Desperate Remedy
Kill or Cure

DESPERATE REMEDY

Mary Kittredge

BANTAM BOOKS
New York Toronto London Sydney Auckland

This edition contains the complete text
of the original hardcover edition.
NOT ONE WORD HAS BEEN OMITTED.

DESPERATE REMEDY
A Bantam Crime Line Book published by arrangement
with St. Martin's Press

PUBLISHING HISTORY

St. Martin's hardcover edition published October 1993
St. Martin's paperback edition / December 1994
Bantam Books paperback edition / September 1997

ISBN 0-553-57591-0

Published simultaneously in the United States and Canada

Bantam Books are published by Bantam Books, a division of Bantam Doubleday Dell Publishing Group, Inc. Its trademark, consisting of the words "Bantam Books" and the portrayal of a rooster, is Registered in U.S. Patent and Trademark Office and in other countries. Marca Registrada. Bantam Books, 1540 Broadway, New York, New York 10036.

PRINTED IN THE UNITED STATES OF AMERICA

WCD 10   9   8   7   6   5   4   3   2   1

DESPERATE
REMEDY

ONE

B Y SEVEN O'CLOCK on the evening of his admission to Chelsea Memorial Hospital and Medical Center, Michael Munson had already smashed a glass upon being refused a drink of whiskey, hurled a bedpan after learning that he was expected to use it, and speculated so accurately and cruelly on the intimate details of his private-duty nurse's sex life that the young woman hurried from his room in tears, to resign his case at once.

Years earlier, the famed sculptor's grudging presence at some art collector's fashionable dinner party, while almost always shockingly disruptive even then, had been enough to make a triumph of his hostess's entire social season. But now he was old and ill, and in the hospital nobody knew who Munson was, or cared. There, he was just an obnoxious old man.

Meanwhile, it was too late to get a new private nurse for him, even if the agency would consent to send one; after what the last girl had told her supervisor, it was doubtful whether any private nurse at all could be engaged for Mr. Munson, now or ever. So the staff nurse in charge on his ward that evening added his name to her own already overlong list of patients, and went down to his room to introduce herself.

A moment later she emerged, pale and shaking. Returning to the nursing desk, she reached for the telephone, pausing only to consult the small engraved business card Mr. Munson had thrust upon her, and refusing to contemplate any further the disgusting remark with which he had accompanied it.

Desperate situations called for desperate remedies; in this case, the remedy was Edwina Crusoe.

Edwina reported all this to her husband, the ex–homicide detective Martin McIntyre, as she prepared to go over to Chelsea Memorial and rescue Michael Munson from the hole he was digging himself into. That the hole could end up being Munson's grave was already apparent to her; it was a sad fact of hospital life that patients disliked by the staff were in danger of receiving somewhat less than perfectly scrupulous care, and despite the remarkable vigor of his profanity Munson's medical condition was so fragile that the slightest bit of neglect could kill him.

"Sounds to me like a dose of his own medicine might do him good," McIntyre observed, glancing up from the books and papers piled before him on the kitchen table.

After twenty years of fishing murderers out of the slime ponds in which they dwelled, only to see too many of them wiggle off the hook once their cases came to trial, Martin had retired from the New Haven police force and entered law school, since according to him there was no point to catching a fish unless you could also fry it afterward.

Edwina turned to look at her husband: a tall, dark-haired man with a lean, hawkish face, a thin, expressive mouth, and an intelligent expression. She sometimes almost felt sorry for the heinous criminals whom he would eventually prosecute; almost, but not quite, having been on the receiving end of a fair amount of criminal heinousness, herself, one way and another.

"Martin," she said now, "Michael Munson is an old friend of my mother's. If anything happens to him, she'll be heartbroken. Besides, he's not as bad as all that. He's angry and frightened, and probably in pain, but—"

"I've overheard you two talking about him," Martin put in. "Is this the same guy who threw an interviewer from *Art News* off a balcony? The same one who went to a rival sculptor's gallery show, got drunk, and shot the arms off four statues?"

"Well, yes, but he's an artist himself. He's very—"

"The same one," McIntyre persisted, "who's had six wives and seventeen illegitimate children?"

"—temperamental," Edwina finished, not sounding convincing even to herself. Michael Munson *was* a terrible old man. Still, she could not very well abandon him; Harriet would have her head.

"Martin, the wives and children were ages ago, and the balcony was a *very* low one. Only about ten feet or so, I think. And the sculptures were worth much more after he shot their arms off, because of the publicity; even the artist admitted it."

McIntyre managed to express what he thought about all this without saying a word, but after a moment he got up and put his arms around his wife.

"You can take the girl out of nursing," he teased as she leaned her head against his shoulder, "but not the nursing out of the girl."

"Oh, no," she protested, pulling away; Martin always looked so good, felt so good, and smelled so good, that it was very dangerous to hug him when one was due so soon to arrive somewhere else.

"I'm retired from nursing, remember? Just visiting a sick old family friend. And I'm retired from investigating, too . . . for now."

She placed her hands over her stomach, which was still relatively flat although it would soon not be so. She supposed that motherhood would prove interesting, once the practical aspects began arising; at present, however, the idea remained unnerving on several counts.

"No nursing, and no investigating. And especially," Martin reminded her, "no murder investigating."

"No murders," she agreed easily, of course not believing

she would encounter any of these during a simple hospital visit.

"Michael, how could you? They're only trying to take care of you. Put your foot out here, now, and let me see it."

"Not taking care of me. Trying to kill me. Damned bunch of snot-nosed ignoramuses." Seated in a wheelchair, Munson thumped his cane on the carpeted floor of his private hospital room.

"Oh, my. This doesn't look too good. Does it hurt?"

Munson glowered. "Can't feel it. That's how I did it. Put my damned cane down on my damned toe. Leaned on it. Smash."

"You were trying to work, I suppose." Carefully, Edwina removed the gauze dressings, frowning at their condition; Munson had for days refused to let anyone near him to administer the care this injury required. Now, if the situation were not gotten under control quickly, things could get ugly.

"Not *trying* to work," Munson growled. "Working. Can't work sitting down. Damned fool doctor. 'Put your feet up,' he says. Stupid bugger, I'll put my foot up his—"

"Michael," Edwina remarked mildly, "you mustn't speak that way to me, you know. It's too shocking." Lifting his foot, she placed it into a plastic basin of warm, soapy water.

"Shocking. Hell." But a grudging glint of humor appeared in his blue eyes. "Did you bring me anything to drink?"

"No, Michael. You're not allowed to drink until this thing is healed up. Your circulation is poor enough as it is."

"Goddammit!" he bellowed, smashing the cane down onto the bedside table. "No this, no that! No, no, no!"

Edwina, whose back had been turned, came slowly around to face him. In one hand she held a stainless steel kidney basin; in the other, a packet of iodine wash and a plastic syringe.

"You could lose the foot," she told him quietly. "At your age, and in your medical condition, it would be very difficult to fit you with a prosthesis. You'd never walk again, Michael. You wouldn't be able to stand up without help. And you would never be able to work. Is that what you want?"

"Oh, is that all?" he inquired bitterly, looking as if he had just swallowed a cup of poison. It was obvious that no one had told him this before—or, more likely, that he had been shouting and pounding his cane instead of listening, when someone tried.

"No, as a matter of fact, it's not." She lifted his foot from the soapy basin, rinsed and dried it, and began sluicing it with iodine wash. "You could die in surgery, or if surgery is unsuccessful, you could die of septic shock. Blood poisoning."

"If they put me on a respirator, pull the plug." His chin thrust out; clearly, he had been worrying about this. Just as clearly, he could be perfectly rational whenever he chose to be.

"Michael, it doesn't work that way. If you want someone to be able to make that decision for you, then you'd better get a lawyer and make a living will, a legal document."

Edwina paused. Probably now was not the time to try explaining all this to Michael Munson. Instead, she finished cleansing and rinsing his foot. Then she covered his injury in bactericidal ointment and applied the dressings. Finally, she secured the dressings, not too tightly, with gauze and strips of tape.

Munson remained silent. Edwina thought he might be mulling over what she had told him, or might even have fallen asleep. But when she looked up, his round, pale face with its stubble of silvery whiskers, its bushy, white eyebrows, and its piercingly pale blue eyes, had twisted into a grimace of rage.

Without warning, he swung his cane, gripping it in both his strong, work-callused hands to raise it high over his head, then smashing it down like a murderous club onto his freshly bandaged foot.

An hour and a half later, Edwina was joined in the surgical intensive-care conference room by a slender, red-haired woman wearing a green operating-room scrub dress and a name tag that read "Alison Feinstein, MD."

Alison's creamy white complexion was dusted with pale gold freckles, and her eyes were the light sea-green of a tropical lagoon. But her expression was cloudy, perhaps because as chief resident on Chelsea Memorial's orthopedic surgery service, Alison was unlikely to have slept for more than four hours in the past thirty-six.

"Well," she sighed, pouring herself a cup of inky coffee and sinking into one of the metal chairs at the long table, "he broke two more of his toes, really shattered one of them, but I think I got all the bone chips back in place."

She sipped the horrid coffee. "Fortunately, you'd padded the injured toe up pretty well, so it's not too much worse off than before. I did a little soft-tissue debriding while I was in there, not too radical, but I sent off a bunch of cultures and it's nice and clean, now. And he's sleeping it off in post-op."

Through the open door of the conference room came the steady beeping of cardiac monitors, the brief, intermittent janglings of respirator alarms, and the occasional tweeting of a pocket pager.

"Did he need general anesthesia?" Remembering his horror at the idea of a respirator, Edwina hoped Munson would not have to wake up and find himself attached to one, even temporarily.

Alison shook her head. "Local. He didn't really even need that. They told me he'd lost some sensation in his feet, but what I saw was quite remarkable. Has he been worked up for this numbness, or whatever it is?"

"I don't know. He's pretty cantankerous. An old family friend. I guess my mother must have given him my card, told him to have them call me if things got difficult in the hospital. Which, knowing him, she'd have realized they would."

Alison swallowed more coffee, made a face, and drank the rest of it. She had been a college student, doing a hospital volunteer project over the summer break, when Edwina first met her. "Yeah, well, I put in for a neurology consult for him. The whole thing seems very weird to me. Hell, maybe it's even fixable. If it is, I wish he were my only problem."

"That's what I thought. You don't look so good. I can keep things under my hat, you know," Edwina suggested carefully.

Alison got up and closed the door. "Maybe you're right. I need to talk to somebody about it. The thing is, I've got this guy on my service, a surgery resident. And he's the best I've ever seen."

She sank into her chair again. "I swear, Edwina, if you're some little twink LPN student on the midnight shift and your hip-replacement patient throws a clot to the lung, he is the guy you'd just better pray shows up when you yell for help. He knows what to do, and he can do it."

Edwina tipped her head. Stories about naturally talented persons were always pleasant to hear, only she had a feeling this one wasn't going to have a very happy ending. "And?"

"And in the OR, he's the same. Fast, accurate, cuts to the chase. He even tells good jokes."

"Sounds great. So, what's the problem?"

"The problem," Alison replied, "is that I'm pretty sure he's running on empty. Cocaine. But I don't *know*. And I absolutely do not know what to do. If I'm right, he's got to be stopped, of course. But if I'm wrong, I could ruin his career because he's tired and he happens to have hay fever. Which is what he says."

"So you've confronted him?"

"Of course I have. He laughed at me. Asked me if I thought he was nuts. No way, he said; he was tired, and he's allergic to ragweed, that's all."

Alison ran her fingers tiredly through her hair. "But the other day, he just about passed out during surgery, nearly fell right into a complicated bone graft. And Edwina, ragweed season is pretty well over."

"I think," said Edwina, getting up, "you should do something about this fellow now. If you're right, he's killing himself, and he could hurt someone else. It is difficult, though, because if you're wrong . . ."

She thought a moment. "Well, it wouldn't be pleasant, but he'd get over it; it wouldn't really ruin his career. But if you're not wrong, you'll be doing him a favor. I mean, if he's using cocaine, then he's buying cocaine somewhere. You don't think he's stealing hospital pharmaceuticals?"

It was a statement, not a question; hospital-grade cocaine was the purest, finest variety of the substance available, but its use and distribution were so strictly controlled that getting at it would involve stealing or duplicating medication-room keys, faking the controlled-substance records, and who knew what else.

"No. He's not that crazy. At least," Alison said, "I don't think he is."

"Then better you should stop him now. If he's buying a lot, somebody downtown probably knows about him." Drug purchasers always thought their transactions were secret, but in truth many of the heavy buyers were well known to narcotics cops, who were only waiting for the proper opportunity to arrest them. "And if they do," Edwina went on, "sooner or later the enforcement people will pick him up and make him help them set up whoever's selling it to him."

Alison stared. "Do they really do that? Threaten them, and scare them, and so on?"

Edwina controlled her impatience. Alison obviously didn't watch much TV or have much experience with life's seamier side. In some ways, she was still very much the wide-eyed college girl; she hadn't had the free time to become anything else.

"Alison, 'scare' and 'threaten' are inadequate words for

what really happens, okay? Jail is . . ." Edwina paused, struggling to find a way to describe just how awful imprisonment was. "People turn in their mothers, hoping for a suspended sentence. I've *met* people who have."

Alison nodded, convinced. "That's another good reason to do what I've got to do." She got up and opened the door between the conference room and the intensive-care unit. As she did so, the voice of the overhead page operator floated from the direct address system, sounding unusually crisp, urgent, and demanding.

"Code Five, Grady Pavilion, operating room three."

"That's strange," Edwina remarked. "Don't they have enough warm bodies down there to handle a resuscitation by themselves? I've never heard anybody call a code in the OR before."

But when she turned, Alison Feinstein had gone even whiter. "The guy I was telling you about? Edwina, I've got a bad feeling his problem was just taken out of my hands. He's assisting on a traumatic compound fracture of the femur, big emergency gunshot wound, down in room three."

Alison made a face. "Or he was, until a minute ago."

Eric Shultz was in his mid-twenties, a short, compactly built young man with a thick mop of curly black hair and an expression petulant even in unconsciousness. His face, which looked as if it might be handsome under other circumstances, was ashen and sweat-beaded; his mouth sagged open and his eyes rolled whitely up into his head. A pit of partly unfolded paper spilled white powder on the tiled floor beside him; perhaps, realizing what was happening, he had been trying to hide it somewhere less obvious than his scrub shirt pocket.

"Jesus," said a tall, gray-haired man in disgust. He wore a green paper surgical cap, wire-rimmed glasses, and a green scrub uniform. Paper shoe covers surrounded his feet.

"He passed out, the stupid little shit. Nearly contaminated the goddamn incision. Get him out of here."

A couple of burly orderlies lifted Eric Shultz's limp body to a gurney, and wheeled him from the room. The patient whose surgery Shultz's faint had interrupted was in another suite, his procedure being completed. And from the look on the gray-haired surgeon's face, Alison Feinstein was about to receive the worst dressing-down of her life.

"You knew!" he bellowed at her, slamming his fist onto the operating table. "You worked with him every day, you must have known he was on something, and you *let it go on.* He's a junkie and you *let him keep working* until he nearly *killed my patient.*"

"Dr. Grace," Alison began, "I'm terribly sorry about this. But I can explain."

Edwina stood quietly at one side of the room, staying out of the way of the aides who snapped off the big metal overhead lights, dragged the rumpled sheet from the operating table, and swept curls of EKG paper from the floor. Bill Grace was a well-known terror around the hospital, as legendary for his explosive temper as for his skill in repairing shattered human bones; his patients adored him, and his co-workers despised him. But Alison faced him calmly, her head held high and her hands relaxed at her sides.

"I suspected. I confronted him," she said. "He denied it. He never gave me any reason to admonish him. There were no absences, no lapses."

Alison paused, evidently remembering what she had just told Edwina. "Nevertheless, I did suspect, and I was about to report him."

Grace's lip curled as if he had just bitten into something rotten. The aides were gone now, and he had not noticed that Edwina remained. "You had a crush on him. So you ignored the *obvious* fact of his impairment. You women, you've all got your brains between your—"

Quietly, Edwina cleared her throat. Grace's head swiveled smoothly around, his eyes narrowing; in that instant he resembled a striking snake. But he was caught, and he knew it; whatever ugly thing he had been about to say, he would not say it in front of a witness.

"Some of your *evidence* is in detox, down in the emergency room," he said, sneering at Alison, "and the rest is going into the safe in the medication room." He scooped up the bit of powdery paper and stalked out.

Alison's shoulders sagged. "Jesus." Then she straightened. "Well, I guess there's no point in putting it off."

"Are you going to file a complaint over what Grace said to you?" Edwina asked, following Alison into the corridor. From here she could see into the postoperative recovery room; this late in the evening, only a few gurneys remained, lined up under the monitors. On one of the gurneys, Michael Munson slept, with the assistance of a light sedative.

"You mean that stuff about women, and why I didn't turn Eric in earlier?" Alison laughed harshly, striding toward the bank of elevators at the end of the corridor. "That's mild compared to some of the things I have to listen to around here, especially from Grace. He'll say anything. And besides . . ."

The elevator doors opened; she stepped in, with Edwina right behind her. The car started down, toward the level marked "ER."

"Besides," Alison finished, so softly that she might have been speaking only to herself, "this time, I'm wondering if what Bill Grace said is true."

Chelsea Memorial's emergency room was almost an entire hospital to itself, occupying the whole first floor of the Grady Pavilion. Edwina accompanied Alison in silence past the pharmacy, the X-ray department, the major-medical and surgical treatment areas, the major-trauma room, the pediatric waiting areas and clinics, and a pair of unmarked doors leading to a temporary morgue.

"What are you going to do?" Edwina asked finally.

Michael Munson probably wouldn't be sent upstairs for another hour or so; until then she might as well stick around with Alison, who looked as if she could use some moral support.

"Well, first I'm going to find out Eric Shultz's condition. Then I'm going to call the chief of staff, and let him know what happened. Also, I'd better redo the on-call schedule. I have another resident who was about to go on vacation, but she'll have to cancel it."

"What happens to Eric?" Ahead, the corridor opened into two big rooms; some of the cubicles lining the rooms were divided from one another by curtains, while others were of masonry walls with locked doors, sparely furnished interiors, and large windows of wire-mesh-reinforced glass. The masonry cubicles resembled large bare cages, which was precisely what they were. A sign on the wall directed one to the left, for the psychiatric area, and to the right for the acute-substance-abuse and detox areas.

"Well, it's not my responsibility to fire him," Alison said. "There'll be a disciplinary hearing first."

In one of the enclosed cubicles of the detox area, a man was bellowing something over and over, hammering with his fists on the shatterproof glass. No one paid any attention to him.

"But I can tell you right now," Alison went on, "he's done for here. I suppose I'd better let him know not to come back to work tomorrow. If he's even awake yet."

Ordinarily, Edwina would not have glanced twice at the man bellowing inside the cubicle. Flushed and disheveled, his face so twisted with rage that his own relatives probably would not have recognized him, he went on hammering and shouting.

It was not polite to stare at a person in that condition. Also, Edwina had been a hospital nurse for fifteen years; the spectacle the man was making of himself was not remarkable enough to pique her interest. Alison ignored him, too.

Only, *something* about him looked familiar: his clothing, Edwina realized. He was wearing a scrub suit.

"Alison," she said, "I think he's awake."

"I'm a doctor, dammit, let me out! What the hell is wrong with you people, don't you understand? I'm a *doctor!*"

The big, gray-haired nurse behind the desk looked bored. "Yeah," she remarked to no one in particular, "I can't wait to have you taking my appendix out."

"I want to talk with him." Alison took the stethoscope from around her neck, placed her pocket pager on the counter, and removed the pens and scissors from her pocket.

The nurse frowned doubtfully at Alison. "You come to take our little pal off our hands?"

Alison shook her head. "No, I'm his chief resident. Whose patient is he?"

A very tall, extremely thin young man in dungarees and a scrub shirt looked up from the end of the desk. "Mine. What the heck happened to him, anyway? They wheeled him down and dumped him. I haven't even gotten any decent report."

At Alison's explanation, the young psychiatrist whistled. "Boy, his goose is cooked. No wonder he's so agitated. Sure, go on in and talk to him. Seems like he's calming down, now that he sees you."

Eric Shultz had indeed calmed down; no longer shouting, he sat on the padded gurney which was the cubicle's only furniture. His feet did not quite touch the floor, and with his ankles crossed and his hands clasped prayerfully in his lap, he looked like a little boy steeling himself to undergo a serious scolding.

Edwina wondered if he realized, yet, how disastrous a thing had happened to him. Unless he was extremely lucky, the closest Eric Shultz would ever get again to practicing medicine would be as an orderly or nurse's aide somewhere, in some little community hospital so far away, his ruined reputation couldn't follow him. It was a big comedown for a talented future surgeon: like the one straight down from the top of a skyscraper.

"Wish me luck," Alison said, smiling wanly, and waited as the nurse unlocked the door of the cubicle, to let her in.

Shultz jumped off the gurney and began talking fast, wheedling and justifying and explaining, a wide, insincere grin spread across his pasty face. Alison listened impassively. The door closed again on the sound of his voice: talking, talking.

Disheartened, Edwina turned away. She had forgotten to ask Alison how long she thought she might be here. But it would only take a minute to walk down to the central admitting desk, see if anyone she knew was there to say hello to, and then walk back.

She asked the nurse to tell Alison this, if Alison came out. The nurse nodded expressionlessly, her eyes on the window of Eric Shultz's confinement cubicle.

Shultz's face had gone flat with denial and disbelief. He seemed to be trying to argue Alison out of something she had just said to him. In reply, Alison only shook her head.

"That boy," the nurse remarked to nobody in particular, "is about to be in a world of pain."

Edwina Crusoe was rich and pretty: tall, dark-haired, and the owner of an inherited fortune so large, she need never have worked for a single minute. But on her eighteenth birthday, without telling anyone, Edwina had enrolled herself in nursing school.

Learning of this, Harriet Crusoe suffered her only recorded attack of the vapors. Billionaires' daughters did not muck about in hospitals. But Edwina's father, E. R. Crusoe, only laughed and settled a million dollars on the girl. Having spent eighteen years teaching her that human beings ought to do things that mattered, he had decided that the choice of which thing to do quite properly belonged to Edwina. The million, he confided to her, was for pocket money.

Twenty-two years later, Edwina approached the central admitting desk in Chelsea Memorial's emergency room with a sense of mingled nostalgia and remembered dread. All the worst things that could happen to people came here, or at least the worst physical things; they came through those doors and past that desk, and some of them, once upon a time, came into the anxious care of a brand-new registered nurse, a rich girl from Litchfield County. Edwina smiled a little sadly, recalling how frightened she had been of doing something wrong, and how determined to live up to her father's opinion of her.

"Lady?" Someone tapped her on the shoulder; it was an orderly in white slacks and white uniform shirt. "Lady, could you move out of the way? We got a trauma coming in."

"Oh, of course. Sorry." She'd been daydreaming. There was no one she knew here tonight, anyway; fewer and fewer of her old friends still worked at Chelsea. Like her, they had moved on. She turned to go, then leaped out of the way as the big glass doors to the ambulance bay jumped aside and a stretcher barreled between them, heading for the major-trauma suite.

It was obvious that the patient was not going to survive. The dressing slapped onto the patient's wound had slipped, mostly because there had been so little left to tape it to; as the trio of medical technicians rushed past, propelling the stretcher, Edwina saw that a portion of the patient's skull was absent, obliterated by an obvious gunshot injury.

As the stretcher disappeared into the trauma suite, the big double ambulance-bay doors jumped aside again, only this time the entrant was not in any hurry. Dick Talbot, Martin McIntyre's old partner from the homicide department, limped in looking disgusted with the situation, only brightening a bit as he glimpsed Edwina.

"You know," he rasped, wincing as he bent to rub the leg a fleeing suspect had shot out from under him long ago, "they're all out there, shooting and stabbing each other as fast as they can. I wonder sometimes, why bother stopping 'em?"

The tough old Irishman paused, laboring to catch his breath. He had thinning black hair, a barrel chest, and the blue-tinged complexion of the chronic emphysema patient; between his bad leg and his bad lungs, Talbot ought to have been on disability years earlier, only he refused to go.

"If you meant that," Edwina told him, "you'd have retired yesterday. You could be in Florida next week."

"Yeah, and in my coffin the week after that." Talbot popped a mentholated cough drop into his mouth and grimaced. "Busting these yahoos is the only thing keeps me ticking. Christ, what a mess. You see her? Just came in?"

"Unfortunately. I couldn't help wondering why they brought her here at all. It looked as if she's . . ."

"Dead meat," he agreed bluntly. "Only of course when *I* catch dead meat, it's gotta be *complicated* dead meat."

He scowled at the trauma suite. "This lady, the one who got shot, her name is Mrs. Clarke. And it turns out her *husband* got shot a couple hours ago, too. Her husband, *Dr.* Clarke. Somebody practically cut him off at the hip, he's walking on the street. Looked like a random drive-by, until now."

"Wait a minute. They brought the husband here?"

That, Edwina realized, must be the traumatic hip fracture repair Eric Shultz's faint had interrupted; even at Chelsea, it was unusual to have two major gunshot wounds in surgery at the same time.

Talbot nodded sourly. "So number *one*," he said, "she's definitely bought the farm, but they gotta bring her in, anyway, go through the motions, make sure her hubby the doc doesn't sue somebody later. And number *two*—"

"Husband and wife wounded in separate firearms assaults within a few hours of each other," Edwina supplied. "Not very likely to be a coincidence, is it? Much as we wish it were."

"Give the little lady a kewpie doll," said Talbot. "*So we*

gotta put a pair of blues on the husband, make sure this wackola doesn't get to try again."

"Edwina." Alison approached from the psychiatric-area corridor. "I've got to get back upstairs. But there was someone from administration looking for you on the phone, down at the other desk. I said I thought you were still around, somewhere."

"*Which* means we gotta pull officers off the street, the department hasn't got the budget for all the overtime," Talbot went on; once he got going, he always kept talking until he was finished, whether his audience was listening or not.

"Administration? What would they want with me?"

Alison's pocket pager emitted a shrill chirp. "Didn't say. Damn, gotta go. Oh, and your buddy Mr. Munson's back upstairs," she called as she hurried away. "Ask him not to clobber himself anymore."

"Right," said Edwina, but without much conviction; in her experience, the aging delinquent generally did the opposite of whatever he was asked, as immediately and defiantly as possible. What made Harriet Crusoe care for a contrary old hooligan like Munson, Edwina never had been able to discover.

"*And*," Talbot said, "*that* means the bad guys will be out there shooting and stabbing people even *faster*, while *I'm* out there limping around, trying to stop them."

The doors to the trauma suite opened and the resuscitation team emerged: nurses, therapists and technicians, trauma surgeons. Ten minutes spent trying to revive an obvious corpse hadn't exactly lifted anybody's spirits.

"Ah, what's the use," Talbot finished disgustedly, "we ought to just give 'em all bigger knives and guns. See you, Edwina."

Flipping out his notebook, he limped painfully off to elicit the details of yet another homicide victim's demise, meanwhile concealing his discomfort at being here at all; Talbot despised hospitals. Probably he *would* die when he retired, just as he said, like an old cart horse that collapsed when taken out of harness.

Thinking this, Edwina heard her name being pronounced on the overhead paging system. Startled, she looked around for a phone, obeying as if by reflex the summons of the page operator.

Moments later she was listening to a familiar voice, while wishing intensely that she were not listening to it. Ned Hunt was a Chelsea Memorial Hospital administrator, an old friend from Edwina's childhood, and the son of one of her mother's dearest chums. Unfortunately, he was also an incompetent with a tendency to panic when anything the slightest bit unusual happened.

"Ned," Edwina began, but the rush of words flooding from the phone could not be stopped. The nursing supervisor had called him about Mr. Munson, Ned babbled worriedly, to see if Chelsea's legal people ought to be informed; could he sue the hospital for letting him break his toe, the nursing supervisor wanted to know? And of course Ned had told her Mr. Munson could, and what else was she doing about this patient? Which was how he learned that Edwina was visiting the troublesome old man.

And, he went on, apparently without taking a breath, then the emergency-room nursing supervisor called, to let Ned know that a well-known local doctor's wife was coming in by ambulance, suffering from a gunshot wound, and the doctor had already been brought in with a gunshot wound. And was there anything special the supervisor should do about it? Because the situation *was* unusual, and besides, the newspapers had already begun calling.

So, Ned finished, sounding upset and as if he were already at his wits' end—which, Edwina thought sourly, was not a long trip even under the best of circumstances— could she possibly stop in and talk with him for a few minutes? She was always so calm and cool-headed in a crisis, while he was such a . . .

Charitably, Edwina did not supply the missing noun.

"Yes," she reluctantly told Ned Hunt at last. "I'll see you in your office in ten minutes."

To Bonnie West, nursing was a career whose ladder was meant to be climbed swiftly. She didn't want to end up like so many of her co-workers at Chelsea Memorial: middle-aged, going nowhere, and not even smart enough to be worried about it. Bonnie knew exactly where she wanted to go: first to an assistant head nurse position, then to a head nurse spot.

By that time, she hoped, she would have her Ph.D. and could snag some sort of high-level consulting work, possibly in the insurance or pharmaceuticals industry. She didn't care just what kind of work it was, as long as it got her out of the hospital. Anything would be better than the plodding, repetitive drudgery of taking care of sick people.

Sighing, Bonnie glanced up at the cardiac monitor, then at the electronic readout on her patient's respirator. Bored half out of her mind, she recorded his heart rate and respirations on her clipboard. After that she took his temperature and blood pressure, noticing with exasperation that his linens were soaked in sweat again. She had already changed his whole bed once, and was damned if she would do it a second time; let the night shift deal with it.

Finally, fighting to keep her eyes from glazing over with the sheer, mind-numbing tediousness of it all, she checked his respirator settings, noting the position of each dial and jotting it on the record sheet. Everything was as it should be, except that the respirator tubings were filling up with water, again; automatically, she straightened the plastic tubings so that the fluid condensed in them gurgled back down into the respirator's humidifier.

Strictly speaking, she wasn't supposed to do that; the condensate could contaminate the humidifier's reservoir. But it was a pain in the neck disconnecting the tubes, emptying them into a basin, and reconnecting them, especially since that also meant refilling the humidifier. Dumping was good enough.

Closing the clear plastic cover that protected the respirator's dials and knobs from accidental readjustment, Bonnie glanced down at the patient: silver-haired, sixtyish, his face slack with the effects of the anesthetics and morphine he had been given. The respirator tubings led to another tube, protruding from his mouth; this tube was secured with strips of adhesive tape. His chest rose and fell with the respirator's cycles; otherwise, he was motionless, his fractured hip padded, taped, and suspended in weight traction to keep it from shifting.

A doctor, according to the brief personal history on the nursing notes that Bonnie had been given; his name was Clarke. Shot through the hip as he was walking along the street.

Bonnie eyed the patient dispassionately: Plenty of doctors deserved to be shot, in her opinion. Anyway, he was still unconscious, and with any luck, he would stay that way until her shift's end. Otherwise, she would have to talk to him, and talking to groggy post-op patients was a drag; all they ever did was complain. Besides, she had studying to do. Her class in the basics of health-care management met tomorrow, and she suspected there would be a quiz.

She reached for the textbook she'd left on the windowsill; one of the benefits of "specialing" a fresh post-op patient was the amount of time it left for other activities, especially when one omitted the nonessential tasks: maintaining respirators and changing damp bed linens, for instance.

Retrieving her book, she looked up and saw a figure reflected in the darkened window glass. It stood a few feet behind her, framed in the doorway of the small private room as if waiting for permission to enter. But visiting hours were over, and anyway, visitors so soon after surgery were never allowed. Bonnie turned, opening her mouth to say so. The figure advanced in a sudden, silent rush, its fingers closing around her throat.

TWO

AT NINE O'CLOCK on the morning after his surgery, Michael Munson sat in his hospital room, eating a soft-boiled egg. From the corridor came the rumble of breakfast carts, a clatter of trays, and the ever-present voice of the page operator.

"Runny," Munson grumped, and swallowed another spoonful, as his pretty young Jamaican nurse snapped a fresh sheet across his bed, tucking it in with practiced skill.

The nurse wore a white uniform dress, white stockings, and immaculately polished white low-heeled pumps. Her black hair was intricately arranged in cornrows, tightly braided to a head so perfectly modeled that it might have been chiseled out of onyx. Clipped to the cornrows was a starchy-white gauze cap, crimped around the sides like a soufflé dish: the mark of a St. Francis Nursing School graduate, Edwina noted with respect.

Glancing at Munson, who looked none the worse for wear after his night's ordeal, she caught the old reprobate eyeing the nurse speculatively, over his egg cup. Certainly his instincts had suffered no serious damage; Munson's fingers twitched mischievously.

"Don't you be thinking of pinching me, now," the nurse said. Her voice, still carrying the hint of a musical island lilt, was rich with confident good humor. "I told you before, if you don't behave, I'll never marry you."

Munson scowled. "Marry me. Hmph." But his fingers closed obediently around his spoon again.

"Marry you, and take you to a tropical paradise," the nurse said. "But definitely not until you shave."

"Can't stand up. Can't shave. Won't shave." Munson thrust his stubbled chin out defiantly. In a pair of tattered flannel pajamas and a robe long overdue for the trash heap, he looked more like the inmate of a shelter for derelicts than a hospital patient.

"And whoever said a man has to stand up to shave?" Light on her feet, the nurse practically danced past Munson into the room's tiny bath cubicle. There were the sounds of water running, and cloths being wrung; a moment later she stepped out again, bearing a basin and an armful of steaming towels.

"Put your head back. I'm going to shave you, but first you must have the moist heat. *Most* relaxing."

Munson's blue eyes widened in consternation, probably at the idea of any female getting near him with a razor. Almost all his relationships with women had ended in their wanting to cut his throat.

"When I finish, you will be a handsome man, not some grizzly old grandpapa."

Speechless with dismay, Munson stiffened as the nurse carefully draped a hot towel over his face, smoothing it with her gentle hands. "There, now. Doesn't that feel good?"

Munson sputtered unintelligibly from beneath the towel.

Unperturbed, the nurse placed a second towel over the first. Munson's protests intensified. But Edwina noted that he was not trying to remove the towels, nor was he trying to get up. What he was doing instead was bitching and moaning, two activities at which he excelled.

Meanwhile, his nurse laid out her collection of grooming tools: a soft-bristled shaving brush, a fresh cake of shaving soap, the basin of very hot water, and a straight razor. Finally she turned to Edwina, her perfect teeth glittering in a smile as bright as the razor's blade.

"You could go now," she invited Edwina pointedly,

"and have a nice, hot cup of coffee. After he's shaved, Mr. Munson is going to have his bath. He is too attractive a man," she added shrewdly, "to go around smelling like an old billy goat."

"Mmmph," Munson objected again from beneath the towels, but with less conviction. Appeals to his vanity, combined with an assertive application of comfort measures, had tranquilized him for now. Edwina thought that for once the old rascal might have met his match.

"I'll be back," she promised.

"Take your time. We'll be getting along fine," said the nurse, whose name, according to her name tag, was Zinnia Martin.

Smiling, Zinnia tested the razor's edge.

There were no chairs by the pay telephones at the end of the hospital corridor, Edwina noted with regret. As long as she sat still, her stomach did not object so much to the breakfast smells wafting from the nearby dietary carts. But moving around brought on a vivid awareness of the eggy plates, sticky cereal bowls, and jammy toast crusts now concealed in those breakfast carts; she knew a few mornings' queasiness was a small price to pay, but at the moment she felt quite ill, and rather lightheaded in the bargain. She dropped a coin into one of the phones and punched in the number of the Litchfield house, hoping her mother would not hear discomfort in her voice. But no such luck.

"Dear child," Harriet interrupted after only a few syllables from Edwina, "you sound green. You must nibble a soda cracker."

Edwina's insides did a slow roll at the thought of nibbling anything, even a soda cracker. "Mother, I'm supposed to sound green. I'm pregnant. And let's not discuss my digestion, if you don't mind. I want to forget all about my digestion. Forever."

"Heavens, what a stubborn little goose you are, worse than your father was. But have it your own way, if you must."

"Thanks, I will. Anyway, I'm at the hospital. Michael broke his toe with his cane last night, purely in a fit of evil temper. I thought for a minute there he was going to bash my brains out. Really, Mother, why you put up with that nasty old man is beyond me."

"Yes," Harriet agreed comfortably, "it is. How is he this morning?"

"Bright as a penny. He's too mean to die. He's got a new nurse, though, and I think she's got his number. She's in there now, absolutely lavishing him with special care as if he's some sort of high pooh-bah."

"That's clever of her," Harriet said, a bit suspiciously. "Michael adores being coddled. Smother him in enough luxury, and you can make him do anything."

"Yes; well, I detect an iron hand in the velvet glove. If anyone can keep him in line, she can." Too late, Edwina realized her unfortunate word choice; Harriet, naturally, picked up on it.

"What are you still doing there, then, my dear? I should think you'd be going back home to rest, after being out so late last night. Or do I *detect* some other situation developing?"

Damn and blast. "I suppose you've read the papers." Of course she had; Harriet scanned more newsprint before breakfast than most people read in a week.

"Indeed. A terrible thing. Such a young girl." Harriet waited.

"Mother, I don't know any more about it. Someone killed her, and tried to kill her patient by turning down the oxygen on his respirator. Luckily, his cardiac alarm sounded before any irreversible harm was done."

"And no one knows who the terrible individual may be?"

"No," Edwina admitted reluctantly. She knew where this conversation was heading, though, and so, unfortunately, did her mother. After fifteen years as a nurse, Edwina had retired to begin another career: the investigation of health-care-related crimes. But that career, too, had been shelved temporarily, as at age forty Edwina smacked up against the realization that motherhood might be a now-or-never project, while crime went on forever.

"The patient was a gunshot victim. So was his wife, as you've probably read by now, and she didn't survive. The police are assuming that whoever shot him in the first place came back to try to finish the job before any guards were placed," Edwina continued unhappily.

She supposed she could have gone on taking cases, but it didn't seem fair. What started out as a civilized investigation into some seemingly not-too-awful wrongdoing could, and often did, turn violent in the end; she felt she might at least let the baby develop its own working life-support system, before putting her own at any more risk.

Rather, she might find out for sure whether the baby was going to develop such a system . . . but this idea was too unpleasant to endure for long; Edwina put it aside, knowing it would return.

"And now," Harriet remarked, "I imagine that hospital security has been alerted, identification is being checked at the entrances, and anyone without proper reason to be on the premises is being questioned and escorted out."

"Yes, Mother. All the precautions are being taken. No one suspicious could even get onto the ward, much less into the patient's room."

"How reassuring," Harriet commented drily. "But why do you suppose the culprit turned down the oxygen? Wouldn't the direct approach be to shut the machine off? To, as it is so vulgarly put nowadays, simply pull the plug?"

Suddenly Edwina knew with whom Michael Munson had discussed the possibility of a respirator. It struck her with a thump of sorrow that her mother was aging, too, right along with the rest of the world; quickly, she dismissed the unwanted mental picture of the two old friends talking about pulling the plug.

"Well," she answered, "it *would* be more direct. But if you don't do it just right, the respirator alarms go off. Someone would come to see why, immediately, so not only would you not do any harm, but you'd be caught."

"Indeed. And someone knew that. How interesting."

"It certainly ... Mother, are you *trying* to get me involved, here?"

Even as she spoke, Edwina's mind raced. To the uninitiated, a respirator's control panel looked as complex as the cockpit of a 747. Yet someone had quickly located the oxygen control knob on Dr. Clarke's respirator and twisted it down to 21 percent, while managing not to set off any of the machine's numerous bells and whistles.

"Get you involved? *Moi?*" Harriet's laugh was silvery, but her voice was unfooled. "Dear child, if you got any more involved, you'd have had to commit the crime yourself. You don't expect me to believe you're still loitering around there out of concern for Michael Munson, do you? Especially now that he seems to have gotten himself the nurse from hell."

"*Mother!* She's a wonderful nurse. She's absolutely what he needs: smart, pretty, and not about to take any guff. And I am not—"

"There's no one so attractive to a certain variety of young woman as a certain variety of rich old man," Harriet pronounced crisply. "With a cough," she added, "although Michael hasn't got a cough. Try to see that he doesn't develop one, will you, dear? Indulge your cynical old mother."

Edwina thought she had indulged her mother enough, at least as far as this conversation was concerned, and said so. But Harriet had not yet quite gotten her final dig in, and after seventy-five years she was not about to surrender the last word to anyone, not even Edwina.

"And dear," Harriet said, "while you're doing whatever it is you're doing, do remember to be careful. I had coffee with Ned Hunt's mother this morning, by the way. Lovely boy, Ned. And *he* tells *his* mother everything. Good-bye, dear."

With that, Harriet Crusoe hung up, leaving Edwina gripping the telephone receiver furiously, as if she could choke the life out of it. Harriet could be the most annoying person on the planet, especially when she was right.

Which she was, in this instance; carefully, Edwina replaced the receiver on its hook, resisting the temptation to bash it against the wall. Breathing slowly and carefully, and not even looking at the dreadfully aromatic breakfast carts, she made her way down the corridor. By now, Ned Hunt would probably be in his office in the hospital's administrative building.

Seeing Ned for the second time in twenty-four hours was not an attractive prospect, but she couldn't very well strangle him over the phone. Maybe on the way there, she would find someone who would give her a soda cracker.

Chelsea Memorial's new administrative offices had fake-burlap walls, carpeting that smelled like chemicals, and low chairs covered in dark gray industrial-strength fabric. The night before, with many of the fluorescent lights turned off, the place had at least had the virtue of being incompletely visible, but now it looked about as inviting as a bank lobby; when Edwina remembered the graceful, vaulted ceilings, marble-tiled floors, and tall, wavery-glassed windows of the Harkness Sanatorium, which had been demolished to make way for the new building, her morning sickness got worse, so she stopped thinking about them.

Ned Hunt's desk, made of some sort of woodlike substance, looked as if it had been extruded from a pulp machine, allowed to harden, and varnished with a particularly obnoxious shade of dark brown hair dye. But from the way Ned kept stroking and patting it, and running his hands along its edges, it was obvious that he liked it very much, just as he did the hideous plasterboard cubicle that was his office.

Probably he also liked the reproduction Currier and Ives prints on the fake-burlap walls, the plastic philodendron in the *faux* marble planter, and the bunch of paper flowers blooming in a vase that was supposed to look like brass, but was really painted cardboard. As far as Edwina could see, there was nothing real in Ned Hunt's office at all, an assessment that included Ned.

"You fink," she told him. "You promised me last night that if I helped you, *advised* you, you wouldn't say anything about it. And then what do you do first thing in the morning but go and blab to your mother."

He'd blabbed things to his mother as a little boy, too, mostly because he thought that if he blabbed them fast enough, he might not be punished, or at least not so severely; his little playmate, Edwina, would be punished instead. That this tactic had worked accounted, Edwina thought, for the level of Ned's character development, which she estimated to be that of a six-year-old child.

"Now, Edwina." His voice, however, had matured: rich and flowing, luxurious as thick oil. "Been talking to Harriet, have you?"

To her face, Ned addressed Harriet as Mrs. Crusoe. Edwina wondered what it would take to wipe the smirk off Ned's lips. Steel wool, probably. Really, he was the most maddening man; at the sound of his voice on the telephone the previous evening, her heart had positively plummeted, mostly because she knew that, maddening or no, she would not be able to refuse his request.

He leaned back in his chair, lacing his fingers comfortably across his ample middle. "Come on, Edwina, we're old friends. No secrets between our families. I stop by for breakfast with Mater every morning, and you know how she loves hearing the news. It's the one small pleasure I can still give her."

Melinda Hunt didn't only love hearing the news; she loved spreading it like rice at a wedding. "*Your* mother was on the phone with *my* mother practically before *your* mother's maid got done rinsing out your orange-juice glass," Edwina said. "Do you still drink out of the one with the bunnies on it, by the way? Seeing as there are no secrets between our families."

Ned drew himself up woundedly, his pink lips pouting.

"No need to get personal. I don't see that that's any of your business."

By which he meant that not only had he drunk his morning orange juice out of a bunny glass, but probably also that his cornflakes had arrived in one of the bunny bowls both of them remembered from his childhood. Stifling a giggle, Edwina wondered if Ned drank his evening brandy out of a bunny snifter.

"Stop it," he complained. "You're always doing that."

"What, Ned? Seeing you as you really are? Well, I can understand why that might make you uncomfortable. But you know, the trouble now is that you lied to me. You knew you weren't going to keep my help confidential; having me on your side even in a minor way makes you look good, doesn't it? Probably you've got one of your flunkies typing a press release about it, right this minute."

Ned Hunt flushed guiltily. He was about as transparent as a windowpane, and his promises were about as sturdy. If she hadn't known him all her life, she wouldn't have wasted another minute on him.

But she had. His face, a smaller, pinker version of its present self, was among her earliest memories. And now there he sat, fat and forty, wanting desperately to do the right thing, but quite not knowing how. A life of prep schools, polo games, and private clubs whose members verged closely upon the mummified had never prepared poor Ned for the rigors of the real world, nor had the indulgences of Mater.

Edwina was about to explain yet again that she did not want her name linked, however distantly, with any crime investigation; if and when she officially began working once more, she would do the linking, herself. But Ned was unwilling or unable to hear her; she'd barely begun scolding him for gabbing about the advice she'd already given, when he began demanding more.

"I've got to have *something* to tell the board of directors," he pleaded, "something to reassure them. It was bad enough Dr. Clarke's getting shot, and his wife killed.

That's all I wanted to talk with you about last night. Just handling the media, and so on."

On that score, Edwina had recommended he let the hospital's public-affairs people do any necessary media-handling, and keep his own mouth shut. Fat chance, she thought, beginning uneasily to wonder what else Ned might have had a chance to do and say already this morning.

"But *that* at least didn't happen on our grounds," he went on. "For heaven's sake, Edwina, we've had a murder here."

"Try telling the board of directors you're resigning," she replied, "effective immediately. That ought to cheer them up."

"Not fair. It's true, my mother put a good word in for me, just to get me a foot in the door around here. I wasn't too proud to take her help when I needed it. But I've gotten all my promotions by myself. On," he concluded haughtily, "the merits of my achievements."

Just for an instant, Edwina debated telling Ned the true reason for his rapid climb up Chelsea Memorial's corporate ladder: Melinda Hunt had made the hospital her pet charity, soliciting enough contributions from her wealthy friends every year to support the economy of Peru. Naturally, a spot must be found for Mrs. Hunt's son, Nedley.

Then, just in time, Edwina remembered a fat little boy of about five years old, who when asked what he wanted to be when he grew up, stoutly announced his intention to become a badger. Probably, he'd have been happier if he had. And he *had* always shared his chewing gum, sometimes even letting Edwina chew it first.

"All right, Ned," she said with a sigh. "What's happened so far today?"

He brightened. "Well, I *think* everything's under control. Security beefed up, of course, and the police are interviewing people. Guards at all the doors, and they've been issued logbooks. Everybody has to sign in and out—"

"Wait a minute. When did you start that?" There hadn't been any logbook at eight in the morning when

Edwina had arrived at the hospital, only the guard looking more carefully at IDs and stopping anyone who didn't have one; fortunately, Ned had supplied her with an ID the night before.

"Nine-ish. Didn't think of it until then. Good idea, though, isn't it? Came up with it myself. And I sent a fruit basket to the girl's parents, had the store put a sympathy card right inside."

Ned beamed, proud of having done so much original thinking, so early in the morning. "I also sent a fruit basket to the guy at the New Haven *Register*, the reporter who's covering the story. I figured maybe it would help to keep us on friendly terms, so he'll take it easier on the hospital when he writes his piece."

Instead of getting her son a job, Melinda Hunt would have done better to have had him assassinated. Edwina cupped her hands to her mouth and intoned through them:

"Earth to Ned: You are an idiot. A dangerous idiot."

"Huh? Why? I'm only trying to—"

"Never mind what you're trying to do. What you're doing is making sure that at three this afternoon, when the day shift goes home and the evening shift comes on, there'll be enough people lined up waiting at those log-book stations so that *anybody* could slip in, in the confusion. Call down and cancel them."

Not that that would necessarily do any good, but it was better than complete pandemonium; Edwina quailed mentally at the thought of an entire shift's worth of Chelsea Memorial workers, lined up to sign their names; by the time they were done, the *next* shift would be arriving.

Ned pouted, but did as he was told. "I suppose everything else I've accomplished today is wrong, too," he complained.

Edwina just looked at him. He resembled a badger, actually: plump and podgy, with small, neat hands, and bright, darting eyes that blinked rapidly when he was nervous, which he was almost all the time. And his rumpled, itchy-looking wool suit was a badgerish shade of tan.

"How did you know where to send the fruit basket?" she asked him. "The one to the dead nurse's parents, I mean."

It was too late to do anything about the one he'd sent to the *Register*. Edwina cringed inwardly, imagining how the crime-beat reporter would react to an attempted bribe of apples and bananas, interspersed with wrapped pieces of cheap hard candy.

"The parents' address was in her personnel record," Ned replied. "They live in California."

Great. It was seven o'clock in the morning in California. The parents could have been out last night. Not everybody in the world had an answering machine. And the mills of justice ground exceedingly slow, especially when they ground transcontinentally.

"You checked first, of course, to make sure they'd already been notified. They're not going to find out their daughter's dead by reading a sympathy card out of a fruit basket."

Ned looked stricken. "Oh, my God. I never . . ."

Edwina got up. Trying to beat common sense into Ned was like trying to make a parakeet learn algebra. "Cancel the fruit basket, too. And don't take any more of these bold, assertive actions. When you see the board of directors, tell them you've placed the whole problem in the hands of the security department and the police, and you're following their advice. Believe me, that will reassure them."

"Oh, my God. Oh, my God, where's the number of that fruit place?" Ned rummaged frantically through his phone book; he had a habit, when he was really anxious, of losing what little physical coordination he possessed.

Crossing the cubicle, Edwina took the phone book from his hands, opened it, and found the number for him.

"And Ned," she added gently, "if you mention me once more in connection with any of the unpleasant events that have been happening around here lately, I'm not only going to stop giving you all this good advice."

Ned gazed up, wide-eyed. "You're . . . not?"

"No. Besides letting you flounder around on your own,

if I hear my name again in the same breath as any of this, I'm going to go over to your mother's house and break your bunny glass. Now, cancel that fruit basket."

Gulping, Ned Hunt reached for the telephone.

"He asked me for help, and I said I would help him. I mean, Martin, the guy is a complete nitwit; his one saving grace is that he sort of suspects it, himself. He's just doing his best with what he's got."

McIntyre frowned at the selections in the cafeteria's salad bar, steam tables, and sandwich rack, then chose an apple and a carton of yogurt for himself. Optimistically, Edwina took a cup of chicken noodle soup and plenty of soda crackers.

At noon, Chelsea Memorial's lunchroom was jammed with doctors, nurses, aides, technicians, visitors, and visitors' babies and toddlers. Edwina got into line at the cash register behind a woman struggling to manage a lunch tray, an infant, a satchel full of baby supplies, and an even rudimentary control over two slightly older children, both rackcting around loudly.

The baby's eyes were huge, dark blue, and not yet focused. It waved a small red fist experimentally and yawned, squirming in its blankets. Its mother snatched once more, unsuccessfully, at the collar of one of the retreating three-year-olds.

"I could hold the baby for you," Edwina offered.

The woman turned, her complexion sallow and her eyes gummy with fatigue. "Oh, thanks." With her hands free, she expertly corralled the toddlers, popped a carrot stick into each one's grasp, and paid the cashier, all with the brisk efficiency of a woman who is accustomed to beating chaos down to a dull roar, its elimination having long ago been abandoned as a lost cause.

Edwina gave the baby back, realizing that she wanted to go on holding it, and looked up at Martin who was watching carefully. "So what are you going to do about it?" he said when they had reached their table. "I thought you'd decided you weren't going to work for a while."

"I thought I had, too. It's only that Ned's so helpless. Do you want me to tell him to forget it? I could, you know," she said, and wondered if she meant it.

McIntyre ate a slice of apple. "Oh, no, you don't. I'll start getting bossy when there's an infant around to boss; that way, I'll have a better chance of winning. For a while, anyway," he added as the pair of three-year-olds ran shrieking by the table.

Edwina confronted her chicken soup. Its noodles slithered wetly in her spoon. She forced herself to swallow them.

"*If* there's an infant," she reminded him. "We still have to get the results of the amniocentesis, and another ultrasound."

"And if there isn't? It's been a while since we've talked about that. Any second thoughts?" His voice was gentle, inviting her to confide in him; McIntyre never pushed.

"Six weeks, four days, and three hours, to be exact. I'm sorry, Martin, I know I haven't been very chatty on the subject. It's just that every time I think about it, I'm ready to burst into tears. Only I can't even do that, it turns out. They seem to stick in my throat."

The tests were to see whether the baby had birth defects, and if so, how severe they might be. The trouble was, it took eight weeks to get the results: eight weeks of swinging from optimism to terror, from nervous prospective motherhood to the possibility of a grief so deep and terrible, Edwina wanted to run from it.

Only, there was nowhere to run; for forty-year-old prospective mothers, or at least for ones with her opinions on the topic, this was the drill: tests; a dreadful eight-week wait; prenatal diagnosis; and (if the diagnosis came back bad) a traumatic second-trimester pregnancy termination.

Resolutely, she turned her mind from the many objections her heart had offered to this last; the knowledge that others would choose otherwise was also irrelevant. Medical science offered an alternative to a blind ride on the genetic roulette wheel; if she had to suffer in order that her child should not, then she would do so. Case closed.

"What we decided then is what I still think," she recited to McIntyre. "There are problems that can be fixed, and ones that can be dealt with. And then there are ones that can't." She looked at him. "It's easier for people like us; we have the money for a special school, corrective surgery, or whatever. We can handle problems better than most. But . . ."

"But if we find out it's only going to suffer and then die anyway, we're not going to have this baby. I agreed with you then, and I agree with you now. I just wanted to be sure we're still on the same page about it, that's all."

McIntyre smiled bravely. He had seen a lot of unpleasant things in his career as a homicide cop, but he hadn't seen the tragedies Edwina had witnessed, down in the newborn intensive-care unit. So at his words she felt a huge burden lift; he wanted the baby very much, even more than she did, and she hadn't been sure how his feelings might change as the weeks went by.

"We're on the same page, all right. But I'm still scared." She tried to smile back at him, but her lip was trembling too hard. "Damn," she said, angry with herself.

He put his hand over hers. "Me, too. Listen, let's deal with things when we have to deal with them. Instead of torturing ourselves, let's try to believe everything's okay until we find out otherwise. Agreed?"

"Agreed." She laughed shakily, and tried another spoonful of soup. It went down easier, this time.

"But that still doesn't help me decide what I'm going to do about poor Ned," she went on after a moment. "He and I used to splash around in a wading pool together. We shook our *rattles* together, for heaven's sake."

McIntyre grinned. "I wish I'd seen that. The wading pool, *and* the rattle. But look, you're going to be hanging around here anyway, checking up on the terror of the geriatric set. I don't see what it could hurt, if you just kept your eyes and ears open. Who knows, you might come up with something."

He scraped the bottom of his yogurt carton. "From what I hear, nobody else has, yet. And it'll keep your mind off other things," he added.

"You really are the most intelligent man." She had, she realized suddenly, eaten a whole cup of soup and half the soda crackers without noticing.

"Of course I am. That's why I married you." Grinning, he loaded her cup and cracker wrappings onto his own tray, and got up. The crush in the cafeteria line had now become the crush at the dish room, everyone trying to hurry out at once.

"You know, though," he said, "if you want to catch up on the background, you'd better get upstairs. I saw Talbot heading up there just as I got here, and from the look on his face I think you'd better have a chat with him. Otherwise, he might be too mad to tell anybody anything, even you."

"Talbot's upstairs? On the surgical ward? Interviewing the doctors and nurses? *Alone?*"

"Uh-huh. And you know how Talbot enjoys the company of health-care professionals, yourself excepted."

"About as much as a poke in the eye with a sharp stick." Edwina snatched the last soda crackers off the tray before they could slide away down the conveyor belt.

"Thanks. See you later," she told McIntyre, and headed for the elevators, unwrapping the crackers as she went.

Mostly on account of his own checkered medical history, Talbot did not think medical personnel were exactly paragons of virtue. He could be quite vocal about this, too, with almost no provocation; one whiff of rubbing alcohol, for example, could set him off on a tirade.

In fact, if she didn't get upstairs right now, the staff on the surgical ward might murder *him*.

"There's only one way to get interns and residents to sit still for any length of time, especially if you also want them to stay awake. And that, my friend, is to feed them."

Arriving on the surgical ward, Edwina had located the

head nurse, taken him aside, and introduced herself. Swiftly, she had explained why she thought her presence might be useful in helping the detective's work go more efficiently. Translated, this meant helping Talbot get out of here before he drove everyone crazy, a project she felt sure the head nurse would endorse.

Talbot himself sat behind the nursing desk, getting madder and more frustrated by the minute, trying to get a young intern to stop scribbling in a chart long enough to answer questions.

"Uh-huh," the intern said distractedly, checking a card from his pocket, then scrawling another note. He had been on service for several months, and looked appropriately exhausted; if it had a bed in it, his attitude said, even a jail cell held no terrors for him.

The head nurse, a blocky blond fellow who looked more like an NFL linebacker than a professional descendant of Florence Nightingale, listened alertly to Edwina. At one in the afternoon a third of his patients still hadn't gotten to the operating room, while another third of them had begun returning from it. The rest of his charges were recovering from previous surgeries, in conditions ranging from critical to extremely guarded.

In short, the ward resembled a war zone; all it needed was the boom of artillery, which if Talbot got any madder it was going to get. The head nurse glanced at Talbot, at Edwina, and at his own clipboard, upon which he had listed all the things he needed to accomplish immediately if not sooner.

"You can handle it? Great. Handle it. Let me know if you need anything." The head nurse had hurried off down the corridor to where a patient-transport aide was trying to get an enormous, enormously confused woman to please, *please* remain seated in her wheelchair, whereupon the woman struggled up again.

Now, with Talbot in the ward's conference room, Edwina put the finishing touches on the table: cups, sugar, cream, napkins, and a deluxe platter of cold meats, cheeses, rolls, pickles, and cherry tomatoes, courtesy of Ned Hunt, who had turned out to be good for something, after all. One thing Ned did know how to do was order from a delicatessen and get the food delivered pronto.

"I don't know why I've got to pamper these punks," Talbot groused. "I'm a cop, for chrissake, they've *gotta* talk to me if I want them to talk to me. I can slap 'em with a *warrant* if they don't talk to me."

"Of course they do," Edwina soothed, "of course you can. But the more you tempt them to stick around, the more they *will* stick around, and maybe remember something useful. Besides, I'll bet you haven't had any lunch, yourself. Here, sit down."

Tactfully, Edwina steered him to a chair facing away from the IV-preparation area. Every time Talbot's gaze fell on the bottles, glass vials, boxes of syringes, and packs of hypodermic needles stored above the stainless-steel prep counter, his eyes widened anxiously, his respirations increased, and little veins began popping out in his forehead. Edwina could only imagine the effort of will it must have taken for Talbot to come upstairs at all.

"Hope they aren't all too polite to talk with their mouths full," he grumbled around a bite of smoked-turkey sandwich, then reached out and speared a pickle with a plastic fork.

"Don't worry about it. This place beat the manners out of most of them a long time ago. Just sit tight; the people you want to talk to can smell food a mile away."

Just then, the intern Talbot had been trying to question appeared in the conference-room doorway. He was in his late twenties, pale and slump-shouldered in an oxford-cloth shirt, frayed tie, and corduroy trousers. A pack of index cards and a bunch of pens stuck out of his ink-stained shirt pocket, and after only a few months of hospital training, he had already hammered most of the useful life out of a pair of Hush Puppies.

Now the intern's gaze lit hopefully upon the table full of food. "Say, could I have some of that?"

Talbot's smile widened slowly, like the one on the face of the tiger just before the tiger pounced.

"Siddown," he said.

The murdered nurse was twenty-six years old, single, and had a bachelor's degree in nursing from Carlton College, in Redwood City, California. Before her death, she had been taking courses in business and health-care management at Quinnipiac College, and had already made overtures to the Yale School of Public Health, in hopes of being admitted to the master's degree program there. Bonnie West, as everyone knew, had had career aspirations.

Bonnie was never late and never called in sick. She never did anything that might have earned her a serious black mark on her employee evaluations. She subscribed to the nursing journals, read them, and even tried her hand at writing for them; her grade-point average hovered around 3.85. She was always neat, clean, and appropriately dressed, right down to her gold Carlton College nursing pin.

But Bonnie was also the most disliked nurse on the ward. She did everything she had to do, never any more; she was a genius at calculating the minimum possible effort required to stay out of trouble. She never volunteered to help anyone, and if there was any doubt over whether a certain task was her responsibility or someone else's, someone else wound up doing it. Also, Bonnie made no secret of her own supposed intellectual superiority, nor did she trouble to conceal her contempt for anyone less ambitious than herself, a category that included almost everyone.

"Bottom line, Bonnie was a little brat," said the tiny, black-haired practical nurse sitting at the end of the table. "I mean, I'm sorry about what happened to her. It's a terrible thing. But . . ."

After questioning the hungry intern, who had turned out to have little to offer other than his appreciation for

the meal, Talbot had worked his way through the chief
resident, assistant residents, and other interns on the surgical ward; as a result, the conference room had taken on
the atmosphere of a party, and the sandwich platter now
held only a few crumbs. But Edwina had put in another
call to Ned, and a tray of pastries was on its way.

None of the physicians had known much about Bonnie
West; she had been neither pretty nor flirtatious, her
manner neither craven nor haughty. To them, she was just
another nurse; Edwina suppressed the twinge of resent-
ment she felt at this, remembering how angry the same
attitude had made her in her own nursing days.

The more things change, she thought with an inward
sigh, and put the idea away as Bonnie's co-workers' atti-
tudes proved to be an entirely different matter. One by
one, they came in and took a sandwich or a cup of coffee,
staying only a few minutes but painting a fairly complete
picture of Bonnie—and damning her in their assessments:

Bonnie told night-shift secretary Clarissa Hale that if
she ever got fat, she would just go out and kill herself.
Clarissa weighed over two hundred pounds, worked two
jobs in order to support six children, and according to the
nurse who remembered the event, had not appreciated
Bonnie's frankness.

Bonnie let a patient wait half an hour for a bedpan,
until the nurse's aide got back from coffee break to deliver
it, while Bonnie sat at the nursing desk working on a
school assignment.

Bonnie saw another nurse make a medication error;
instead of telling the nurse about it, she informed the
supervisor, and had the offending caregiver put on report.
Both nurses had wanted the same day off, on the same
upcoming holiday. The other nurse had more seniority,
but Bonnie got the holiday.

In short, Bonnie was the sort of nurse the other nurses
all would have liked to murder; none of them, however,
had. With the exception of the hefty Clarissa, who was
home in bed with the flu at the time, and the head nurse,

who had been home, too, walking the floor with his colicky infant daughter, none were physically large or strong enough to have overpowered Bonnie with their bare hands, strangling her swiftly.

But that was what had happened to Bonnie West, and if no one particularly mourned her, no one wished it on her, either. In their voices, Edwina heard the fear they all felt.

It had happened to Bonnie, and it could happen to any one of them. In a linen closet, an empty stairwell, the nurses' locker room, or any of the many other places in the hospital where a nurse might suddenly be alone, someone had been hiding where no one was supposed to be able to hide.

Someone had gotten at Bonnie and her patient. The patient, they all knew, had been the real target; otherwise, why had his wife been murdered that same night? And why, after killing Bonnie, stick around to tamper with the respirator?

About Victor Clarke, the physicians on the ward did prove somewhat more knowledgeable. Clarke had a thriving practice in general medicine; he was not a surgeon, so the surgical ward was not his usual stomping ground. Still, he referred patients who needed surgery to specialists at Chelsea Memorial, and all the doctors of whatever specialty glimpsed one another now and then at various social, philanthropic, or local medical-association events.

"Fine man, Clarke. Hope he can hang in there," said a surgeon clad in rumpled OR greens. He popped a bite of pastry into his mouth and washed it down with coffee, glancing at his watch. "Has his faults like anyone, of course."

"And what might those be, sir?" Talbot asked, scribbling in his notebook. Only the faint tightening of his fingers on the pen betrayed his heightened interest.

All the other surgeons had likewise painted Victor Clarke as a fine fellow: no bad habits, no enemies; none, anyway, that they knew of. They catalogued his clothing (dark suits, or slacks and cashmere sweaters), praised his

well-known generosity to charity, and categorized the care
he took of his automobiles (black Lincoln Town Car, red
Fiat Sport Spyder) as excellent. In fact, Dr. Clarke sounded
unnaturally fine, almost too good to be true. But now that
Talbot had found someone who seemed to know Clarke
better than most, and had run into mention of Clarke's
flaws, there was a chance the detective was hitting pay dirt.

"Well, he's a rotten golfer," the surgeon offered.

Talbot looked up. "Yes, sir," he replied in a voice like a
whip's flick. "Anything else? Besides the lousy golf game, I
mean." His pen paused over the notebook.

Pale, unhealthy-looking, and dressed in a cheap plaid
sport jacket and shiny trousers, Talbot looked more like
an aging racetrack tout than an experienced homicide cop.
The surgeon, in contrast, was tanned and fit; it was clear
from his manner that he was accustomed to respect from
everyone. At Talbot's tone, the surgeon frowned; after all,
Talbot was a public servant, wasn't he? With emphasis on
"servant."

"Somebody tried to kill Victor Clarke," Talbot said.
"They killed his wife. Renata, *her* name was," he added,
glancing at his notes. "And they killed a nurse right here in
your hospital." His voice grated down a little harder on
that "your," as if implying some responsibility.

The surgeon flushed. "See here, that's none of my
affair, I don't have to—"

"Sorry, sir, but I'm afraid you do. You know he's a bad
golf player. I guess that means you must socialize with
him, you don't just see him here at the hospital. Right?"

"Occasionally. I don't see what that has to—"

"Did you know Renata Clarke? Or the rest of Victor
Clarke's family? Ever visited Clarke at his home?" Talbot
rat-a-tatted the questions.

When he hit his stride, Talbot was perfect at this sort of
thing. Now the surgeon, however offended, would be so
concerned with demonstrating his lack of involvement that
he would answer all Talbot's questions, and probably
some that Talbot didn't yet know enough to ask.

"Ever mention any trouble?" Talbot pressed. "Business, financial, marital? Maybe a patient who was angry with him?"

It worked like a charm. Edwina covered a smile with her napkin, pretending to dab at her lips.

"Look here," the surgeon responded more amiably, trying to defuse this pushy cop's pesky assertiveness by taking another tack, "you've got the wrong idea. We're talking a few Saturday morning golf games, not buddy-buddies."

"Yes, sir. Of course, I understand." Abandoning his quick scribble, Talbot printed a note in his book; even from across the table, Edwina could read the words: "Not close acquaintance." Watching, the surgeon relaxed visibly.

"Why don't you tell me what you do know, then," Talbot said. "Just any little items you remember. You could be very helpful to the investigation."

The touch of flattery, combined with the removal of threat, opened a floodgate. The reluctant surgeon actually knew both victims fairly well, and soon a clearer picture of them emerged. In their sixties, athletic and at least superficially sociable, they lived in an expensive suburb on the outskirts of New Haven. He ran five miles a day, played tennis, and was an avid golfer despite his indifferent skill at the game. Well thought of by his colleagues, he was board certified in internal medicine and made it a point to keep his knowledge current, attending four or five medical conferences every year.

"And not the kind where all you do is hang around," the surgeon added. "Some of the ones the pharmaceutical companies run, there's not much real education involved. They just put you up at a fancy resort for a long weekend, maybe have a couple of slide shows, to try to get you to prescribe their newest drug. But Clarke only went to the serious, legitimate conferences. He even had a big paper he'd been working on, to present at one of them. This guy is committed to his profession."

"Yes, sir," replied Talbot, who had never been to a

resort, expensive or otherwise, and whose idea of a long weekend was one during which he did not get to go home, except to shower and change clothes, from Friday until Tuesday.

The doctor's dead wife had been just as active, involved, and seemingly unimpeachable: An accomplished horsewoman, she kept a Thoroughbred stabled in a neighboring rural town, rode often in shows and for pleasure, swam most mornings and afternoons at the country club. Dressed well, took good care of herself; of course she was no spring chicken, the surgeon added, but she was a good-looking woman.

"Known them long?" Talbot asked.

The surgeon shrugged. "Twenty years. As I told you, not as close friends. But that's long, in my book. Met him a couple of years after they both moved here—some party at the club or some such thing. He'd already been in practice a while then."

"And where was he before that?" Talbot flipped another page in his notebook.

The surgeon frowned. "You know, that's the one funny thing. The two of them were about the most normal people I've ever met. Only I don't know where they were before they came here. Not that I knew them really well, as I said. But I don't remember them ever talking about it, or even mentioning it at all."

If Talbot thought anything was odd about describing as normal a fellow who lived in a swanky suburb, wore silk suits, kept expensive cars, belonged to a country club, and supported a wife whose hobby involved the upkeep of a large, valuable animal, he managed to conceal this opinion.

"So you don't know where he went to school, or where he got his training. You don't know where they lived before they moved here."

It was, as even Talbot knew, unusual for a physician not to talk about these things; like cops, doctors liked to regale one another with war stories, even years after their bone-crushingly miserable greenhorn days had ended.

"No," said the surgeon, "and I remember wondering about it, once, at a gathering at their house. They had a sort of gallery of photographs in frames, on a grand piano. Anniversaries, shots of the two of them on vacation, a studio portrait of her. That sort of thing. And it was odd."

"What was odd about it, sir?" Talbot kept writing. Anyone who did not know him would have thought he could be capturing at most one word in five of what the surgeon was saying. But Talbot took shorthand at the rate of 130 words a minute, a skill he had acquired by attending secretarial school on his own time. At the end of the interview, he would have in his little notebook every syllable that had been spoken, plus pertinent comments on the interviewee's tone and expression.

"This can't possibly be important," the surgeon said. "It's just some quirk of theirs. But you know, they had a photograph of themselves for nearly every year, going back fifteen years or so."

"The get-together you're talking about, sir, how long ago was that? What was it for? And was it the last time you were in their house?"

"It was about five years ago. And no, I haven't been in the house since then. They entertained mostly at the club, but he was president of the local MA group that year, and there's an annual thing at the president's home. Sort of an ongoing custom. But what was funny was, they didn't have any earlier photographs. None from the time before they came here."

"No earlier photographs," Talbot repeated blandly.

"That's right. I remember thinking, it was as if the time before that hadn't existed. Or . . . as if they didn't want it to."

The surgeon got up, glancing once more at his thick gold watch. "Well, I'm sure that's all very useless and melodramatic, but you did ask me for my impression. And now, if you'll excuse me, I've got a customer waiting, down in the operating room."

"Yes, sir." Talbot closed his notebook. "Important case?"

"L.O.L., L.O.L.," the surgeon replied, gripping Talbot's wiry hand in his thick, tanned one. "That's surgeonese for 'Little Old Lady Lying on Linoleum.' It's how they're usually found," he explained with a grin, "when they fall and break their hips."

"I see, sir." Carefully, Talbot removed his hand from that of the surgeon, who strode jauntily off to operate. When the surgeon had gone, Talbot looked down at his hand and began wiping it with a paper napkin, as if to remove the coating of invisible slime he apparently felt must still be clinging there.

"Now, Dick, he was only trying to be funny," Edwina said. "Surgeons get hardened over the years, seeing so many people in so much pain. It's just their way of protecting themselves."

But Talbot wasn't having any. Possibly it was because his own arms were bumpy with the marks of dozens of venipunctures, or perhaps he was feeling another twinge from the repair of his old gunshot wound. Maybe he was remembering the origins of the faint white marks still showing on the sides of his neck, where big IVs had been run in under pressure in an attempt to supply his bullet-punctured body with new blood even faster than it was hemorrhaging out the old blood.

Or maybe it wasn't any of those things at all. You could never tell for sure, with Talbot. Grimacing, he crumpled the paper napkin and tossed it at the wastebasket.

"L.O.L., my ass," was all he said.

THREE

"**S**NAPPERS," MICHAEL MUNSON growled later that afternoon, scowling at the row of red, wrinkled little faces visible through the glass of the nursery viewing area on Chelsea Memorial's maternity floor. Each bassinet on the other side of the glass held a small pink or blue stuffed bear, a pink or blue rattle, and a brand-new baby.

"Useless. Me, too." Munson glowered at his bandaged foot, which stuck out before him on the leg support of his wheelchair. Much of his day had been occupied by the battery of neurological tests and examinations Alison had arranged; now it was past three, Zinnia had gone to attend change-of-shift report, and Edwina was only waiting for Harriet to arrive before going home, too.

"Of course they're useless, Michael," Edwina said. Getting the old man out of his room had been a chore; he complained about everything, objected to everything, and made as much unnecessary fuss as he could about everything. But he seemed content at present to sit in his chair, his sharp, disapproving old eyes taking in every detail of his surroundings.

"But they won't stay useless," she continued, "and neither will you."

Privately, she was not so sure of this; the results of the neurology consult were not yet known. To avoid possible questions from Munson on the topic, she peered intently through the glass. The baby in the end bassinet looked different from the rest, with its unusually round face and tiny jaw, too small even for its rather small head. Jerking suddenly awake, it began to cry, producing a high, thin sound like the mewing of a cat.

A nurse came in to it, smiling reassuringly through the pane as she lifted the infant and placed it against her shoulder; the infant quieted. With a pang, Edwina turned away, propelling Munson's chair back toward the nursing desk and the elevators beyond. She had thought seeing the babies might amuse Munson, but it had been a mistake to come here.

"Poor snapper," he said suddenly. "What's wrong with it?"

Edwina hesitated. She did not want to talk about birth defects. But this was the first time Munson had expressed any interest in anything other than himself; if by some chance it indicated a trend, she supposed she might as well encourage it.

"Cri-du-chat syndrome. Small head, funny round face, and that strange cry, like a cat. It's mentally retarded. It will have other problems, too, probably very serious ones." She maneuvered the chair onto the elevator, and pushed the *Up* button. Harriet would surely be here by now.

"Mmmph. What happens to 'em? Die?"

She eyed him, surprised: Why all this sudden interest in an afflicted child he had never seen before and never would again? Morbid curiosity, no doubt; he was an intensely selfish old man. But she answered his question.

"No. Or at least not right away. Babies with the syndrome don't eat well, and a lot have heart defects. Some go home for a while; others go to institutions, if the parents aren't able to cope with them, do all the special things they need. They can live a few years, and they can be very difficult to care for. Expensive, and—"

"Had one," he interrupted harshly. "Fourth wife. Long time ago. Died."

Edwina stared at the back of the old man's head, wishing she could see into it. He must have known all along what the baby's trouble was. What in the world could he be thinking?

"Die then. Die now. Progress," he spat. "Damned fraud." He thumped his cane, which he had refused to give up although he was still forbidden to walk; Edwina kept a sharp eye on it.

The elevator doors opened and Harriet stood there, in a nearly visible cloud of perfume: Pears soap, pinkish scented face powder, and Joy cologne.

Harriet wore a forest-green plaid wool skirt, razorishly pleated; an ivory silk blouse with a jabot of French lace; and a cream boiled-wool jacket. With her silver hair elaborately coiffed, her makeup perfectly if generously applied, and her tiny feet shod in hand-dyed green alligator pumps, at seventy-five years old Harriet Crusoe looked as if she had just stepped down from a fashion runway in Paris.

She would probably have been welcome there, for Harriet was not just a best-selling romance writer; she was a worldwide phenomenon, an arbiter of taste and of the romantic imagination. In her trademark rope of pearls too huge and perfect to be real (Harriet's funny little secret being, of course, that they *were* real) she regularly supplied to the popular press comments ranging from her opinions on the wisdom of premarital sex (she was against it) to her notions on the nature and existence of the hereafter (she was for it).

In fact, Harriet might easily have slipped into caricature; her salvation was that she meant every word, including the twenty-five hundred she wrote each morning on a yellow legal pad in blue fountain-pen ink. She meant them from the bottom of her heart, the wisdom and generosity of that noble organ being, Edwina believed, the true reason behind Harriet's enormous popularity.

"Darlings!" the old lady said, bending to put her arms around Munson's neck as Edwina wheeled him from the elevator. "Oh, how glad I am to see you, and looking both so *well*."

The alligator pumps made Harriet's legs seem slender as

a girl's. Edwina put her cheek against her mother's soft, powdered one, as Harriet straightened. Posture was another of Harriet's strong points.

"Hello, dear heart," she said. "And how is this irascible patient today?" Reaching down, she patted Munson's cheek with her plump, perfectly manicured hand.

"Paugh," spat Munson, turning his head away sharply. "Too much perfume."

"Yes, dear," Harriet replied, seizing the handles of his wheelchair and gazing down indulgently at him. "And aren't we fortunate, both of us, that we can still smell it? Now, Michael, I want to hear all about this new nurse. Just how besotted are you with her?"

Beaming, the old lady bore Michael Munson away. In the next half-hour, she would no doubt rearrange Munson's room, scan and criticize his list of medications, scrutinize his treatment plan, and demand a special menu for him, creative meddling being yet another of Harriet's talents.

Still, Munson actually looked happy, tipping his head to chat as amiably with Harriet as if he were a normal person, and not some sour old hospital patient from hell.

"Good-bye, darling," Harriet called over her shoulder. "Do come and see us before you go, won't you, please? I can't bear not to visit with you a little more. Say, in an hour or so?"

Mother, Edwina thought, *you awful schemer. Why, you're as bad as he is.* Which perhaps explained as well as anything the friendship between the two.

No doubt Harriet had been conferring with Ned Hunt's mother again. Melinda would take help where she could get it, especially on Ned's behalf. Thus, given by Harriet's design a little longer in the hospital on her own, Edwina got back onto the elevator. Change of shift was over, and the acute surgical ward would by now have settled quietly into its three-to-eleven-P.M. routine.

At least, she hoped it had settled quietly—a hope that was emphatically dashed as she stepped out onto the surgical floor.

• • •

"I want those X rays! I want those X rays! I don't care what time it is. I *ordered* them *ten minutes* ago!"

Edwina sighed, hearing William Grace bellowing out his demands from somewhere on the ward. Some physicians simply never understood that evening shifts ran differently from day shifts, mostly on account of their notoriously meager staffing. Tasks that were not quite of life-or-death urgency were deferred, sometimes, in favor of tasks that were, and this naturally led to occasional disagreements, such as the one that was occurring now.

"What the hell is the matter with you people? Goddammit, *I want those X-rays!*" Grace roared unashamedly. He did not care how or why the hospital ran, only that he got what he wanted.

Still, as she approached the nursing desk, Edwina was not prepared for the chart that sailed past her head, hit the wall, and sprang open, scattering lab slips, progress notes, and order sheets everywhere. Grace hadn't even looked to see where he was flinging it; now he hammered his fists on the ward secretary's counter, irrational as a thwarted child.

Abruptly he stopped, stiffened, and stalked off the ward, brushing past Edwina without a word. Stunned nurses and aides stared silently after him; there was no getting used to Grace's explosions, however often one witnessed them.

But he really did seem to be getting worse: In the old days when Edwina had been a staff nurse, a younger William Grace had occasionally thrown things in the operating room, but never on a patient ward. Muttering, Grace strode into the elevator; the doors closed. The heavy bang from inside the metal car must have been his fist, slamming the wall.

"Whoo-ee," said one of the nursing aides, bending to gather up the scattered records. "He *has* got a hitch in his git-along."

"Yes," Edwina said, scooping up some of the papers

and the chart folder, and handing them over. "He certainly does have a temper."

The aide was a small, slender woman in her sixties, with salt-and-pepper hair clipped very close to her head. Her blue cotton uniform, ironed to military perfection, smelled of bleach and laundry starch; her shoes, a cracked, elderly pair of Nurse Mates, were powdery with white polish.

"Temper? Honey, he ain't got a temper. He's got a *fuse*. I ask him yesterday if he mind if I get by him, get into a room for some work I got to do. You know what he did?"

The woman's eyes widened at the memory. "He come around at me and *clutch me by the throat*. And, honey, I don't got to take that kind of treatment. Huh-*uh*."

Edwina listened, astonished. "What happened? I mean, what happened then?"

The aide got up, her hands full of disarranged papers. "He kind of focused his eyes on me after a second, and he let go. But he has got the devil in him, and that's a fact."

Alison Feinstein sat at the nursing desk, writing a post-op note. "So, what did you think of the 'Dr. Bill Show'? Is he getting to be a pip, or what?"

Edwina sat beside her. "I guess so. Is what that aide just told me true, about him grabbing her by the throat?"

Alison frowned, and scrawled her signature at the bottom of the note. "I hadn't heard that one. This morning while I was assisting, he threw a trochar. The man's a nut case."

She snapped the chart shut. "And speaking of nut cases, my little friend Eric has disappeared. Signed himself out of the ER as soon as he was lucid enough to talk them into letting him go, and nobody's been able to get in touch with him since."

"Oh. Alison, I don't know what to say. That's terrible."

"Is it?" Alison's green eyes narrowed with unhappiness. "I suppose it is. I had all these great plans for getting him into rehab, maybe even getting him back into a residency. Trying to be his friend, you know? Giving him some support. God knows he isn't going to get any from anyone else around here."

She slotted the chart back into the rack. "But it looks as if Eric doesn't want help. So maybe it's just as well he's taken off. At least I won't have to watch him crash and burn," she finished bitterly.

"Look, maybe he'll show up. It could be he's too ashamed to face anyone right away, or maybe he's afraid he'll get arrested. Although I doubt anyone here would make a criminal complaint. The publicity for the hospital would be too bad."

"Yeah, or it could be he's off somewhere stuffing his nose full of coke, convincing himself it's all somebody else's fault." Alison massaged her temples tiredly. "Anyway, I've got to get back down to the recovery room. Thanks for stopping by."

"Alison, listen, I came because I need a favor. Grace's patient, the gunshot wound from last night? The one whose—"

"Whose nurse was killed," Alison supplied flatly. "As if we needed more trouble around here. Poor kid," she added, seeming to realize how she must have sounded. "What about him?"

Edwina shrugged. If she'd known the answer to that, she wouldn't have been there. "I want to see him. Just . . . have a glance at him. But I don't want to look as if I want to see him; I don't want to seem involved. Do you have any excuse to go into his room, and I could just be with you, sort of tagging along?"

Alison looked skeptical. "Not much to see. Unconscious guy on a respirator with his leg in the air, going nowhere fast. But I could stop in; he's on my service, so technically, I'm still in charge of him."

"Technically?" Edwina strode down the corridor alongside Alison, whose quick step was even quicker than Edwina's own. Alison had once said she moved so fast because she was always so tired that if she ever slowed down she might fall asleep.

Now she chuckled without amusement. "While my case is under review. Grace didn't only bring a case against Eric. He also brought one against me. Failure to supervise; failure to report. In a few days, I'll find out if I get disciplined. Or fired."

She stopped in front of a private room. The only sounds from inside were the whooshing of a respirator, and the beep of a cardiac monitor. A uniformed police officer sat by the door to the room, reading the New Haven *Register*.

COPS PROBE HOSPITAL NURSE DEATH, the headline blared, and underneath: "Security Gaps, Safety Measures Criticized." Edwina guessed the reporter really hadn't liked Ned's fruit basket, or maybe just hadn't liked Ned.

The cop outside the room looked up, recognized Alison, and allowed Edwina to pass also; Edwina was not surprised. Had she seemed in any way as if she didn't belong here, the guard would have stopped her, but challenging everyone who went in and out would be just too cumbersome, especially when the patient was as sick as Victor Clarke.

Clarke's eyes snapped open as the women entered. Lurching up, he tried to raise his arms, which were secured to the bed rails by loops of gauze. His face twisted as he struggled to speak around the plastic tube protruding from his throat; at the increased pressure, the respirator alarms beeped wildly.

Then, as if the effort had exhausted him, he fell back; a moment later, he was unconscious again. His nurse, a grim-faced woman in her forties, reset his respirator and cardiac alarms.

"He does that every time anyone comes in," the nurse said. "We should have transferred him to another room. Who knows what the poor man saw in here last night?"

"There isn't another room, and I doubt he saw anything." Alison's tone indicated that the subject was closed. Briskly, she checked Clarke's day sheet for his vital signs, then laid a finger against the exposed top of his suspended foot.

"Circulation's still okay. Let's hope it stays that way, or Grace will have something else to bitch at me about."

The nurse's pink-painted lips tightened at the profanity. "I'll be right back," she said, and huffed out.

"Silly twit," Alison remarked without emotion, easing aside the dressings to inspect the surgical site.

The room was little more than a cubicle, with just enough space for the respirator and a bedside table, plus a single chair. To one side, a tiny built-in sink with a mirror and an outlet for an electric shaver occupied a niche in the wall; there was also a small built-in closet. There would not have been much area to maneuver, in an effort to escape a killer.

But probably Bonnie West had not had time to try; there had been no sign of struggle, no disarray, only a dead nurse and a misadjusted respirator.

"How can you be sure he didn't see anything?" Edwina asked. "And why is he still so out of it? The police are dying to talk to him." *And so am I,* she added silently. Even major surgery shouldn't have kept Victor Clarke so nearly comatose for so long.

"Edwina, if this had been an ordinary hip replacement, he wouldn't be so sick. But as it is, he could be out of it for weeks. We're talking big-time trauma, here, you know, not a nice clean elective procedure."

Alison sighed, replacing the dressings, and motioned Edwina to the doorway, out of Clarke's hearing. "The wound was a mess—the bullet bounced around and pulverized everything, and of course it was dirty, so he's got an infection cooking. And he's no youngster to start with; the shock alone would have killed him if he'd been any farther from the ER when it happened."

She eyed the iron traction weights and the cord that suspended them, appearing to find the apparatus satisfactory. "*And* we transfused in half his blood volume," she went on, "which was what he'd lost. So now he's got respiratory distress syndrome on top of it all. We're stuck with keeping him snowed on Demerol and morphine, just so we can ventilate him, and we could stay stuck for a long time."

As she spoke, she crossed back to the bedside table and re-moved something from its top drawer. "Here, put these on."

Edwina removed a pair of horn-rimmed bifocals from the leather eyeglass case. Blinking through them, she experienced the strong sensation that her eyes were being magnetically drawn out through a spot just above the bridge of her nose.

Hastily, she removed the glasses. "Gad, these are high-powered. He must be nearly blind without them."

Alison surveyed the patient, his monitors, and his trac-tion apparatus again, and scanned the respirator panel. "Yep."

She picked up the clipboard hanging from the side of the respirator, read it, and replaced it with a grim frown. "He might have seen something when he was first shot, of course; probably he was wearing his glasses then. But he's not going to be identifying anyone any time soon. Assuming he . . ."

Alison stopped. Just because Clarke seemed uncon-scious didn't mean he couldn't hear. "Assuming he makes it," Alison meant, but she knew better than to say so in front of Clarke. Also, she cared enough not to, which was one of the reasons Edwina liked the young surgeon.

"Even if he did see anything," Alison corrected smoothly, glancing at her watch. "Damn, I've really got to get down-stairs; I've got a patient in post-op who's so unstable, he'll fall apart the first time someone looks at him wrong. Where's that nurse, anyway? If Grace finds out this guy was left alone, he'll go absolutely ballistic."

As if in answer, an enormous crash sounded from somewhere down the corridor. The cop in the chair out-side the door sprang to his feet, his hand moving reflex-ively toward his sidearm, as Alison and Edwina peered past him toward the nursing station.

A medication cart lay in front of the desk, its drawers and contents scattered. Smashed glass vials leaked their potent fluids; pills and capsules rolled, and ointment tubes squished out their gooey contents beneath the feet of people rushing to help.

Sitting smack at the center of it all, looking if anything

rather proud of herself, was the large, confused woman who had not wanted to stay in her wheelchair earlier. Apparently she had not wanted to stay in it again, and had tried to haul herself out of it by grabbing onto the medication cart, conveniently stationed where she could reach it.

Unfortunately, the cart had responded to 275 or so unevenly applied pounds by obeying the laws of physics. Now a half-dozen nurses and aides scurried around, trying at least to sweep up the broken glass before attempting to move the patient. Among the scurriers was the nurse who was supposed to be special-dutying Victor Clarke.

"Oh, shit," Alison Feinstein said. "Grace'll kill me if I leave, and he'll kill me if I don't."

Her face looked drawn and terrible, with huge, exhausted circles under her eyes, and worry lines etched into her forehead, her teeth gritting so hard that her jaws looked wired together.

"Alison," Edwina said, "he's killing you, now. Don't let him, and don't let hindsight make you think your feelings clouded your judgment about Eric Shultz. You told me the story, and I don't think so. And you know I'd tell you if I did."

Alison's shoulders relaxed. "Thanks. That's the first sensible thing anyone's said to me today."

"You're welcome. Go on downstairs. I can baby-sit this guy until his nurse gets back."

"You're sure?" Alison paused, clearly doubtful but not wanting to be insulting.

"You think my skills might be getting a little rusty? Let's see, now." Edwina frowned in pretended thought. "Chest goes up and down, heart goes lub-a-dub, pulse goes thump-thump-thump. If any of those things stop happening, I yell for someone, quick." She looked up innocently. "Excuse me if I'm being too technical. But is that still the gist of it, or has vital-sign monitoring changed more than I realized?"

"That's the gist of it," Alison smiled. "Only, about *this* patient, there's one more rule. . . ."

"I know. Don't let anybody murder him."

• • •

With Alison gone, Edwina stepped to Clarke's bedside, to assess him. His heart rate was ninety-five, fairly regular, with a few premature atrial contractions. His pulse was decent and his color was okay, considering the dreadful circumstances, and his temperature only a couple of degrees above normal; this was to be expected, and he was on Tylenol and antibiotics. His IV bottles were full, and no medications were due to be given for another hour, nor did vital signs need to be recorded until then.

In short, nothing officially needed to be done for him, and there was nothing untoward in Edwina's simply staying with him until his own nurse returned, as long as she did not give actual nursing care. Still, even a visitor could sponge a patient's forehead; wringing a cloth at the built-in sink, she proceeded to do so, since if there was anything she hated seeing on a patient, it was a sweaty forehead.

Moving to the other side of the bed, she noted the settings on his respirator, which was cycling at a rate of fifteen times per minute at 75 percent oxygen, with very large tidal volumes. There was a lot of end-expiratory pressure dialed in, too; that kept his lungs from collapsing every time he exhaled, but also put quite a lot of pressure on his circulatory system.

Edwina made a face at the respirator's settings: They did indeed indicate severe respiratory distress with, at best, an iffy prognosis. Then she turned to examine the rest of the room.

Ordinarily, there might have been tidying chores: cards to open and display on the windowsill, flowers to arrange, plants to water, even coats or other belongings of visitors to put away. But except for Clarke and his necessary medical supplies, this room was quite bare.

From down the corridor, voices still cajoled and threatened the recalcitrant patient, who seemed to regard the wheelchair as something akin to the rack and the Iron Maiden. Rinsing the washcloth and hanging it on the bar by the sink, Edwina thought a slice of chocolate cake from the cafeteria might do the trick, perhaps accompanied by a scoop of ice cream and a glass of milk. She had used this lure several times, herself, over the course of her nursing career, and found it effective in persuading the most obstinate among her charges.

But now no one was asking her advice, and besides, she did not want to leave Clarke unattended. So, having nothing else to do, she sat down to read the nursing notes on Clarke's clipboard. And among these, she discovered an interesting fact.

"Martin," Edwina told her husband that evening, "no one has called to check on his condition. He has not had one card or visitor. His nursing notes would say so, if he had, but that section is entirely blank. It's as if he never existed, yet he's supposed to be a popular, well-thought-of physician. He even belongs to a country club, for heaven's sake. Wouldn't you think someone there would care about him?"

McIntyre, whose opinion of country clubs was about on a par with his opinion of toxic-waste dumps, looked skeptical as he applied a sharp knife to a large yellow turnip. He apparently felt that if he might soon be asking an innocent little child to try new vegetables, he ought to begin trying them himself.

"Well, his name wasn't in the paper. They didn't have ID on him confirmed in time. Could be people don't know what happened to him yet."

He frowned down at the turnip cubes. "How long are you supposed to boil these, anyway?"

"Eight or ten hours, at least," Edwina replied. The turnip, she felt, was an excellent food, if you happened to be a barnyard animal. "Then you drain them and mash them and butter them well. And then you throw them out."

Martin looked long-suffering as he dropped the turnip cubes into boiling water. "Funny no one from his office even stopped by, though," he said, pouring himself a glass of white wine from the chilled jug in the refrigerator.

Edwina averted her eyes and took a swallow of her seltzer water, comforting herself with the thought that at least she had not had to give up smoking; unloading two vices at once would have been too excruciating.

"And what about his family?" she agreed. "Maybe they didn't have children, but wouldn't you think one of them would have a relative who would show up, even just to see what's going on?"

McIntyre opened the refrigerator again, removing a plate of sole fillets. Carefully, he sprinkled them with a mixture of lime juice, herbs, and a few drops of olive oil.

A *very* few drops. Harriet had told McIntyre that a very plain diet cured morning sickness, and McIntyre had believed it. Boiled turnips and fat-free fish, Edwina thought. Yum, yum.

"Nobody's been to the house, either," McIntyre said. "The forensics people have been there since last night, working up the scene."

Sniffing, Maxie the black cat strolled in from the living room, where he had been shredding a sofa pillow. A few telltale threads of upholstery still clung to his front claws.

"Maxie," Edwina scolded him, whereupon he leaped to her lap and rubbed his face against her cheek, purring as he settled.

Secretly, she wished that Maxie would hurry up and ruin the rest of that sofa; once he did, she would get the new sofa she really wanted, and Maxie would get a catnip-scented scratching post, which was what *he* really wanted.

Then she realized what McIntyre had said. "Wait a minute, how come you know so much about it?"

Maxie sprang down and began parading, tail switching, back and forth in front of the counter, just below the fish dish.

You can have mine, she thought at him, whereupon he stopped, swiveled is glossy head, and gazed at her, so of course she had to get up and give him a tiny piece.

Meanwhile McIntyre tried to act innocent, which he was not; there was no way he could know when the forensics team was at the Clarke house, unless he'd made a point of finding out. McIntyre wasn't in the loop anymore, unless he put himself in it.

"Well," he said, his back turned as he measured rice into a cup, "I happened to be talking to Talbot. He says you're an okay broad, by the way."

Edwina grinned. This, from Talbot, was high praise.

"Did the forensics people give him any idea how the perpetrator entered?" Hearing herself, Edwina winced inwardly; hanging around with Talbot even for an hour always made her use words like "perpetrator" and "entered."

"Knocked on the door. She answered. Shot her where she stood, Talbot says, shoved her body aside, and shut the door again."

Edwina shivered, suddenly wanting a cup of hot tea instead of the iced seltzer. "The sensitive type," she commented.

"Right. The house is out of the way enough so no one heard the shot. She might have stayed there a while, only a neighbor was out looking for his lost dog, went up to her door to ask, and saw the blood spattered on it."

Maxie, licking at the olive oil on the fish, suddenly encountered a patch of lime juice and recoiled offendedly, shaking his paw in distaste.

My sentiments exactly, Edwina thought as he headed back to the predictable, if flavorless, comforts of his sofa pillow.

"You haven't said why you were talking to Talbot. It wasn't by any chance anything to do with me, was it? Checking up on the little woman, making sure she doesn't get in over her head?"

"The little *mother*," McIntyre corrected, and ducked, laughing, to avoid the potholder she sailed at him. "But yeah, I asked if he thought things might get rough again." Edwina's name and photograph had been in the papers often enough and in connection with enough successfully prosecuted murder cases to make any killer reasonably anxious at her interest. "Stupid question, though," McIntyre added, straightening. "How's Talbot going to predict a thing like that?"

"Maybe I should ease myself out," she allowed. "Let Ned hire some private people, if he wants. I could recommend some good ones to him."

McIntyre took the broiler pan out of the oven. The aroma of the cooked fish, which ordinarily she would have enjoyed, now more resembled the ripe emanations of low tide; pregnancy, having already ruined her appetite, had apparently also scrambled her olfactory sensations.

Briskly, McIntyre slid her plate before her: fish, rice, and turnips. "Mmm," Edwina said; convincingly, she hoped.

Maxie appeared in the dining-room entryway, noted that the menu had not changed, and shuddered delicately. *You've got that one right,* Edwina thought at the cat.

Maxie was lucky. His dry kibble didn't glisten. It wasn't moist, and horridly yielding beneath a fork. And it didn't smell so much like fish. Tentatively, Edwina put a tiny bit of the fillet into her mouth, chewed it quickly, and washed it down with water.

"I asked Talbot that, too," McIntyre said, tucking into his meal with evident pleasure. "About you staying away from the hospital for a while, just to be on the safe side. You know what he said?" McIntyre chuckled, remembering.

"No, what did he say?" Only about two hundred little bites of fish to go, Edwina calculated miserably. And then the turnip; good heavens, look at all that turnip. She put a bit of fish and some turnip together; maybe the tastes would cancel each other out.

McIntyre hunched his shoulders, squinted, and rasped out a credible imitation of Talbot's voice: " 'Hey, the broad's gotta have a life too, you know.' "

Edwina blinked. "Really? Talbot said that?"

McIntyre ate some rice, swallowed a sip of wine. "Uh-huh. I think he meant it, too. You know, for a dumb Irishman, Talbot is actually pretty smart."

McIntyre did not think that Talbot was a dumb Irishman; he only said it because it was what Talbot said, himself. Edwina didn't think so, either, and her already high opinion of Talbot's intelligence had just gone up another notch.

Also, she didn't think the turnips were all that bad, which surprised her; she had always hated turnips. Experimentally, she took another bite. Very odd. Fish, which had always been one of her favorites, now smelled and tasted awful, while turnips . . .

That was it: The sensory scrambling had gone in her favor, for once. Happily, she considered the possibilities. Stewed okra, and tofu. Liver sausage and smoked anchovies. She had always despised anchovies. Meanwhile, she continued cleaning her plate, mixing the fish and rice with the *excellent* vegetable while McIntyre watched, clearly bemused.

Why, boiled turnips were positively *delicious*.

"Martin?" Edwina said into the darkness a few hours later.

"Hmm?"

"Somebody managed not to set the alarms off, and found the respirator's oxygen knob without trouble, but didn't disconnect the respirator altogether."

"So?"

Edwina drew Maxie snugly into the crook of her arm. The cat wriggled luxuriously, and slept again.

"Well, it would have been more effective. And it's easy to disable the alarms, if you know how."

"Mmm. Somebody didn't know how."

"Or wants everyone to think so."

"Turning the oxygen down's not so complicated, is it?"

"It doesn't sound complicated, but there are lots of dials on the front of that machine."

"So maybe someone knew how to disconnect it, but didn't do it."

"Right. Because having that much knowledge, and a reason for using it . . . well, it could be potentially damning, couldn't it? Down the line when we start getting some possibles."

"We?" McIntyre chuckled sleepily.

"When the *police* do," Edwina corrected, and sat up. Sleep was just another of the little luxuries, like eating anything even halfway resembling a normal diet, that her body had decided to renounce for awhile.

Probably, she thought glumly, *it's to prepare me for what the nights are going to be like* after *the baby is born. If it's born.* But as usual, each time she tried confronting this idea, her mind skittered away from it like a frightened animal.

"After all," she said, "you're right: You could argue that anyone who can read can also find an oxygen knob on a respirator. It *is* marked. And respirators have alarms. Anyone might think of that, and try to be careful to avoid them."

"Or not think of that, and just avoid them by dumb luck."

Edwina frowned in the darkness. "Right. Anything any more technical, though, and we start getting into the guilty-knowledge department. And I just wonder if somebody realized that, and I'd still like to know why Clarke hasn't had any visitors."

McIntyre snored softly, leaving her to ponder the other question that continued bothering her: Why? What had Clarke and his wife done to make somebody hate them so much? The plan, clearly, had been to kill them both, only the plan had gone awry.

And that seemed strange, because in spite of his work, their hobbies, and their social activities, the overwhelming impression Edwina had received while listening to descriptions of the two of them was that neither had ever really existed at all.

Cars, horses, golf, the country club. Nothing about family. Nothing about close friends. No cards or calls, and no visitors, not even a minister.

It was as if, even before someone tried to kill them, the Clarkes had already been ghosts.

• • •

Eric Shultz sat huddled on the bus stop bench across from Chelsea Memorial's main entrance. It was late, and a chill wind fluttered in the flyers and announcements taped to the walls of the bus shelter: "Happy Hour Friday Night." "Healthy Volunteers Wanted for Metabolism Study." "Crystallography Dept. Dance Party: Be There or Be Cubic."

Eric shivered, crouching miserably deeper into his jacket. With a woolen hat pulled forward on his head and his collar up around his ears, he looked like any other poor slob heading home after the medical library closed. But when the medical school's shuttle bus came by, Eric did not get on. As it pulled away in a cloud of exhaust, he remained gazing brokenly into the hospital lobby.

The lobby was glass-walled and brightly lit; Eric could see the upholstered sofas in the waiting area, deserted at this hour except for a security guard in a blue blazer. Behind the guard were patient-admitting and information desks, the elevators, and corridors leading to offices, labs, the gift shop and cafeteria, and the emergency pavilion. Eric knew the whole place by heart; he could have gotten around it with his eyes closed.

Upstairs, many of the patient-room windows were dark; a few still flickered dimly with the glow of a television, or flared with the bright white overhead lights that meant something out of the ordinary was going on: a midnight admission, a resuscitation. Two nights ago, that light in one of Eric's own patient's rooms would have made him curse, even as he sprinted toward it; no one understood how tired he always was, as if his blood were thick with some slow-killing poison. After a while, only cocaine had kept him awake, kept him alert and moving through the never-ending nights, until last night when he had gotten careless with the stuff.

Now, after twenty hours of a sleep so deep it was like a kind of death, he would have done anything to cross the street, walk into the hospital as if nothing had happened, and go back to work. Instead he sat and stared, growing colder by the minute, brushing an occasional droplet from the end of his nose. Chelsea Memorial was only a few steps away, but for him it might as well have been on the moon.

Footsteps shuffled in the fallen gingko leaves on the sidewalk behind him. Turning, he saw three people coming up the street. Two were women, one gray-haired, the other younger, holding hands and walking together very fast, with determined faces and frightened eyes.

Eric knew the look; they'd gotten the midnight call. "A turn for the worse. We think perhaps you'd better come."

The women crossed the street, their shoulders unnaturally straight, as if stiffened against a coming blow. Behind them, a man in a black hat and overcoat paused on the curb, then glanced briefly at Eric before crossing, too. Eric hunched deeper into his jacket.

In the lobby, the women spoke to the guard, who allowed them to pass at once. Next, the man in the hat and overcoat went in, and was admitted with equal swiftness. He got into the elevator with the two women, and the doors closed in front of them.

Eric sat and watched. Tomorrow he would go out and score. Not a lot; things had gotten out of hand. Obviously, he would have to be more careful. Maybe it was even a good thing, what had happened.

He was sure he could make them take him back. There must be some kind of disciplinary probation, something. They couldn't dump him, not after all he'd been through. And once he *was* back, they would be watching, just waiting for him to screw up again.

Which would help him be more careful. And that was all he needed, wasn't it? To be more careful.

Things had gotten a little out of hand, was all.

FOUR

IT WAS PAST ten o'clock the following morning when Edwina eased her car to the curb in front of the Clarkes' sprawling suburban ranch house. The low fieldstone structure stood on an enormous landscaped lot curving around a blacktop cul-de-sac, with copper beeches, cedars, and blue spruces towering over a still-green lawn. In the side yard, a gray slate terrace bore clay pots of ivy and geranium, cast-iron patio chairs, and a glass-topped, cast-iron patio table with cast-iron grapevines twining up its legs.

A gray squirrel perched on the table, chattering as Edwina got out of the car. She walked up to the front door, viewing with a careful lack of emotion the faint stains remaining on it, then followed a slate-paved path to the back of the house.

The scene team had finished, and no one was around; the yellow crime-scene tape had been taken away. Edwina had thought there might be a housekeeper; someone, at any rate, had tried cleaning the blood from that door. But the rear windows of the house were without life or movement behind them, and the house had already settled into the stillness of a long vacancy.

The wide, deep backyard was quieter than the front; only an occasional distant hum of traffic out on the main road broke the silence. A black walnut fell with a sudden, soft thump; the squirrel eyed it brightly. Everything seemed almost unnaturally perfect, as if the place existed under a glass bell. Edwina stepped up to the back door, and peered in through the window.

A man's startled face peered back at her.

"Good God, but you gave me a scare. Who are you, anyway?"

Edwina took her hand away from her heart. "I didn't expect anyone, either. . . . That is, I *hoped* someone would be, but . . ."

She stopped, composed herself, and began again. "I'm Edwina Crusoe. I happened to be in the emergency room, the night . . ."

It was a completely inadequate explanation for her presence, but the man didn't seem to expect more, so she didn't offer it. She wasn't even certain, herself, why she had come, only that she had thought she might have a quiet look at the place. After half a morning of wandering around the apartment, she had finally given in to the impulse.

The man went on staring at her. He was tall, about thirty-five, with dark hair and very dark brown eyes, dressed in a pair of gray slacks and a navy blue jacket. He had the sort of face that showed five o'clock shadow at ten o'clock in the morning, but he was otherwise so intensely well-groomed that he might have been polished with emery paper.

"I'm terribly sorry," Edwina said. "Are you their son?"

He gave a short, unhappy laugh and returned to his task of loading manila folders into a cardboard box. "No. They don't have any children. No family at all, so far as I know, either of them. I'm the doctor's office manager. The police said we could come this morning and get some things we need."

No family; that explained, at least in part, the lack of hospital visitors. "I see. Of course, there must be a lot to do. I'm sorry, but I'm afraid I didn't catch your name?"

Edwina held out her hand, smiling pleasantly, and waited. All but the most boorish of persons generally responded to this, if one simply waited long enough.

She and the man stood in a linoleum-tiled hallway; to one side, beyond a pair of opened French doors, were a kitchen and breakfast area. The built-in appliances were new, and a lot of shiny, unused-looking gadgets lined the countertops: an espresso machine, a food processor, an electric mixer. Small knickknacks crowded the windowsills.

"I apologize," the man said at last, taking Edwina's hand and shaking it. "I'm Peter Garroway, and I'm not usually this rude. I'm upset, that's all."

He shook his head hopelessly at the box of files. "I'm not sure if it's that I'm a terrible manager, or if he's terrible at being managed, but whatever it is, you're looking at one hell of a mess, and it's all mine. Wouldn't you think he could at least have *alphabetized* them?"

Edwina smiled sympathetically, noting as she did so that there were no glasses in the kitchen sink and not so much as a bottle of dishwashing liquid on the drainboard. The only trash repository in sight was a small, plastic-lined straw basket.

Also, the place was as free of food smells as the model kitchen in a home-improvement center. Perhaps the doctor and his wife were unusually fastidious; more likely, meals cooked in this kitchen came frozen into the compartments of little tin trays, as odorless as they were flavorless.

"It does look like an awful chore," Edwina commiserated with the young man. "These are patient files you're taking away? But why did he have so many of them at home?"

Garroway sighed. "Don't ask me. I didn't even know they were here until I went looking for them at the office. He had—*has*, darn, I keep doing that—some research he's working on. A paper he wants to write, I think, but I don't know much about it. He doesn't talk to me about that kind of thing."

He stuffed more files into the box. "Whether the magazines in the waiting room are up to date, and whether the billings went out on time, which they always do, and whether the patients' restrooms have toilet paper in them. That he can talk to me about. But not that he's got all these files at home, and they're not in any *order*."

"Oh, my. That must be very frustrating. Have you worked for the doctor very long?"

Edwina stepped a little farther along the hall, so that she could see beyond it. Garroway was so intent on his unhappy chore, he didn't seem to care who she was or what she was doing here, and of course this suited her perfectly.

"About five years," he said. "And I shouldn't talk about him that way, especially now. I like the job and he's an okay guy, really, only . . . Hey, where are you?"

Edwina stepped back into the hall. "Sorry. I was looking at the . . . at the painting."

For an instant, his expression was sharp and unpleasant, but at her words it cleared. "Yeah. Quite an object, isn't it?"

The phrase did not even begin to do justice to the enormous canvas, dominating the living room with its garish slashes of orange and green. Edwina could not imagine what it represented, nor why anyone would want to look at it all the time.

"She painted it," Garroway said. "One of her hobbies. He wanted to hang it in the office waiting area, but there isn't a wall big enough." *Fortunately,* he did not add, but his tone made this clear.

"Do you mind if I examine it more closely?"

"Suit yourself." Garroway frowned at another folder, sighed heavily, and stuffed it into the box.

Remarkable, Edwina thought; he still hadn't asked her why she had come. But from the look of things, he had a lot on his mind. From the hall, she stepped onto a thick green wall-to-wall carpet that extended through the long, wide living room and into the dining room.

Both were filled with more furniture than Edwina had ever seen in one place before: sofas and settees, rockers and lounges, desks and chests and tables littered with more knickknacks, some quite expensive-looking: a crystal inkwell, a Fabergé egg, a small gold clock.

Glass-fronted cabinets in the dining room were crammed with china, crystal, and a forest of silver candlesticks. Tapestried chairs crowded up to the mahogany table, under a chandelier big enough for a hotel lobby. Silver bowls full of wax fruit on the sideboard were flanked by a glittering collection of cruets and decanters, lorded over by a pair of parchment-shaded lamps, resplendent in ruby Bohemian glass.

So many *things;* Edwina tried imagining the grasping hand, in its act of reaching for them. Was it the same hand that messed orange and green onto an enormous canvas?

The only books in sight were ornamental ones: Gilt-trimmed bindings of leather were ranged in sets behind leaded-glass bookcase doors in the living room. A few newspapers, a *TV Guide,* and a remote control lay on a coffee table in front of a big color TV. No pens or papers, no letters to be answered; no reading or writing things at all were in evidence anywhere.

Possibly those items were in the little office; Garroway had said the doctor was working on a paper. Perhaps his wife had a room of her own, too, where she read or answered mail. Possibly she even had a painting studio, where another angry, never-to-be-completed canvas awaited a furious finishing touch.

Outside the windows, the day remained bright, but a chill had begun seeping into the still and silent rooms. A swinging door led from the dining room into the kitchen. On one counter lay a handwritten bill of some kind. Through the open French doors into the linoleum-tiled back hall, Edwina could see that the box of folders was gone. It struck her suddenly that there had been no car but hers, out on the blacktop cul-de-sac.

The bill was from a housecleaning service, for work done this morning between the hours of seven and ten. The bill also totaled hours of similar work, two mornings each week, for the previous month. "Thank you!" the slip concluded brightly.

Gently, Edwina put the paper back down on the counter. The cleaning people must have departed just before she arrived. Thus the smears of blood removed, though inadequately, from the front door; thus the civilized appearance of the place, which had been the scene of a particularly uncivilized crime.

No further sounds of shuffling papers, boxes being moved, or file drawers being manipulated came from the linoleum-tiled hallway. Peter Garroway might have parked his car on the main road, beyond the cul-de-sac, perhaps not realizing that he would end up having to carry a heavy box.

A telephone hung on the wall in the breakfast area. Edwina pressed the numbers for the cleaning service, listed at the top of their billing slip. The pleasant woman who answered said that yes, they had indeed been notified of the tragedy; someone from the doctor's office had called early this morning, asking them to come only once a week until the doctor returned home, but to come today as usual. They were awfully sorry, the woman said, about the way the front door still looked; probably it would need repainting.

"Fine," Edwina said smoothly, "that's just right. I only wanted to be sure you'd gotten the message properly. Oh, and one other thing: Have the people who cleaned here this morning gotten back to your office, yet? I have one quick question for them."

The woman at the other end covered the phone for a moment; then a younger woman's cautious voice came on.

Cleaning help were always being accused of breaking, eating, stealing, drinking, or otherwise misappropriating the belongings of their employers. Edwina made her own voice as unthreatening as she could; frightening people only made them lie, sometimes even when they had nothing to lie about.

"I'm at the doctor's house trying to clear up a few things," she said, "and I wondered, when the doctor's office manager came by here this morning, did you let him in, or did he use his own key? Because someone seems to have forgotten a key out here," she lied fluently, "and I just thought it might be his."

"Office manager?" The woman's voice sounded puzzled. "I didn't see the office manager. Was I supposed to?"

"Oh, I'm sorry, I must be confused. Everything's so badly disrupted, of course, on account of the tragedy, but I thought Mr. Garroway said that he was going to . . ."

There was another muffled consultation, in the office of the cleaning service. Through the doorway to the dining room, Edwina could see the grand piano, with the framed photographs arranged upon it.

A tanned, white-haired man of about sixty, steadying a golf club. The man and an ash-blond woman with a tight, paintbox-brilliant slash of a red mouth and narrowed, ferocious-looking eyes. The same woman, seated astride a handsome Thoroughbred.

The cleaning woman came back on the line. "Mr. Garroway," she said distinctly, as if speaking to someone not quite bright. "He didn't have a key. He knocked, and I let him in. I always keep the doors locked when I work alone in a place."

"Very wise of you," Edwina said, but the woman kept talking, trying to straighten Edwina out.

"Only, Mr. Garroway isn't the doctor's office manager. I've met her, I *know* who she is."

Peter Garroway did not reappear in the hall where sunlight fell silently onto the linoleum tiles. By now, Edwina knew he wouldn't.

"Mr. Garroway came straight from the airport in a taxi," the woman went on instructively. "As soon as he heard about what happened, he flew in. And I felt so bad for him, he was *so* upset about his stepfather and even worse about his stepmother . . ."

The woman stopped. She cleaned houses with the doors locked but she had let Peter Garroway in, because he was the stepson of the murdered woman and the injured man.

"Who did you say *you* were, again?" the woman asked, the unease in her voice heightening a notch.

I'm not their son. They don't have any children.

Quietly, Edwina hung up.

"Let her look," Talbot told the officers over the telephone a little while later. Alerted by the suspicious cleaning woman, they cruised into the cul-de-sac and approached the house with caution. But a quick talk with Talbot defused their mistrust; fortunately, Edwina had been able to reach him.

Now they sat outside on the cast-iron lawn chairs, drinking coffee out of paper cartons and enjoying the sunshine while they waited for her to be finished. *Which I was before I started,* she thought irritably.

Bankbooks with surprisingly low numbers in them, statements for payments to the same creditors every month, and to a great many charities; checks to a stable, to the country club, and for membership in a number of horse-related associations, plus a pair of regular checks made out to cash for walking-around money every week constituted the only financial records Edwina could find. There was nothing suspicious about any of them; only the high amounts of the charitable donations and the low bankbook balances made Edwina blink.

Slowly, she walked once more through the quiet house, noting clothes all neatly hung in their closets and folded into their dresser drawers, toiletries in the bath, and a bundle of firewood on a hearth in a paneled den, which like the living room was exhaustingly overfurnished and watched over by the gray, unwinking eye of a giant-sized television set. There was also a TV set in the kitchen, and one in each bedroom, as if anywhere the Clarkes might go, they wanted to be sure of distraction.

But there was nothing really odd or interesting to be seen. Edwina wandered back to stare at the painting again, idly running her fingers over the yellowing ivories of the grand piano. A half-dozen sour, untuned notes informed her that nobody played it. Like the rest of the costly stuff with which she was surrounded, the instrument was window dressing.

Only Mrs. Clarke's painting studio seemed truly functional; a large, bright room at the rear of the house, it smelled sweetly of paints and turpentine. But there too, the acquisitive touch was in evidence: more brushes, sketchbooks, colored pencils, and tubes of paint than anyone could use, ranged around the neatly kept room.

Lots of things, lots of televisions, lots of money spent or given away, and no books anywhere except for the doctor's medical books in his little office; the people who lived here were experts at distracting themselves from something, but from what?

"You done?" The officers relaxing on the lawn chairs got up, crushing their paper coffee cups in their big hands. From a branch above, the gray squirrel chattered angrily at them.

"Yes. Thanks for being so patient. The door locks when you shut it, if you fix it from inside. Do you want to watch me?"

The two officers observed her tolerantly as she locked up; they had been ordered by Talbot to put up with her, she had done nothing to alarm them, and she had provided them with some easy duty. They wished every morning could be like this: comfortable and quiet. Only the back door slamming was loud as a gunshot.

"He was so smooth, I never had a clue that he wasn't who he said he was. You're quite certain he's not anyone you know? Or perhaps someone the doctor knows?"

Edwina had come straight from the Clarkes' house to Victor Clarke's office. The suite was a set of modern cubicles: pastel walls, beige upholstery, and mass-produced prints of soothing water scenes. Easy-listening music burbled from hidden speakers; the air smelled of soap and disinfectant.

"I'm certain I don't know him," replied Marion Glick. Victor Clarke's real office manager was a brisk, business-like woman of about forty-five, dressed in blue gabardine. She was tall and muscular, with broad shoulders, a squarish, solid body, and heavily boned wrists, her only jewelry a thick gold wedding band.

"Obviously, though, the doctor must know him, or at least he knows the doctor," she said.

"I'm afraid I don't quite understand." Edwina trailed the woman down a corridor whose doors opened onto examining rooms, a small, neatly kept culture laboratory, an X-ray-reading room, and a file room. The whole place seemed so clean, well organized, and well equipped, it might have come out of a kit labeled "Contents: One (1) Doctor's Office."

Mrs. Glick ran her hand along a row of manila folders, dozens of shelves of which completely filled the file room. She appeared to find nothing out of order.

"I mean," she said, repeating the process at another shelf, "there's no other reason for him to have been there. Is there?" she demanded, turning to Edwina with a small, grim smile. "He wasn't stealing valuables, after all. He wasn't just some ghoul who'd read the obituary and the newspaper stories, and decided to ransack the house when he knew it would be empty."

She stepped out of the file room, and snapped off the light. "He went there for something he knew about, something the doctor kept in a file folder. Or something he thought the doctor kept there. Which means," she continued, "that whoever it was knew the doctor. Otherwise, how did he know about the files, and why did he think he wanted something from them?"

"Yes," Edwina murmured, thinking for an instant that if Clarke did not recover enough to practice medicine again, his rather forbidding but quick-on-the-uptake office manager might like a job as a private investigator's assistant.

"So, what do you think was in those files?" Edwina asked.

"Possibly the doctor's research. The actual paper isn't there; he writes here, on the computer. But it was a historical paper he was doing, not a clinical account. I don't see why anyone would want to steal anything related to that; there's nothing secret about it. All the information comes out of medical journals; anyone could learn it, who wanted to do the labor involved. And there are no patient records missing from here."

Mrs. Glick looked up, and glimpsed an expression Edwina was not able to hide.

"I know there are a lot of files," the office manager said. "But believe me, I'm very familiar with each and every one, and I would notice a gap if there were one. It is my job, you see, and I take some pride in doing it well."

Edwina had no doubt of that. "Well, then, I am sorry to have wasted your time. You must be busy, what with referring the doctor's appointments and so on." She got up to go, then decided to play a small hunch; Marion Glick was so *very* businesslike.

"And I'm sorry for what's happened," she added as Mrs. Glick accompanied her to the waiting area. "From what I've heard, the doctor is a fine man."

For a moment, the office manager seemed to be thinking of something else. "Yes," she uttered brokenly, "he is. Immensely dedicated, tremendously generous. Too fine for . . ."

She glanced worriedly over her shoulder to the business area of the office, where two women in pastel uniforms were phoning the doctor's patients, referring them to other physicians, and marking them off Victor Clarke's appointment calendar.

"I understand," Edwina said quietly, "that Mrs. Clarke was somewhat . . . forgive me. One mustn't speak ill of the dead. But that she was difficult, in some says."

Actually, Edwina hadn't particularly understood it, not until she saw the photograph on the piano. But those ferocious eyes, and that slash of a mouth, and all the greedily collected *things* in the house made her quite sure, and

Marion Glick wasted no time in confirming Edwina's opinion.

" 'In some ways'?" The office manager laughed bitterly, causing the women at the telephones to glance up. "In all ways," she went on, no longer bothering to moderate her tone. "Why, I could tell you stories. . . ."

Edwina smiled. "Could you, indeed?"

One of the women got up from her chair. "Mrs. Glick? This is Dr. Grace's office on the phone. They want to know what to do about the wrist fracture and the shoulder repair Dr. Clarke referred to them last month. Should they send those patients to another medical office for good, or just give them a temporary referral? And . . ." The woman paused, glancing at Edwina.

"What is it?" Mrs. Glick asked impatiently.

"Well," the woman said, covering the mouthpiece of the phone with the palm of her hand, "she's not *asking*, exactly, but Dr. Grace's nurse is angling around, wanting to know why we haven't sent any patients to them lately."

Marion Glick flushed. "Tell her we haven't had any surgical candidates to send them. Not that it's any of *her* business," the office manager added to Edwina. "Anyway, I haven't been able to bring myself to go to the hospital, to see Dr. Clarke like that," she went on, changing the subject.

Edwina cursed the woman's professional decorousness. A single burst of emotion on the topic of her employer's difficult wife might be one thing, but a gossip session was another, the office manager seemed to feel.

"And the other staff don't know the doctor well," Mrs. Glick said. "I suppose we ought to send a card, but that seems *so* impersonal, and . . . well. Probably he wouldn't want me to go, anyway. The doctor is a *very* private man."

Then without warning she paused, lowering her eyes. "I know I'll have to tell someone what happened," she whispered.

Good heavens, was the brisk, businesslike woman getting ready to confess an affair? "We all admire our co-workers, when they're good at what they do," Edwina ventured, thinking to make it easier. But the other woman looked appalled.

"Oh, no, it wasn't *that*," she said.

Edwina sighed inwardly, wondering what in the world it could be, then, and feeling that it was time to snap the reins a bit; for one thing, her breakfast was settling poorly, after several hours of not settling at all.

"Look here, if you've got something to tell me, I wish you would just go ahead and say it. I only came by to let you know some files were missing, only now they aren't missing."

She took a deep breath, and steadied herself on the counter between the waiting room and the business area.

"So if you don't mind," she said, the words coming out in a rush she absolutely had not planned, "I'd like to go home right this minute and collapse, because I am quite miserably pregnant at the moment, and I don't feel like dancing around with you."

Gathering herself immediately back into a bright, sharp bundle of professionalism, Marion Glick fixed Edwina with a gaze that was one part clinical, one part female, and one part positively no fool whatsoever.

"Come with me," she said.

Half an hour later, Edwina reclined on the leather couch in the doctor's private office, with her feet propped on a cushion and a cold cloth on her forehead. On a table by her elbow stood a paper cup of ice chips and a paper plate with crackers on it.

"First one?" Mrs. Glick asked. "Shocking, isn't it? All your life you've been a person. Suddenly you're just some sort of *vehicle*. How are you feeling now?"

Edwina sat up experimentally. "Better, I think. I appreciate your help. Do you have children of your own?" She took a few of the ice chips, letting them melt on her tongue.

"Eight," Marion Glick replied. "All grown now, married or in college. Except for my daughter," she added with sudden pride. "She's on tour. Emily's a professional skater."

She drew a laminated snapshot from the pocket of the gabardine suit and handed it over. The dark-haired young woman in the photograph was tall and slender, wearing a pink tulle skating outfit. The scars puckering her right thigh were just barely visible, and whatever their origin, they appeared to be causing her no difficulty now, as fast-action caught her spiraling over the ice in a complicated, perfectly executed jump. She was beautiful, and obviously very happy.

"Lovely," Edwina murmured, handing the photograph back.

"Thank you. And my husband is a salesman, traveling a good deal, you see." Mrs. Glick's expression sobered again. "So I don't have as much to occupy my mind as I used to, what with Emily doing so well and the others out of the house. I suppose that's why I took it into my head to . . ."

She paused, seeming to struggle with herself. "To concern myself with the doctor's personal affairs. To snoop through his things and find something," she said at last, "something nobody else knows, not even the police."

"Because if you told anyone about it, you'd have to say how you learned it," Edwina supplied, feeling as if a bit of the puzzle had just snapped into place. "And you're ashamed to."

Marion Glick nodded, her words pouring out now that she had decided to speak them. "He was *so* anxious. The doctor, I mean. I'd worked here for twenty years; I knew when something was wrong with him. Hardly anything ever was."

She lifted her muscular hands with their short-clipped, bare nails. "He loved his work, he adored his wife, monster that *she* was. I shouldn't say that, but she *was*, and if he drove himself too hard, it was so she could have all the things she wanted. I thought it was awful, to tell you the truth, but if it made *him* happy, who was I to say so?"

"But then something did go wrong." Edwina swallowed a few more ice chips. She no longer felt ill; it was as if a brief, violent squall had passed by, and now the sun was out again.

Marion Glick nodded. "He'd seemed . . . unsettled, not himself for several weeks. Then a few days ago, I opened his mail as I always did, and brought everything in here on a clipboard for him, as I always did. Except for one envelope. That I didn't open, because it was marked 'Personal.' I put it on top of the opened things, on the clipboard, and I left it."

The cold cloth wasn't necessary any longer; Edwina removed it, and accepted the linen handkerchief Mrs. Glick offered. It was a beautiful thing, Edwina noticed after patting her forehead with it; large and crisply white, with a pale gray whip-stitched edging and the initials MG ornately embroidered in one corner. The embroidery was too ornate, in fact; still, the handkerchief was a lovely object.

"And sometime during the day, the doctor read his mail?" she asked.

"Not sometime. Exactly at eleven. Like clockwork. After that, he would have his coffee. From eleven-thirty to one, he saw appointments. Shortly after one o'clock, he ate lunch: tuna salad, no mayonnaise, on whole-wheat bread."

"A man of regular habits," Edwina observed.

Marion Glick looked gratified. "Exactly. So when he didn't come out for coffee, I thought something must be wrong. When he finally did come out, he canceled that afternoon's appointments. He had never done that before. And his lunch . . ."

She paused, remembering, and sighed heavily. "I found the plate and the sandwich in the wastebasket later. He hadn't even unwrapped it."

"You asked him if he was feeling well, of course."

"Of course. He looked right through me. And the *way* he looked . . . well. Miss Crusoe, when you've had eight children, you know there's enough to do and worry about in this world without imagining silly ideas. But I looked into that man's eyes, and I thought, *He's a dead man.* It was my exact thought. His eyes looked . . . dead."

"And after that?" Edwina asked. "How was he the next day?"

"He went through the motions, followed his routine. But it was as if he was just waiting for something terrible to happen."

Edwina got up. "So you went looking for the reason. You hunted for that letter and you found it. Where was it, Mrs. Glick? What did it say, and where is the letter now?"

Marion Glick sank into one of the leather armchairs and lowered her face to her hands. "What I did was wrong," she said through her fingers. "I found it, folded up small, in a pocket of his briefcase. He was with a patient at the time. I smoothed it out and read it."

Her fingers plucked the edges of the tissue she had taken from the box on Dr. Clarke's desk. "It said he was a murderer, and he was going to lose everything unless he kept quiet about everything. 'About everything'; those were the exact words."

"What did you do with the letter?"

The office manager sat up straight. "I put it at the exact middle of his blotter, where he would be sure to see it. I meant to tell him what I'd done. He might fire me, but I meant to make him go to the police. Obviously he took the letter seriously; it was eating him alive. So I took it seriously, too."

"What did he say? When he saw what you'd done, I mean. He didn't fire you, clearly. Why didn't he go to the police? And what finally happened to the letter?"

Marion Glick looked down at her square, clean hands, still methodically tearing apart the tissue. "He never knew. While he was with his last patient that day, one of the office nurses let a pharmaceutical salesman in here to wait, without telling me. At least, he *said* he was a pharmaceutical salesman. I'm supposed to screen people who come in here, so when I heard about it, I came to check, but the 'salesman' was gone, and so was the letter."

"The doctor never mentioned missing the letter?"

Mrs. Glick shook her head. "Perhaps he didn't look for it again, until after he'd left the office. At any rate, he never said a word about it to me, and after what I'd done, I was afraid to bring it up. But now I wish I had. Maybe if he'd been able to talk to someone, thing would have turned out differently."

"Did you ever see this so-called salesman?"

"No. I questioned the nurse about him. But she wasn't much help. Tall, dark-haired, and very clean, she said. She made a big point of how clean he was, as if that excused her letting him in here."

Edwina thought that if more people read the financial pages of their daily newspapers, fewer of them would believe that a clean shirt and a clean face guaranteed a person's honesty. But Mrs. Glick's next remark drew her attention back.

"That's another reason why I feel so terrible," the office manager said. "The letter specifically said Dr. Clarke should keep quiet."

"But then there the letter was, right out in plain sight."

"Yes. And now I think the phony salesman must have been the man who wrote it; when he saw it there, he must have thought the doctor wasn't following his instructions. He took the letter and left, and only a few hours later . . ."

Out in the office a phone rang; a file drawer slammed. A keyboard clicked rapidly. "You know you'll have to tell this to the police."

"Yes. That's why I decided to tell you: to make sure I would be able to. Without," the office manager added quietly, "breaking down."

"And the man who took the letter? Can you tell me anything else about him at all?"

"Well," Mrs. Glick said consideringly, "from the description the office nurse gave me, he sounds like your mysterious Peter Garroway, doesn't he?"

"Yes," Edwina agreed, "he certainly does."

A few minutes later, Edwina left Dr. Clarke's office, having given Dick Talbot's number to Mrs. Glick and extracted her promise to recite her story to him. Not until Edwina opened her bag for her car keys did she discover that she had tucked the linen handkerchief into the bag.

Turning, she took a few steps back toward the office. Then she stopped; Marion Glick would want her handkerchief returned. It was large and rather masculine, more like a man's thing than a woman's, really, except for the ornateness of the monogram, and probably expensive: too fine to give away casually. But there'd been something a bit glib about the office manager's story, hadn't there? Somehow, it felt manufactured.

And when people told manufactured stories, they often forgot bits or changed parts, given a little time. Edwina decided to keep the handkerchief for a while. She could always return it later.

The visitor sat by Dr. Clarke's bedside, reading silently from a black leather-bound book. It was wonderful how devoted he was, Ellen Biedermeyer thought warmly. Late last night, and since a little before lunchtime today, just sitting there as if he had nothing else to do but comfort the poor, injured man.

Of course, any ordinary visitor would have been questioned, and perhaps not even admitted, but a Catholic priest was different; even the young cop sitting outside the room understood that much. The priest had spoken briefly to the guard and come right in, just as he had the night before.

Ellen knew the priest had come last night, because she had been here and seen him; she was working a double shift today, on account of one of the regular nurses calling in sick. With the mortgage due and her husband only recently back to work after a long layoff, Ellen needed the extra money. That sixteen hours on duty was turning her into an utter zombie was beside the point; at least she would be a zombie with a roof over her head.

Loudly, Ellen yawned, then caught herself. "Excuse me," she said with a smile of embarrassment, then noticed the warmth of his deep brown eyes, as he smiled back at her.

"Long night," he remarked—softly, so as not to disturb Dr. Clarke. Really, he was wonderfully considerate and kind, Ellen thought. He held Dr. Clarke's hand when Clarke woke, speaking to him in low, soothing tones, unbothered by Clarke's terrible agitation, which no amount of morphine could completely quell and which made him very difficult to care for.

Also, the priest was sitting in the room's only chair, which was in fact a kindness; Ellen knew that if she were to sit in it, she would fall asleep, and if it were vacant the temptation might be too much.

"I could watch him for a minute," the priest offered, "if you'd like to run down and get some coffee. Or," he added quickly, seeing her inner struggle (dear *God*, how she wanted a cup of coffee!), "I could go and get some for you."

"Oh, would you?" she replied gratefully. "That would be so kind. Here, I'll give you the money."

He waved her off. "My treat. I've seen how hard you work." He took his coat, a beautiful black woolen one, from the little closet. "I think I'll run across the street to the coffee shop. The stuff in the cafeteria," he said with a smile, "isn't really coffee."

"More like battery acid," she agreed, laughing. Gosh, he was nice. Good-looking, too, and so clean. He smelled exactly like fresh laundry, and his fingernails practically gleamed.

But then the patient-transport people arrived to take the patient downstairs for X rays, a process that involved moving the bed, the traction, the cardiac monitor, and the respirator. None of this would have been so bad if all the respiratory therapists had not been busy with two resuscitations, a major trauma in the emergency room, and another transport.

Sighing, Ellen prepared to move the patient herself, with only the help of the two transport aides. It was a pain in the neck, but it could be done . . . she hoped.

Just for a moment, it occurred to her that she had not seen one of the transport aides before; a new employee, probably. Luckily, the police guards weren't too overbearing about letting people in and out of the room, as long as the people seemed to belong there and wore hospital uniforms—or priest uniforms, which of course amounted to practically the same thing.

"Okay," she said, "let's put the cardiac monitor down at the foot of the bed. Wedge it in by the footboard. I'll ventilate him and push the IV pole."

"Who's going to push the respirator, then?" the new aide asked. "It takes both of us to handle the bed."

Ellen had already disconnected the respirator tubing from the patient, and pushed the button that disabled the alarms temporarily. Now, with one hand full of the patient's Ambu-bag and the other gripping the IV pole, she couldn't even get around the bed to pull the power plug and unhook the compressed-air and oxygen connectors, much less push the respirator itself.

With the power still running, the machine's alarms switched back on and sounded a high, shrill *thweep* that to Ellen's sleep-deprived brain sounded like an air-raid siren. The priest, who had been about to leave when the transport aides arrived, reached out and pressed the disable button again, then glanced doubtfully at Ellen.

"I saw you do it," he explained, in apology. "Of course, I would never . . ."

The priest had introduced himself, naturally, when he came in, but his name had disappeared in the fog of fatigue blurring Ellen's thoughts. Feeling wooden with tiredness, she wondered if there would be an empty stretcher in the X-ray corridor, and if so, how she would keep from crawling onto it, herself.

"Don't worry about it," she told him. "Do you suppose . . . I mean, if I tell you what to do, could you help? It's just that I'm kind of up the creek, here."

In reply, he pulled off his black coat, tossed it onto the chair, and rolled his sleeves up. "Okay, ready for orders," he said a bit nervously. "I just hope I can do what you want."

"Sure, you can. It's easy. First, press the alarm-disable button again. Good, now turn off the power switch. It's there, at the bottom right-hand side of the panel. Now grab those high-pressure hose connectors. Twist the plastic collars, and they'll come out of the wall outlets."

Each connector sprang from its outlet with a little popping sound. The priest looked pleased with himself.

"Great," Ellen said. "Now, unscrew the screws that hold the power plug into the electrical outlet, and pull the plug."

Dr. Clarke was becoming agitated, probably because of all the noise and activity. "Look," Ellen told him a bit harshly, "I'm doing the best I can here. When we get downstairs, I'll give you some more morphine, but for right now, you're going to have to chill out."

Amazingly, Dr. Clarke quieted. Ellen felt bad about scolding him; his eyes, when they met hers, had been frightened if a bit unfocused. But she couldn't help it, and if she'd scared him a little, it was only for his own good.

Meanwhile, the priest continued trying to disconnect the respirator. "I'll be darned," he said proudly at last, holding a pulled plug in his upraised hand. "I did it."

Suddenly, Ellen did remember the priest's name: Garroway. He was Father Peter Garroway.

FIVE

"MARBLE FROM A quarry. Great damned blocks of it, white as mother's milk. Drill it out, winch it out, set it on a flatbed. Watch it all the way home, the damned fools don't drop it."

Michael Munson thumped his cane for emphasis, and with enjoyment. Zinnia had stationed his wheelchair in the early-afternoon sunshine near the window in the solarium, placed a cup of tea and some cookies on a tray by his side, and gotten out her needlework.

Seated beside him, she stitched swiftly and expertly, offering interested comments and questions; unnoticed in the solarium doorway, Edwina watched and listened, amazed. Munson, who usually spoke two or three words at most—and one of those a profanity—was actually having a conversation with Zinnia.

"How do you ever get a huge thing like that in your house?" the nurse asked, her fingers moving ceaselessly as her needle flew.

Munson shot a narrow glance at Zinnia, perhaps suspecting that he was being humored. But whatever he saw in her face reassured him. "Not house. Studio. Great damned roof door. Lift it in, with a crane."

He scowled ferociously at the cookies, took one, and bit into it. "Good," he commented grudgingly, washing it down with a slurp of tea, and took another.

Zinnia said nothing, only smiled, as Edwina came in with the magazines she had bought for Munson after leaving Dr. Clarke's office. In brand-new blue flannel pajamas, a dark blue velour robe, and what appeared to be a new, fleece-lined leather slipper on his uninjured foot, Munson was the very picture of the well-groomed hospital patient.

"Your mother," he said by way of greeting. "Damned meddler. Nosy old snoop."

"Mr. Munson," said Zinnia, in mild reproof. "Mrs. Crusoe is only looking out for your best interests."

The needlework was reverse appliqué: intricate silhouettes snipped into bright fabric, and the fabric fastened by a variety of many-colored stitches to black background cloth. The result was a stylized, richly textured design; reverse appliqué was highly prized among collectors of Caribbean folk art.

Noticing Edwina admiring the piece, Zinnia spread it out on her lap. The top silhouettes were of suns, moons, and stars; below were dogs, horses, and people, and at the bottom, fish.

"It is for Mr. Munson," Zinnia said, "so he has something to remember me by, when he is home and well again. Then all this hospital time will be only a bad dream, won't it, Mr. Munson?"

Munson glowered, grabbed a cookie, and chomped irritably into it. "Dream," he muttered.

Zinnia only smiled sweetly at him again, while her fingers turned cloth bits into a work of art. "Now, you must forgive my ignorance. But tell me, are you the kind of sculptor who carves a horse, and it ends up looking just like a horse?"

Munson straightened, thumping his cane again. His eyes flashed, his chin lifted, and his pale, pouchy face grew youthfully firm; Edwina could imagine him stomping about the marble quarry, questioning everything, criticizing everything, and demanding to be let down into the shaft, shouting orders and threatening dire consequences if they were not obeyed.

"By God, yes!" he snapped. "Nature! What good is a horse if it looks like a kindergarten scribble? Damn it, my horses are so real, they eat *oats!*"

"My goodness," remarked Zinnia, seeming as enthralled as a child hearing a fairy tale. "And do you carve these little oats individually, or a whole feed bag of them at once?"

Munson laughed, a rich, real-sounding laugh that filled the whole solarium. Suddenly, Edwina realized that Zinnia had been right: Munson was a handsome man. What had looked like selfish, miserable spite was really his creative vitality, cut off and pushed down, thwarted by his ill health, until it sprang back and began strangling him like some invisible, poisonous vine.

But now he looked ... happy. Quietly, Edwina left Munson and Zinnia in the solarium, where in his gruff way he was regaling her with stories of his early career triumphs: competitions and prizes, travel and acclaim. Zinnia, unlike any of Munson's other acquaintances, had not heard these stories a dozen times before; her musical voice lilted frequently in laughing appreciation.

No wonder Harriet was worried; no wonder she had begun to do and say things Munson perceived as intrusive. For if Edwina knew the warning signs (which she did; and so, apparently, did Harriet), Michael Munson was falling in love.

"I don't know," Alison Feinstein said. "All I know is, the last time I saw that cocaine, Bill Grace was taking it to put in the lockbox, in the medication room. And a couple of hours later when the security people came to get it, it wasn't there."

Alison slumped at the nursing desk on the surgical ward, where Edwina had gone to check on Victor Clarke's progress. "And the disciplinary board seems to think I know where Eric is, courtesy of Dr. Grace, who's developed some kind of vendetta against me, although why, I'll never know. I've saved his bacon more times than I can count. Maybe that's why he hates me."

"I see," said Edwina, placing a cup of steaming coffee in front of Alison. Alison hadn't mentioned rescuing any situations for William Grace, before. As a motive for hatred, it was pretty irrational. But then, so was Dr. Grace. "So, what's the *bad* news?"

Alison chuckled mirthlessly. She had been told that she was being summoned to a meeting, and had expected to answer questions about the events of two nights before, as well as about her own previous knowledge, if any, of Eric Shultz's drug problems.

But the gathering had in fact been an inquisition, directed at herself. After getting a whiff of the brimstone hanging in the conference-room air, Alison had quite sensibly refused to participate further without benefit of legal counsel, and had departed.

"The good news is, I don't know where Eric is, and I have no idea what happened to his little drug envelope. But I can tell they don't believe me."

She took a sip of coffee, cradling the cup in both hands. "And all the time, in their eyes I can see it: I'm the canary, and they're nothing but a bunch of hungry cats. All they want, and I mean *all* they want, is someone to hang the blame on, never mind if it makes sense, so they can say they've done something about an instance of hospital drug abuse."

After leaving Munson and Zinnia in the solarium, Edwina had spent an hour or so writing up notes, a sort of progress report to give to Ned; having things in front of him in black and white always seemed to reassure him. Now, at nearly change of shift, she sat beside Alison, trying not to notice how many patients' call lights were blinking.

The only other person at the desk was the ward secretary; the rest were in afternoon report. But patients always needed something at change of shift; it was a law of nature. Somehow they sensed the desire of the tired nurses to get out of there and go home, and it set off desires in themselves. Of course, what they really wanted was to go home, too; whatever they asked for, when all the flickering call lights finally got answered, was only a substitute.

"I don't get it," Edwina said. "If you've helped Grace out, he should want to keep you. Could he really be so insecure that instead it makes him despise you?"

"I don't know," Alison repeated. "But since the other night he's been intolerable. He wants to get rid of me and that's all there is to it. I'm going to get my walking papers, I just know I am. He's going to make sure I do."

Edwina frowned thoughtfully. "I wonder if he only said he put the cocaine in the medication box. You don't suppose he just tossed it out instead, so he could accuse you?"

"I haven't got a clue. And guess what? Pretty soon, I'm not going to care." Alison placed her palms flat on the desktop and pushed herself up. "I'll go do relief work in some godforsaken place where they don't give a damn who you are, as long as you've got food in one hand and medicine in the other."

Edwina got up, too. "Oh, I doubt it's going to come to that. People know how valuable you are, Alison. When push comes to shove, they're not going to let Grace railroad you."

Alison hoisted her satchel, grabbed a bunch of photocopied journal articles she would read in her few free moments over the next thirty-six hours, and straightened her slim shoulders.

"All I ever wanted was to be a surgeon in a big, university-affiliated hospital medical center. Be right on the cutting edge of things, you know? But there are plenty of other places to practice surgery, Edwina. Places where everything you accomplish doesn't come with a big, heaping helping of counter-productive crap."

She brightened as what looked like an army of aides, nurses, X-ray technicians, and other helpers came onto the ward, pushing a bed with what looked like all the medical technology in the world loaded on it. "Here comes your buddy. Looks like he survived his trip to the X-ray department. Wonders never cease."

At the head of Clarke's bed, squeezing an Ambu-bag with one hand and pushing a wobbly IV pole with the other, was a nurse whose plump face looked pasty-gray and who appeared to be in danger of actually toppling into the bed at any moment; the patient had slid or been moved so far toward the footboard that she had to extend her whole body and totter on tiptoe just to keep the Ambu-bag connected to his endotracheal tube.

Back injury, Edwina thought, remembering the number of good nurses she had lost to extended sick leave in her own days as a nursing supervisor.

"Wait a minute," she said, and the whole procession came to a halt. "Mind if I give you a hand, pulling him up? Easier to do it here than in that little cubicle of his."

"Such leadership skills," Alison murmured wryly; then her beeper went off. "Damn, duty calls. See you later, assuming I live through the night." She strode off down the corridor.

At Edwina's approach, a few grumbles came from the techs and transport aides, none of whom had been planning to do more than roll the bed back into the patient's room and get out of there before their own sacroiliacs came into harm's way. But the nurse looked so grateful at the prospect of assistance, Edwina thought the poor thing might be getting ready to faint.

"Why, he's even got a draw sheet. How convenient," Edwina remarked cheerfully. Seizing one edge of the sheet upon which the patient lay, she smiled her special smile and waited.

Reluctantly, under the influence of that smile, the aides and techs all took their proper positions: one at each corner of the draw sheet, and one in the middle, across from Edwina.

"One, two, *three*," Edwina pronounced, whereupon everyone lifted and pulled on the draw sheet, sliding it and the patient about eighteen inches up toward the head of the bed.

"Wonderful." Edwina stepped back, pleased to find that her nursing-supervisor smile, which in the old days she had honed to the bright, sizzling intensity of a ruby laser, still worked as well as it ever had. "Thank you very much, everyone."

The procession moved on. When they had all passed, Edwina spotted a small black leather-bound book on the floor in front of the nursing desk. For an instant she frowned after Dr. Clarke's bed, now being maneuvered into his room. But it could not have come from there; he was in no condition to read. Some other patient's visitor must have dropped it. Flipping its pages, she found that it was a prayerbook.

Edwina's own prayers tended to be made up on the spot; she had little use for prayerbooks. Still, it was a very nice one, and almost brand-new; its owner would want it back. She propped it up in plain sight on the nursing-desk counter, so that whoever had lost it could find it again.

Then she headed for Ned Hunt's office, partly to deliver the notes she had written up for him, and partly because the sight of Michael Munson and his nurse socializing so happily together had given her an idea.

Ned was the kind of fellow who would rather drink a cup of poison than face an argument, even an imagined argument. At Edwina's suggestion that he escort her to dinner that night, his eyes widened frightenedly.

"I'll call Veronica for you," she said, forestalling his chronic, unnecessary objection to anything even the slightest bit outside his domestic routine.

That Veronica Smythe had married Ned Hunt at least partly in order to enjoy his money was obvious to everyone who knew her, a fondness for idiots not being one of Veronica's major failings. But after marriage, she had not grown bitter, as did so many of the female fortune-hunters in Harriet's romance novels; instead, Veronica had accepted her situation in a spirit some people might have found cruel, had they not understood one other important fact.

"Hi, Veronica," Edwina said into the telephone. "I'm in Ned's office, and I want him to take me out to dinner. You don't mind if I steal him from you for the evening, do you?"

Veronica laughed throatily; Edwina pictured her with a cigarette in one hand and a martini in the other. "Darling, I'd kick up a fuss about it, but I know you wouldn't believe me. I'm in the middle of a ghastly delicious spy novel, and I'm going to go on reading it until my eyes bug out, dinner on a tray. You don't happen to want him overnight? Because if you do, I'll send the chauffeur down with his teddy bear."

Watching Edwina's face, Ned relaxed visibly. Far from being insulted by Veronica's attitude, he found it a relief; he was the sort of fool who equated honesty with love, and in this instance, he was correct. Veronica might make fun of him the livelong day, but let anyone else start giving him trouble and she would impale the offender's head on a spike.

"I don't think bears will be necessary," Edwina replied. "Ned's just busy finishing up something in another office, so I thought I'd call."

"Ned's sitting right there with you, listening to every word," Veronica said without rancor, "and you called because he was afraid to. I swear, the minute they invent them, I'm going to get that man signed up for a backbone transplant. There must be some genetic problem in the Hunt family: All the males are born without spinal columns."

Edwina thought the males in Ned Hunt's family were all born perfectly well equipped with spinal columns; the problem was that the Hunt family females, Ned's Mater in particular, were so good at removing them. After the upbringing he'd had, Ned was lucky to be able to stand upright.

Veronica's voice grew serious. "You are helping him out on this, aren't you, Edwina? Whatever's going on in the hospital? Because I don't know, it sounds a little . . ."

Beyond him, she meant. *More than Ned can handle. The sort of thing that takes a cool head and a keen eye, neither of which Ned has.* But these were things Veronica would never say aloud; she loved her foolish husband.

". . . not exactly up Ned's alley," she said finally.

"No," Edwina agreed. "That's why I'm borrowing him. But don't worry, I'll send him home before midnight."

"Oh, good," Veronica purred. "That way, he won't turn into a pumpkin. Let me speak with him a minute, will you, dear? And say hello to that gorgeous husband of yours. Ta."

Edwina handed the telephone to Ned. As he listened, a deep flush climbed up out of his collar. "Good heavens, Veronica, I'm not alone here, and . . . yes. Yes, that would be fine."

A shy smile twitched the corners of his mouth, even as embarrassment made him writhe; Edwina turned tactfully away, and pretended to be examining his Currier and Ives prints. As Ned hung up, Veronica's wicked laughter was still coming out of the telephone.

If only Veronica Hunt could be cloned, the lives of a lot of rich men would be vastly simplified, Edwina thought as she picked up the receiver, still damp from Ned's palm. Moments later, she had informed McIntyre that she and Ned would soon arrive at the apartment to freshen up before they went out.

"Fine," McIntyre said distractedly; he had been studying. "I'm up to my orifices in case law, here, so I'll just feed Maxie and order in Chinese for me. Where are you two going?"

Ned Hunt's eyes widened again as she pronounced the name of their evening's destination. "Good God," he said.

"I don't see why we're doing this," Ned complained a couple of hours later. "I just don't see it at all."

"That's why I'm driving and you're riding," Edwina told him, neglecting to add that this had been a metaphor for almost every aspect of their relationship for the past forty years, so why do things differently now?

Smoothly, she pulled the champagne-colored Alfa Romeo sedan up to the portico of the country club, having negotiated a row of speed bumps and passed the gate hut where a uniformed teenager shivered in the autumn evening chill.

"Yes, ma'am," the inadequately dressed teenager had said, barely managing to keep his teeth from chattering while the gold braid of his uniform trembled on his narrow chest.

Edwina thought that if year-round New England establishments were going to make their outdoor employees dress like Napoleon, they ought to do a bit of research into the costumes employed by that worthy general for his winter campaigns. She made a mental note to mention this to the club's commodore, or whatever it was they had here, should the occasion arise. Then she surrendered the car to the silver-haired gentleman who came around to relieve her of it, and resting her hand on Ned's ample arm, proceeded up the steps of the green-shuttered, white-clapboarded building that housed Victor Clarke's country club.

"I *still* don't know what we're doing here," Ned whispered.

"Just don't open your mouth except to put food into it, and you'll do fine," she replied *sotto voce*.

"So nice of you to invite me," she added in normal tones as a man in a black tuxedo approached. "I hadn't realized you were a member here, Ned." Of course, she actually had: Melinda Hunt belonged to everything that was anything, from Maine to Florida.

"One of our most valued members," the tuxedoed man put in unctuously. "Good evening, Mr. Hunt, so nice to see you again. Your mother is well, I trust?"

"She's fine, thanks. This is Miss Cr . . . er, Mrs. McIntyre," Ned said, remembering Edwina's instructions just in time. The quasi-legitimate ownership of two different names, Edwina found frequently, was handy when snooping among social types; most of them were so proud of their own old names, they never dreamed a person might fail to flaunt an even older, snootier one.

The club had once been an inn where travelers ate and rested on the crushingly long and uncomfortable stagecoach trip up the Connecticut valley to central Massachusetts, Vermont, and (for the superhumanly desperate or determined), points north. Now it retained its colonial air while boasting modern revenue-producing improvements: cocktail lounge, tennis courts, golf course, swimming pool, exercise facilities, and a baby-sitting service, children under the age of twelve not being considered suitable companions for adults bent on the pursuit of pleasure.

Sipping her lime and seltzer while Ned applied himself with dispatch to his martini, Edwina took in the large, warmly lit dining room of the grand old club. The tables were covered in white linen, decorated with candles and flowers, and glimmering with crystal and silver. Around them, prosperous, well-dressed people ate poached salmon, tiny parsleyed potatoes, and steamed baby carrots with orange-caraway sauce. Wine bottles gurgled discreetly; now and then a champagne cork popped. The waiters glided silently and efficiently among the tables, like well-oiled automatons running on stainless-steel tracks.

It all reminded Edwina of how, when she was eighteen, her privileged surroundings had felt about as appealing as a quicksand swamp. Even now, what she really wanted was her cozy flannel dressing gown, a nice cup of tea, and perhaps some of McIntyre's Chinese food; his favorite Szechuan dishes had always tasted horrible to her, so she supposed that in her present condition she might like them a lot. That she was not going to get any of these things anytime soon was brought home to her by one of the waiters, who bent reverently to proffer a tray of canapés.

On it were halved deviled eggs, their yolks as carefully decorative as wedding-cake flowers. There was nothing really wrong with the eggs, Edwina reminded herself firmly; only her uneasy digestive situation made each half-egg resemble a puffed yellow eye with a bloodshot drizzle of red caviar at the middle of it.

"No, thank you," she managed, and reached for a melba toast, discovering too late that someone had thoughtfully doused it in enough garlic to repel an army of vampires.

"You all right?" Ned inquired, popping his martini olive into his mouth.

"Fine," she gasped, and drank some water. "Why *did* I ever want to come here, anyway?"

"I think I'm beginning to figure that out," he replied, "and now that we *are* here, you might as well enjoy yourself. But you never much liked being a rich kid, did you? I'll bet this place just reminds you of all that."

Edwina stared. It was as if an inflatable Joe Palooka doll had bobbed up to deliver a knockout punch. "You're absolutely right. But how did you know?"

Half a deviled egg followed the martini olive. "Oh," Ned said carelessly, "I'm not so dumb all the time. Anyway, see that guy over there? He's the kind of guy you want to talk to here. People who know Victor Clarke and might gossip about him, right?"

Edwina turned, glanced quickly, and turned back. The object of Ned's attention was a lean, well-muscled man with bushy eyebrows and the sort of golden complexion that came from twice-weekly trips into the coffinlike interior of a tanning bed. He was sitting with a tall, blond, positively gorgeous young woman, also athletic-looking and beautifully tanned, and with another couple who, although they would have been perfectly decent-appearing on their own, looked white and flabby next to the golden pair.

"You're pretty quick on the uptake lately, aren't you?" she observed to Ned.

Ned just shrugged. "He's sort of the club jock. You

know—runs the marathons, gets his name in the club's newsletter, takes about a million vitamin pills every day. Kind of guy I always hated, back when I was in school."

Edwina ventured another swift glance at the fellow, just as the waiter arrived with two dinners: smoked salmon, potatoes, and carrots for Ned, and another plate for Edwina. Steeling herself, she kept her gaze averted as the waiter removed the silver cover; she had gotten herself into this, she was going to have to behave properly, and the quicksand swamp of childhood privilege had at least taught her how to do that. Polite people smiled, ate, and sipped water between bites; if necessary, they sipped like mad.

Surprisingly, though, the aroma that greeted her nostrils was not appalling; she looked down. On the plate were a half-dozen steamed oysters, a tiny dish of pickled onions, eight anchovies, and a small mound of stewed tomatoes. Along the plate's edges were arranged four flawlessly split Vermont milk crackers, and some slices of what could not possibly be, but in fact did turn out to be, Limburger cheese.

Ned Hunt smiled shyly. "Is that all right?" he inquired. "They can fix you something else," he added in earnest tones.

Edwina drank some seltzer water, being at the moment quite unable to speak. Of course one could not be a dinner guest of Ned's, on however short notice, without getting a dinner one could eat. After all, he too had emerged from the swamp of privilege, and in his case the swamp had been positively infested with good manners; Melinda Hunt had seen to that.

"No secrets between our families," she managed.

Ned smiled, meanwhile communicating to the waiter that he would like a little more butter, that the lady's plate was very acceptable, thank you, and that he would indeed have a glass of wine, all with about as many words and minute gestures as the ordinary person took to brush a fly off his shoulder. Once you got Ned out of the hospital and into his own milieu, he actually did function perfectly well; hungrily, Edwina ate an oyster.

"Who is this fellow you wanted me to look at?" The oyster was tasty; so were the onions, the tomatoes, and especially the Limburger.

Ned took a bite of poached salmon, chewed, swallowed, and had a polite drink of water. Dabbing his lips with his napkin, he smiled pleasantly. At the other table, the golden fellow took the golden girl out onto the dance floor as the orchestra at the other end of the room began the first number of the evening.

"Well, besides being the club's big athlete, Mitch Frankau is Victor Clarke's accountant," Ned said. "And the pretty girl with him is Sandra Carr; she rode horses with Mrs. Clarke."

Edwina would have liked to break her abstention from alcohol with a thimbleful of crème de menthe; after the dinner she'd eaten, her breath could probably have knocked over a lamppost, not to mention an accountant. She settled instead for a hasty toothbrushing in the ladies' lounge, and then hurried back to the dining room, where Ned had wandered over to Mitch Frankau's table.

Frankau was regarding Ned with the brand of amused boredom often used by the bright and physically attractive on the dull and physically less impressive, especially when the bright, more attractive one is also a snotty little jerk. Edwina nailed a smile to her face and approached the table.

"I thought I'd lost you," she said, putting a hand on Ned's arm and managing to convey, by the warmth of her expression, that this would have been a tragedy indeed.

A subtle ripple of interest went around the table: Who was this woman fastening herself to Ned Hunt's person as if she owned him? Certainly she was not his wife. As their glances flickered at her and away again, or, in Frankau's case, appraised her with unconcealed interest, Edwina had a moment to feel pleased with the care she had taken in her grooming, and with the concealing cut and fit of her dress, which made her look decidedly unmotherly.

"Huh?" Ned said, and then caught on, clumsily pressing her hand with his own rather damp one. "Not much chance of that. I just came over to, uh . . ."

"Wasn't that charming of you." Edwina turned on her *you're so wonderful* look, the one McIntyre had compared to the powerful flashlights poachers used to paralyze little animals just before they shot them. Combined with an artfully delicate application of cosmetics and the undeniable glow of pregnancy (although, thanks to the dress, not pregnancy's shape), that look certainly did the trick tonight; the orchestra had barely gotten through the first eight bars of "Stardust" when Frankau was on his feet.

"You don't mind, old man, do you?" he asked Ned, and without waiting for an answer took Edwina onto the floor. He had, of course, not asked her if *she* minded, but since getting him alone was exactly what she'd hoped for, she ignored this telling little lapse.

Clasped a bit too closely in Mitch Frankau's arms, Edwina let her feet move into the familiar rhythms; fortunately, he was a good dancer, so she didn't have to think about it. At the same time, she applied to Frankau a technique she knew very well, but had not used since finishing school.

"Making Boys Feel Comfortable," it had been called, and like the other girls she had studied it as if her life depended upon it. Later, she had abandoned the technique along with almost all of the boys, deciding that if they were not already comfortable, who was she to try to make them feel so?

Still, the lesson had stuck. Batting her lashes, smiling prettily, Edwina relaxed into the music and into the dance. "So, tell me all about yourself," she murmured, whereupon, of course, Mitch Frankau did.

•   •   •

"Mitch is very nice," Edwina said to Sandra Carr twenty minutes later. The two women sat in the ladies' lounge, fixing their makeup; Sandra was also smoking a cigarette, having lit it with a humorous, defiant air that Edwina liked immediately.

Sandra shrugged. "He's all right. He tries too hard. But that's okay—I'm used to men who don't try hard enough." She grinned at herself in the mirror, and applied more mascara. "Either that, or they want to design my dresses. Which is nice, too, but in my experience it's not exactly marriage material."

Edwina thought that if Sandra Carr really wanted marriage material, all she needed to do was walk out into the middle of the dining room and raise her hand; the resulting crush would probably require a squad of ambulances. Sandra wasn't just pretty; she was drop-dead gorgeous, and pleasant, besides.

"He was telling me about Victor Clarke, the doctor who was shot. One of Mitch's clients. What an awful thing."

Edwina eyed her own reflection critically. She didn't really need any more makeup, but she was going to sit here and apply more until she looked like Clarabelle the Clown, if need be, as long as Sandra Carr kept sitting here, too.

"Awful," Sandra agreed. "I have a horse up at the stables where she kept *her* horse. Saw her practically every day, and the two of them here pretty often." The girl dabbed a bit of stray mascara from her eyelid. "She was a weird person, though. Nice to the animals, but if you were a human being, watch out." She brushed some pencil onto her eyebrows. "I mean, I guess I shouldn't say this, after what's happened. But she was the kind of person who almost seemed to have it coming to her."

Sandra Carr made apples of her pretty cheeks, and applied more color to them as carefully as if she were retouching the Mona Lisa. "Not that I could have predicted it," she went on, "but once it happened, I realized I was expecting something all along. Like, sooner or later someone wasn't going to put up with her." Sandra put away her blusher and got out her eyeliner.

"Mitch said there's something funny about Clarke, too." Edwina examined her eyebrows, located a stray hair, and after some consideration plucked it.

Actually, Mitch had said no such thing. He had, however, drunk a fair amount of champagne, and probably wouldn't remember that he hadn't said it even if Sandra happened to mention it. Edwina blotted a layer of lipstick from her lips, and began applying another layer.

"Oh, him," Sandra said with a dismissive sniff. "She led him around by the nose like one of the horses. If she said jump, all he wanted to know was off which cliff."

"So, he must have been devoted to her?" Blast, what else was there to do to one's face? Frowning, Edwina found a tiny freckle and began covering it as if it were a blemish.

"I guess. I mean, sure, she was good-looking for her age, and he married her, so I guess he must have loved her. You know, wanted to please her. But he acted like she had something on him or something. Like he was almost afraid of her. Everyone at the club hated her. In fact, everyone pretty much stayed away from them both. They had, um, *acquaintances,* you know. But I don't think they had friends." Sandra snapped her compact shut. "It was like they didn't want anyone to get too close. I mean, you'd have thought they had something to hide."

As if the time before that hadn't existed, the surgeon at Chelsea had told Talbot. *Or as if they didn't want it to.*

"What about you?" Edwina's lashes were now so covered with mascara, they felt like bat wings. "You must have known her a little, if you were around her so much. Were you afraid of her?"

Sandra got up to face the full-length mirror, giving herself the once-over. "Nope. She could really give you the rough side of her tongue, especially when she got a couple of drinks in her. But I wasn't having any of that, you know; my mother didn't raise any doormats." She tugged at her short, smooth skirt. "One time, she had a few more than a couple and started yelling at him, and I was the one who walked her in here. I told her it was a shame the way she treated him, right out in public, and she'd better sober up."

"Really." Edwina ran a comb through her hair. "How did she take it?"

Sandra made a face at her reflection in the mirror. "It was awful. She started crying and blubbering out a lot of nonsense. Said he only put up with her because he had a guilty conscience, he was no better than a murderer. All a lot of drunk stuff, you know, the way people do when they're totally smashed. But the next day she acted like she'd forgotten all about it, so I did, too."

She turned, appraising herself from behind. "Do you think I look fat in this?"

Edwina burst out laughing. Sandra's legs went just about up to her earlobes, and in midnight-blue velvet she looked slender enough to slip through a keyhole with plenty of room left for the key. "You don't really think you look fat, do you?"

Sandra wrinkled her nose. "Nope. You're right, I guess I don't." Grinning, she put out her third cigarette. "We'd better get back out there before the boys send a search party. Although," she confided, "I like it better in here. There's something so relaxing about ladies' lounges."

There was, too; the atmosphere of cozily shared feminine intimacies was about as durable as one of the tissues from the box on the counter, but it was fun while it lasted, and for all her enviable gorgeousness, Sandra was a very nice young woman.

Edwina held the door as they stepped out into the carpeted hall leading back to the dining area. "What do you suppose Mrs. Clarke meant, about his being like a murderer?" she asked Sandra, carefully not seeming to be much interested in the answer.

"I don't know," Sandra replied, spotting Mitch

Frankau from across the room. "God, does he have to wave like that? I mean, you'd think I was the Holy Grail, or something."

Edwina giggled. Mitch Frankau *was* a little . . . intense. In their dance together, he'd outlined his childhood, his schooling, and the list of social, fraternal, and business groups to which he belonged, and informed her that he was a millionaire. A *self-made* millionaire, he'd emphasized, as if when a man told a woman that he had a million dollars, she was going to care a lot about where he'd gotten it.

As it turned out, though, he'd gotten some of it from Victor Clarke, whom Edwina mentioned as soon as she was able to get a word in edgewise, and whose accounting needs Frankau described as interesting. And after being plied with another glass of champagne and coaxed into yet another dance, Frankau had gone further:

Victor Clarke, it seemed, lived a very expensive life. His generosity to charity was more than laudable; it might fairly have been described as self-destructive. Mitch Frankau's main employment for Clarke consisted of keeping the bill collectors from the door: What with his charities, his cars, his clothes, his house, his wife, her horse, and her other expenses, Clarke didn't have a dime. There was, Frankau had confided, just enough on hand to bury her; if *he* should die, arrangements would have to be made even to provide him with a decent coffin.

"Mitch *is* okay," Sandra said now. "If I can't get rid of him, maybe I'll marry him. What the heck, I could do worse: He's straight, he's working steady, and he's got a blood pressure."

"And a million dollars," Edwina drawled.

"*And* a million dollars," Sandra agreed, laughing. Then she looked frankly at Edwina.

Sandra's big, blue eyes were wide and guileless; behind them Edwina could practically hear an efficient little brain, swiftly processing its way through everything that Edwina had said and asked in the previous twenty minutes.

"Dr. Clarke couldn't have been an actual murderer," Sandra murmured, "no matter what his wife said. Want to know why?"

Edwina nodded. Ned was getting up to pull out her chair, while Frankau bore down on Sandra with the bright-eyed, manic intensity of a game-show host on amphetamines.

"Because," Sandra said, "if he were a murderer, he'd have killed *her*."

And that, Edwina thought, was really quite interesting, considering that someone had.

"What if Clarke hired someone to do it? To wound him and kill her, only he got shot a little worse than he'd planned. Maybe to collect on her insurance? If she even had any; Frankau didn't know. Because it's pretty clear no one else has a money motive: There's no money."

It was late; Ned Hunt had gone home, and even McIntyre had closed up his lawbooks for the night. Edwina lay in the middle of the big canopied bed, drinking chamomile tea and watching him arrange the contents of his pockets on the dresser.

Keys, nail clippers, change: McIntyre stacked the quarters, dimes, and nickels neatly, putting the pennies aside to drop into an old milk jug. When the jug was full, he would spend a Sunday afternoon rolling up all the pennies while watching a football game. He usually got about thirty dollars out of the jug that way.

"Doesn't work," he said now of Edwina's theory. "Because whoever it was really did have another serious try at Clarke." He dropped the pennies into the milk jug. "Never mind that turning down his oxygen didn't kill him; it nearly did."

Edwina relaxed against the pillows again, while McIntyre sat down and began removing his shoes and socks. He put the shoes on his shoe rack and his socks in the hamper just inside his closet. When the hamper was full, he would empty it and wash his clothes; he had done these tasks for himself for years, and after marriage had simply gone on doing them.

Sleepily, Edwina considered the idea of calling Sandra Carr and advising her not to marry Mitch Frankau. He was the type who would not take care of his own socks, because he was a busy man and had a million dollars. He would expect Sandra Carr to do it.

On the other hand, Sandra was a smart, funny girl with a more-than-adequate mouth; she was the type who would tell Mitch where to stick those socks, and her first suggestion would not be the laundry hamper. So Edwina decided to let Sandra marry Mitch Frankau, in the unlikely event that she ended up wanting to.

"But the main thing is the gun," McIntyre said. Settling against the four pillows he allotted himself for his regular half-hour of recreational reading, he looked to make sure he had his necessary equipment lined up on his bedside table: glass of 7-Up, dish of frozen yogurt, six gingersnaps, and an aspirin tablet. Martin said an unvarying evening routine was the key to getting a good night's sleep.

From the way he always slept like a dead person all night until just before the alarm went off, Edwina thought this was probably true. But then, most of the things he said were true, including many that Edwina had never heard until he said them.

"Martin? What *about* the gun?"

He held up five fingers and began counting off on them, not taking his eyes from his book. He was reading Armistead Maupin's *Tales of the City,* which he said was the perfect antidote to law school.

"*If* you were hired to fake somebody's murder, *and* you went out to perform this thrilling task, *would* you do it with a large-caliber weapon, *so* your client would probably end up not being able to pay you the second half of your fee? Or at least not for a long, long time?"

Edwina sighed. "Nope. I'd do it with a .22. And even then, I'd try not to get a hip shot. All those big fat juicy arteries down there. And I still wonder about that nurse, too. Why kill her? Maybe she recognized the killer?"

"Or only saw him, and he didn't want to take the chance she could identify him later. I'm assuming it was a he," McIntyre added, "because of the size of the weapon and the way the nurse was killed."

"A big, strong woman could handle a heavy handgun *and* strangle Bonnie West," Edwina objected, thinking without much wanting to of Mrs. Glick and her powerful-looking hands. The office manager had phoned Dick Talbot as she'd promised, a quick call to Talbot had revealed. But Talbot had not been happy with her story; like Edwina, he sensed something false about it. Besides, even if Mrs. Glick was telling the truth, Talbot liked stories that simplified things, not the reverse.

Now Edwina frowned. "The trouble is, whether it's a man or a woman, that gives us one killer and three methods: shooting, strangling, and tampering with the respirator. And that doesn't seem right, either."

McIntyre nodded. "The really versatile types, the ones who will use any method that comes to hand, are usually the top hired people. Or wackos, not that there's a lot of difference. But a good hitter wouldn't have missed Clarke the first time, and certainly wouldn't have screwed up twice."

He thought for a moment. "What you could have, though, is some second-string shooter, local punk—somebody paid him to do the crime, but the punk messed up half the job."

"I see," she said slowly. "And then whoever *hired* the punk might have hurried in to try to finish Dr. Clarke off, but he—or she—couldn't do it right, either. That would account for all the different methods."

She sighed. "Actually, at this point I'm not sure we *have* to account for them, but I'd just feel better if . . ."

"Account for them," McIntyre said, turning a page. "Take it from an old homicide cop—and believe me,

Talbot's thinking about it, even if he's not saying it, yet: Two different methods almost always means two different bad guys. Either that, or a nut case. Hell, most perps, if they were smart enough to *remember* two different methods, they wouldn't be perps in the first place."

Edwina nodded thoughtfully again. "Okay. One of them would have to be able to get in and out of the hospital fast, though, and without attracting any particular notice. Especially on the late shifts, people who don't belong there stick out."

"A medical type, maybe." McIntyre turned another page.

"Uh-huh," Edwina agreed unhappily, still thinking about Mrs. Glick. "Which goes along with my idea that someone knew more about the respirator than how to turn down the oxygen, but didn't want to advertise the fact; a medical type trying to seem unmedical wouldn't tamper with a respirator in an obviously skilled way." Another visit to Clarke's office manager was definitely in order, Edwina decided.

McIntyre drank some 7-Up. "So, what it comes down to is this: Either Clarke hired a rotten shot with a crazy disposition and a cannon to kill his wife *and* fake his attempted murder, or whoever's behind this whole thing was serious and probably still is. What do you think?"

Edwina shivered, snug in her warm, safe bed. "I think maybe Victor Clarke is in a lot of trouble, and so is Chelsea Memorial, because whoever wants Victor Clarke dead is probably going to try again."

"Right," said McIntyre, and ate a gingersnap.

SIX

BOB WHITESIDE, HEAD nurse on the surgical ward at Chelsea Memorial Hospital, pulled his five-year-old Toyota sedan off the I-95 connector and into Chelsea Memorial's big ugly concrete parking garage. The thick walls of the garage turned WFAN's early-A.M. radio program into a hiss of static, and the car's transmission howled as the vehicle struggled up the ramp.

Not too many more miles in this baby, Bob thought as he slotted his card into the parking clock. He wanted to keep the car running, if he could, though, and for as little money as possible; he and his wife had bought some property in Georgia, and were saving every penny to build their dream house.

The red barrier bar at the top of the entry ramp rose automatically, and Bob drove through; it was six-twenty-five A.M. Maybe the next time he had two days off, he would get out the repair manual and have a look at the Toyota's transmission. After all, how hard could it be? It was auto mechanics, not brain surgery.

Parking the car and locking it on the top level of the garage, Bob hitched his canvas attaché higher on his shoulder and headed for the elevator penthouse. Early in the morning, it was beautiful up here, high above most of the city and looking out over Long Island Sound. Most mornings, before the haze settled in, he could see Port

Jefferson, but today a dark cloud bank sat on the horizon, covering the line between land and sea like a child's gray crayon scribble.

Bypassing the elevators, Bob swung into the stairwell and took the damp gray concrete steps down two at a time. He had twenty minutes to gulp a quick breakfast in the cafeteria and work on the staffing schedule for the holidays; the idea, while prudent, made him frown. As usual, the hospital would be short-staffed on Thanksgiving, and the census would be full; at least a few nurses would be sure to call in with half-assed stories about having the flu, and on a holiday, unscheduled admissions were practically a given. Nothing like big, salty ladleful of turkey gravy to put Grandma into the acute episode of pulmonary edema her doctor had been warning her she'd better watch out for, or a rousing dinner-table argument to pitch good old Pops into the heart attack he'd been threatening for years that Mom and the rest of the family were going to give him.

Bob shrugged mentally, his footsteps echoing in the concrete stairwell. Hey, one way or another, holidays made people sick. If worse came to worst, he figured he could volunteer to come in and work the Thanksgiving holiday himself; his wife wouldn't like it, but his bank account would, and at least it would get him away from his in-laws.

Thinking of that almost made him decide to work the holiday, no matter what the staffing situation turned out to be. The brief telephone conversation he'd had with his father-in-law the night before still had Bob's blood boiling. The guy was a moron who thought all male nurses were gay, who had not been convinced otherwise even by the birth of his own granddaughter, and who made no secret of his opinion that Bob's white uniform made Bob look like "some kind of pretty boy."

Bob, who had survived two tours in Vietnam and who had noticed that gay guys shot guns and hurled grenades as accurately as straight ones, didn't care if his father-in-law thought he was as pretty as a ten-dollar Easter bonnet, just as long as his wife knew he wasn't. But he hated the comments about his uniform.

Sprinting down the concrete stairs, he avoided brushing against the walls so as not to get grime on his razor-pressed, pristinely white uniform pants, and stepped carefully over the puddles of dirty water that collected in the landings' low spots, to keep the polish on his white shoes spotless. There was such a thing as pride in appearance, after all, and even now Bob was among the few and the proud.

He slowed, in case someone happened to be coming into the first-floor stairwell at the same time as he was barreling out of it. At six feet and 215 pounds, Bob exercised for half an hour every morning, and was pleased to believe that at age forty-three he remained as serious a collision hazard as he had been back when he was slogging through the jungle.

Which, he thought, his father-in-law was going to find out, if he kept having that smart mouth on him.

Someone was standing at the bottom of the stairs, on the stairwell's landing. There was no one outside the stairwell at all; it was still too early for the night shift to be out, or for much of the day shift to be arriving.

Bob took the last few steps at a sprint. To his left was a door leading to another stairwell; to his right was the one leading to the hospital. Only a few yards away in the cafeteria were Bob's bacon-egg-and-cheese on a toasted hard roll, his coffee, his orange juice, and his prune Danish. *Eat a better breakfast, feel better* all *day,* he thought, looking forward to it.

" 'Morning," he said, and reached for the door on the right. The figure on the stairwell landing turned; in that instant, Bob knew that he had made a mistake.

He felt the impact just behind his left ear, but he didn't have time to decide whether or not he believed it. For a split second, he thought he was back in Vietnam, where nothing was ever what it seemed and any minute could turn into a nightmare.

Ambush, Bob thought, really massively ticked off now. Distantly, he realized that he had been shot, and that only another fraction of a second had gone by, but time seemed to be moving slowly and he understood that he was becoming confused.

The walls of the stairwell landing slid past him like wet cement. Bob wondered how they had gotten that much cement all the way from the supply terminals, way out here into the jungle, and what the hell they thought they were doing with it, anyway, and then he knew the answer.

Damn, it wasn't *his* guys' cement; it was *their* guys' cement. It was *enemy* cement, and he was being buried in it.

"Victor Clarke was born in Cleveland. Went to public high school, and then into the army. After that, college and Johns Hopkins Medical School, internship there, too. When he was forty-two, he married. Same year, closed up his private practice and moved, lock, stock, and barrel, to Connecticut."

Edwina looked up from the sheet of information Talbot had handed her, at the scarred metal desk in the noisy squad room. At a few minutes after seven in the morning, men and women just off the night shift were smoking cigarettes, talking on telephones, and typing up their arrest reports on old manual typewriters. Only Talbot's desk sported a red IBM Selectric which he had bought and set up in the office, himself. It was twenty years old, but here in the squad room it looked like a rocket ship sitting in the middle of a Stone Age encampment.

"Dr. Clarke seems like an ordinary enough guy," Edwina said, "except for the sudden move to Connecticut. Anything about why he did that?"

Talbot shook his head. "Maybe the little woman had a yen for New England," he said sourly. "All that time gone by, who knows anymore what he had in mind? Who's even around, remembers enough so I can ask? There was nothing in the newspapers about him, I know that much. Bank records and tax stuff were all in order. He did have a lot of debt, but he cleaned that up right after he got married. Nothing in the newspapers but his wedding announcement. Then, bingo, he's outa there like a greased pig."

"What about her? Maybe you're right, and she was the one who wanted to get out of town."

Talbot scowled. "If she did, it was on account of she had too many parties to go to. Her, the newspapers were full of, in the society pages. Chairwoman of this, fancy-pants of that, bigshot organizer of the other. Her old man—the first old man, I mean—had a lot of bucks. And he had quite a story on him, too, only not hooked in to her, that I can see."

Talbot took a swallow of coffee so black it looked as if it had been drained out of the crankcase of a hot rod. "Guy found out he had the big C, didn't like the news. So he took his boat out on Lake Erie and shot himself. Body went into the water, they found the boat drifting a couple of days later, gun with only his prints on it, lyin' on deck. Never did find the body, but hey, it's a big lake."

Edwina sat up. "Really? How do you know that?"

Talbot laughed quietly. " 'Cause I know a guy on the force in Cleveland, he owes me a favor. I called him up and told him I wanted some twenty-year-old dirt, and when I say dig, he makes like a backhoe."

"That's how big a favor this guy owes you?"

"That's how many years inside he'd be doing now, I'd have given a sworn statement, all the things I had on him. That's why he's not around here anymore, either. I assured him, as a fellow officer, that he would like some other town a whole lot better, and he picked Cleveland."

Talbot delivered all this in flat, matter-of-fact tones. "Anyway, he sent copies of the newspaper clippings. Says he's going to try to get more stuff, too, but he's not sure there is any. Afterward, I guess, who cared? The guy was dead, looked like a suicide, case closed."

The copies were the slippery, shiny, muddy-looking kind that came out of microfilm-copying machines, but they were legible enough; the main story was a long, schmoozy feature on the dead man's successful life and tragic end. Edwina scanned the lead sentence of each paragraph, paused to read a few paragraphs more thoroughly, then turned to the obituary.

Finally, she looked up. "Dick, have you read these articles thoroughly yourself?"

He shook his head. "Just opened the envelope when you came in. Glanced at 'em." His pale blue eyes narrowed with interest as he grabbed for the sheets. "Why, something here?"

"Two things, actually." She reached across the desk, aiming a scarlet fingernail at the last paragraph of the suicide's obituary. "It lists survivors of Mrs. Clarke's first husband as his wife and his twelve-year-old stepson."

Talbot blinked. "I'll be damned. So where is he now, his mother's at the funeral home?"

"I've got a feeling he's here. I'll bet that's who I saw, out at the Clarkes' house, *and* who Victor Clarke's office nurse described. He'd be about the right age, anyway. But it's not his mother, Dick, it's his stepmother. In the feature piece, it says the kid was the suicide guy's stepson by a previous marriage of *his*."

"Oh, Christ on a lightning bolt. Doesn't anyone get married and stay married anymore?"

Talbot scowled at the newspaper articles. Having been raised in an orphanage himself, Talbot had strong opinions on the sanctity of the nuclear family, while his ideas about romantic love had been sullied, over the years, by the sight of a lot of recently deceased husbands and wives. If the wife was dead, usually the husband had done it, and if the husband was dead, the wife had. Talbot said it was cheaper and safer just to go out and get a dog, since a dog might bite you but if you didn't go overboard on the training routine at least it wouldn't be able to shoot you.

Now he shook his head in pained comprehension. "So he ain't the doc's kid, and he ain't her kid. They both just inherited the poor little bastard from her first husband, who got him from someone else. Where's the real parents, now, I wonder, tending bar and waiting tables on the moon? The whole bunch is starting to sound like they're from outer space."

Edwina scanned the newspaper articles again. There was no mention of the boy's name. The feature writer had called him "the deceased man's stepson." The obituary had called him "a stepson by a previous marriage," also without naming him. Probably this had been out of some imagined sensitivity to the bereaved child's plight.

"Kid must've felt like a freakin' Ping-Pong ball," Talbot groused.

Edwina put down the copies. "Did your friend in Cleveland send all the clippings? Did he send the social-page stuff about Mrs. Clarke?"

"He's not my friend. He's a guy. And yes, he sent all the clippings. Why, you want to know what kind of tea she drank at the charity ball?"

"If what I've heard about her is right, she wasn't drinking tea. Have you got the Clarke wedding announcement?"

Talbot handed it over; Edwina scanned it for the list of people in the wedding party. Mrs. Clarke's stepson would have been an usher, or possibly a ring bearer if he hadn't yet had a growth spurt. And from the rest of what she had heard about Mrs. Clarke, as well as from the length and detail of the wedding announcement, Edwina guessed that the boy had probably been presented with a simple choice: He could appear as a little gentleman in his stepmother's high-society wedding to a prominent local doctor, or he could eat bread and water and sleep on park benches for the rest of his so-called childhood.

And there he was, in the third paragraph, right after the champagne satin bridesmaids' dresses and the bouquets of roses and stephanotis. The boy's name was Peter Garroway, and the wedding had taken place just six months after the tragic death of the bride's previous husband.

But even that wasn't the most interesting thing about the wedding of the new Mrs. Clarke. Edwina turned from the society pages to the feature article and back again. This was simply too delicious to be true, as Harriet would say.

But it was true. "Hey, Dick, guess who her old husband's doctor was? The one who was treating the poor guy for cancer, only instead he went out on his boat and shot himself and fell into the lake?"

"You're kidding. Tell me you're freakin' kidding me."

Talbot's face was a long, lean collection of wrinkles, old acne scars, and liver spots. Most of the time, he looked like fifty or so, going on a hundred and twenty-five. But at the moment, he resembled a kid who had just gotten a puppy for his Christmas present.

"I love it," he breathed. "Clarke. Christ, I love it."

Just then, Talbot's telephone rang. "Yeah," he snapped, and his face changed.

No, Edwina thought, knowing perfectly well that thinking that never did any good. It didn't this time, either.

"Yeah," Talbot said again, grabbing for a notepad and scribbling on it. "South Frontage Road, first floor, stairwell of the parking garage. Okay, got it. Be there in five." He put down the phone, breathing hard and looking all at once like the chronically ill person he actually was.

"Son of a *bitch,*" he rasped, and swept all the newspaper microfilm copies to the floor. "You know, this jerk-off is really starting to burn my freakin' tail."

Twenty minutes later, Edwina sat in Ned Hunt's office. "They're trying to find out what car Garroway might be driving, whether he has any arrest record or military service, anything to say whether his fingerprints might be on record anywhere. They're locating his credit card records, and they're getting the description I gave them printed up, so the guards at the entrances will have it. Ned, they're doing all they can."

"Bob Whiteside," Ned Hunt said softly. "He was a fifteen-year employee. I gave him the award pin myself, at the employee dinner. He wore it, too. Not many of the employees wear their award pins."

In the half-hour after he learned of the most recent death, Ned had delegated to other people everything having to do with the murders. The public-affairs department was handling the press and reassuring patients and their families; security and legal were setting up safety sessions for the staff; grief and anxiety counseling was being arranged; and a special committee had been formed to expedite the deceased nurses' final paychecks and insurance benefits.

Now Ned fiddled aimlessly with some papers on his desk. "I'm being promoted again, did you know that?"

"No, I didn't. It's wonderful—congratulations."

"Mater's behind it, of course," Ned said sadly. "I think she wanted to get me out of the line of fire, what with all that's been happening. I'm going to be vice president in charge of special projects."

"That's . . . wonderful," Edwina repeated, knowing as well as Ned did what sort of special projects he would be in charge of: making paper-clip chains, folding paper airplanes and sailing them at his wastebasket, entertaining corporate visitors whose pompous blowhardiness was equaled only by their uselessness to Chelsea Memorial.

"Well." Ned made an effort to sit up straight. "My wife says I'm a hero, anyway."

Good old Veronica. Edwina made a mental note to take the wealthy socialite to lunch, somewhere rowdy and semi-dangerous. Veronica adored slumming. Ned pulled a tissue from the box of them in his desk drawer and blew his nose loudly.

"She says," he went on, "that when a shark swims with the sharks, it's no big deal, but when a guppy does, it's something. But Edwina, I don't want this promotion."

"But why not? It couldn't be . . ." *Any sillier than what you're doing now,* she almost said, but that would have been too cruel. ". . . any more work than you've already been handling," she amended.

"Uh-huh. But I'm used to this job. And the people here are used to me. I've figured out how not to get in anybody's way. Nobody makes fun of me." Ned looked glum. "In a new job I'll have to start all over being Mrs. Hunt's rich, dumb son, and people might *never* stop making fun of me. Sometimes they don't, you know," he concluded plaintively.

His talk of getting promotions on his own merits, Edwina realized, had been just that; he had known all along the source of his advancement. "What are you going to do?"

The words were out of her mouth before she considered them; clearly, what *he* was going to do was not the issue here. The news of his imminent move upward, along with his shedding of all real responsibility for handling anything connected with the murders, had brightened her spirits for a brief, foolish moment; if he didn't need her help anymore, she could abandon further snooping into what was becoming a most unpleasant situation.

But now she realized: Ned wasn't telling her all this just to make conversation. He wasn't looking for sympathy, either. "I mean," she corrected herself, "what do you want *me* to do?"

Ned brightened; those were the magic words. "Well, if all of a sudden there weren't any more trouble, Mater might change her mind about the promotion. She might decide I'm better off where I am." His voice grew earnest. "I *know* I'm better off where I am, Edwina. I just can't take any more promotions, but every time I try telling Mater that—"

"No more trouble," Edwina repeated evenly. "I don't suppose you'd also like me to abolish war, poverty, and famine? Ned, the police are *working* on this. They're much better equipped than I am, especially now, to . . ."

She stopped. Ned was looking at her with an expression she remembered all too well, having last seen it on the face of a five-year-old boy who wanted more than anything in the world to go on a sleigh ride with the rest of the children.

Only, there had been no seats left. The memory of that winter evening's sleigh ride, which Edwina had spent stuffed uncomfortably into one child's worth of space with Ned (he had been sucking on a particularly sticky peppermint candy cane at the time) was eclipsed only by the memory of his ecstatic sigh as the sleigh topped a moon-lit hill.

At the bottom of the snow-covered hill lay a lake, not yet frozen. In the moonlight, it resembled a sheet of foil. From it, as the horses' bells jingled brightly and the sleigh runners creaked on the packed snow, had risen a flock of geese. Honking, the birds flapped slowly across the round, white moon, while Ned's equally round eyes followed them wonderingly until they vanished into the darkness.

The sleigh had gone on, full of laughing children—all laughing except for Ned, who said nothing for a long time. Finally, his voice had piped up right beside her, his warm, minty breath gusting into her ear:

"Thank you, Edwina," he'd said solemnly, "for letting me come along." And he had broken off half the candy cane for her.

Well, *almost* half.

"I'd feel a whole lot better," Ned said now, "if I just thought you were going to go on paying attention to things. I mean, even if I *do* have to take the promotion. It would . . . it would help me. I'd feel better about Chelsea's employees, for one thing. I'd feel I was taking care of them better."

Edwina got up. She had a medical appointment scheduled for later in the day, and was trying not to think about it. "Okay, I'll keep an eye on things. If anything happens, I'll let you know about it."

She gathered her things and prepared to go, but Ned stopped her. "Edwina, do you remember that time you and I were playing hide-and-seek? Out in the barn, behind my mother's house?"

Edwina blinked. She remembered, but she hadn't thought Ned did; he was turning out to be a regular little fund of unexpected awareness lately. Perhaps she had been underestimating him all these years.

"Yes," she replied cautiously. "I remember, but what does it matter now?"

Ned looked up at her, his pale, plump face lighted with the pleasure of the reminiscence, even as his forehead furrowed worriedly. "I messed up the straw at the foot of the hayloft, and I left my glove on the third rung of the ladder, so you'd be sure to know that's where I went."

She nodded, smiling in spite of herself. "And that's how I knew you didn't. You made it so easy, I never even bothered looking up there. Of course, I knew you pretty well by then. I knew you were just laying a false trail for me."

Ned nodded slowly. Suddenly she remembered the rest of what had happened that day: Ned *had* been hiding in the hayloft.

"I guess there's probably some reason," he said now, "why someone wanted to kill Dr. Clarke and his wife. And even Bonnie West was right there, wasn't she? In the way somehow, probably. But Bob Whiteside . . ."

His voice trailed off as he stared at his hands, clasped on his desk. When he raised his eyes again, they were terribly sad. "What if there wasn't any real reason to kill Whiteside? What if it was just to lay some sort of a false trail, get everyone going in the wrong direction?"

Of all the things in life that bothered Ned, cruelty was the thing that disturbed him the most. He was the only person Edwina knew who kept a bottle of ether in the glove compartment of his car, so that if he should ever hit an animal and injure it irreparably, or come across one that someone else had hit, he could put the poor creature out of its misery.

"There's a reason, Ned," she consoled him, "and when we find out who's doing all this, we'll find out what it is."

Not that it would make Whiteside's death more acceptable, or any of the others', either, but the idea seemed to bolster Ned's spirits somewhat. He managed a shaky smile as she rose to go.

So she didn't have the heart to mention the other memory his hayloft story had triggered. In those days, the Hunts had owned a small red terrier who lived in the barn and whose job it was to exterminate rats, a task it had performed with great enthusiasm. Edwina, who was afraid of rats, had always admired the little terrier until one day in the barnyard when, looking for Ned, she had come across the dog killing an old, arthritic tabby cat.

It took only a few seconds; the dog seized the cat unawares by its scruffy nape and, in a couple of violent shakes, broke its neck. Even that might not have been so bad, but the dog went on growling and flinging the cat's limp body around, long after the cat was obviously dead.

And as she watched, Edwina had understood: The dog did not kill rats because rats were undesirable, or because doing so was its job. Both those things were entirely true, of course, and perhaps in the beginning they had provided some motivation.

But at heart, the dog had killed because it liked to.

"We'll find out why, Ned," she promised him again, hoping to herself that it was true.

Michael Munson waited in his wheelchair, in the solarium on the surgical ward. He was alone in the solarium, and that pleased him. A man who needed the constant yammering of other people did not end up becoming an artist. Besides, it was Zinnia's day off, and if he couldn't have her around, then he didn't want anyone.

From the window, he could see straight out over the jumbled buildings of the medical center, down into the street. At the center of it all stood the once-proud structure of the original Chelsea Hospital, with its red brick chimneys, tall, arched windows, and graceful granite façade. Massive in its time, its building had been financed by the wealthy, influential, and forward-thinking young men of a youthful city.

Now it was dwarfed by taller, more modern buildings

of metal and space-age glass, flashing like the knives of barbarians. Sadly, Munson gazed at the old-fashioned little hospital, once a symbol of scientific progress and the limitless future, now a relic of a bygone era.

Like me. Oddly, the thought no longer angered him. As always, he had risen early, cursing the doctor who had forbidden him his usual eye-opener of black coffee with a tot of brandy. By six, he had been out of bed and dressed, skipping the wash and shave, as he had begun to do lately. He was an old man, by God, and if he stank, who the hell cared?

Stumping about the strangely unfamiliar room with the help of his damned unfamiliar cane—what the hell had happened to his foot, and more to the point, whose fault was it?—he had begun shouting out for Marie, his old housekeeper, and Vincent, who for years had been his houseman, and demanding to know where the hell all his things had gone to. And where was Buster, the flea-bitten mongrel who bounded into his room every morning like a barking emissary from hell, but for whose stupid, slavering grin Munson would cheerfully have stepped in front of a speeding truck?

Michael Munson had slammed his cane down onto the strange, institutional-looking bed. Wrong, wrong; everything was wrong, and somebody soon, by God, would be made to answer for it.

And then, terrifyingly, he had remembered: Buster was dead. Marie was dead, and Vincent, too: Marie of a heart attack in her cottage in Florida, where she had retired, and Vincent of AIDS. Munson had paid for Vincent's care, although nobody else knew this: first in the hospital, then in the guest cottage by the pond that Vincent had always loved, in the garden behind Munson's house. He had been sitting by Vincent when Vincent died.

Vincent hadn't said anything. By then, the houseman had not been able to say anything. Michael had simply sat there and held Vincent's hand, his heartbreakingly skeletal, helpless hand, like a twig, in his own big, callused one.

But Vincent had left him a note, to be opened after his death.

"I have been happy in your house," Vincent's note said, "and I will see you again. When you think of me, do not cry."

Michael Munson had followed Vincent's wish, though at times it had been difficult. But now, in the solarium of the surgical ward at Chelsea Memorial Hospital and Medical Center, he began to weep. How could he have forgotten that Vincent was dead? How could he have forgotten Marie, and Buster?

I'm afraid, he thought. *I'm an old man, and I'm afraid.*

Not of dying, but of living; after he had realized who and where he was, he made a telephone call. Then he had washed and shaved, and put on the pajamas that Zinnia had bought for him, and the new robe to go over them. Seating himself obediently in the wheelchair, remembering that he was not supposed to walk, he had wheeled himself to the solarium. In a while, someone had brought him breakfast, which he ate dutifully.

Now he looked down into his lap, where Zinnia's gift lay. It was a single small block of very fine hardwood. Despite the few hours that she had known him, Zinnia seemed to understand: He had no time for mistakes. There was no second block of hardwood. She had accompanied the block with a set of small, sharp knives, appropriate for carving hardwood.

Munson turned the objects over in his hands. Zinnia was not here, but her gift to him was here. He touched the hardwood and handled the wonderfully new, mysterious-feeling knives with their bright, sharp blades. What might he make of these new and yet familiar sensations? What to cut, after a long life of cutting, into this strange, new stuff he had been given?

A providence, that he had been given it. Surrendering himself to whatever should result from this, Munson looked about and prepared himself, his fingers moving over the material and the tools, learning them by heart in a living instant, so that he might cut properly into the heart of the hardwood.

He had become, without noticing, a very old man. He had, he knew, little remaining time. He began to work.

After a while, the visitor he had summoned with his phone call appeared in the doorway of the solarium. Chris Whitsun was a young, very earnest lawyer, and not half the man his father had been. But old Whit had been dead for almost three years now, and Munson was not about to go hunting for another law firm at this late date.

Besides, the boy had grown up on Michael Munson stories, working around his dad's office in summers and after school, or wandering curiously about the studio when Whit came out to the house with papers for Munson to sign. By the time he was sixteen years old, Chris Junior had probably known more about the laws governing artists' creative and intellectual property, and their messy divorces, than many practicing attorneys.

Thus, in his own green way, the young lawyer understood what Michael Munson was all about. Certainly he'd had no trouble comprehending why Munson wanted him this morning.

"Hello, again, Mr. Munson," Chris Whitsun said, smiling and offering his hand. "Sorry you haven't been feeling well. They treating you all right here?"

Munson shook hands. "Never mind the frills," he growled. "You're as bad as your old man. Talked so pretty, he could make a jury think a cow pie was a chocolate cake."

Saying this, he noticed the gleam of pleasure in the young lawyer's eyes. "But watch it," he added. "You've got a ways to go before you're anything else like your old man."

"Yes, sir," Chris Whitsun said respectfully, which pleased Munson. "I know that, sir. Now, you mentioned wanting to draw up a living will. Can you tell me exactly what you want done, or not done, in the event you become . . ."

Whitsun paused, searching for the proper phrase. Munson had no difficulty supplying it for him.

"Die, you young idiot, if it looks like I'm going to die. That's what old men do, see? They get sick and die. And I don't want anyone stopping me."

Chris Whitsun blinked, but recovered swiftly. "I see, sir. And by drafting a living will, I'm to prevent anyone from stopping you."

"That's right. Brilliant, like your father. Only I want one other thing, besides."

Munson leaned forward. It was important that the boy get this right. His father would have gotten it immediately, even enjoyed it. But, just as his father had predicted to Munson, the one thing it didn't look as if Chris Junior was going to develop was a taste for the jugular. Well, one took what one could get.

"I want you," Munson said slowly and clearly, "to prepare a codicil to my regular will. In it, I instruct that if I get any goddamned tubes down my throat, or goddamned electric paddles on my chest, or any *other* goddamned things like food tubes, respirators, and so on, the rest of the will is null and void, and my entire estate is to be sold."

"Sold, sir?" Chris Whitsun's tone was inquiring, but his expression was becoming more enlightened by the minute. Maybe the kid had more of old Whit in him than Munson had thought.

"Sold, and the proceeds used to sue the *ass* off the hospital where any of those things happened to me. Sue 'em nine ways from Sunday, until they lie down and holler uncle. Got it?"

"Yes, sir, I've got it. And I'll make sure this hospital knows about it, too." Chris Whitsun closed his briefcase and got up. "You don't only want teeth in your living will. You want a set of poison fangs."

Munson eyed the youngster standing before him. In the light slanting palely through the solarium windows, he could almost believe he was looking at old Whit: yellow hair, deep-set eyes, the familiar outline of old Whit's stubborn jaw.

Only, Whit would not have said "poison fangs," and

certainly not with such relish. "You'll make a liar out of your old man," Munson murmured, feeling his mind beginning to wander again, as it had been too often lately; the exchange had tired him.

"Pardon me, sir?" The boy—could he really be forty years old, now? Munson remembered him in his cradle—tipped his head politely.

"He said you'd never be a cutthroat. He was wrong."

Chris Whitsun smiled again, more broadly this time. "Yes, sir. I'll have these things back by the end of the day, for your witnessed signature." He strode off to accomplish what had been asked of him.

When he was gone, Munson leaned back in his chair. Whit would have enjoyed the glint in the boy's eye. Maybe sometime soon, Munson would see old Whit and tell him about it, face to face. Or maybe not; information about the afterlife, Munson believed, was dispensed on a need-to-know basis, no matter what that dogmatic old scribbler Harriet Crusoe thought. Picking up the block of wood and one of the small, bright knives, he began to work on his carving again, feeling pleased with his morning's accomplishments, overall.

At two that afternoon, Edwina sat on the edge of an examining table in Chelsea's high-risk prenatal clinic. The physical exam, as always, had been deft and efficient, the drawing of blood from her arm quick and painless. All of it was familiar and unfrightening; still, her heart raced embarrassingly.

"A little nervous?" asked the obstetrics resident doing the routine checkup. He was tall and freckled, with carroty hair and thick glasses, wearing white running shoes, white slacks with a green scrub shirt tucked into them, and a leather belt.

If she had suspected anything immediately wrong, Edwina would have asked to see her own regular physician. Otherwise, she took whoever the clinic had on staff at the time she found convenient for her appointments.

"Very nervous," she confessed as he pumped up the blood-pressure cuff. She watched the column of mercury rise, felt the thumping of her quickened pulse fade as the mercury reached 120, and felt it resume again as the cuff's pressure was released and the column dropped back past 70.

"I don't know why I should be," she added, "except that I know all the things that can go wrong. Probably I'd be better off if I didn't."

The resident folded the blood-pressure cuff back up. His eyes behind their thick lenses were kind. "Ignorance is bliss," he agreed. "You realize the likeliest thing is that you will have a perfectly normal, healthy baby. Most women do, in spite of what you read in the medical journals." He smiled. "Besides, I'd rather have a healthy forty-year-old mom who's taking good care of herself than a twenty-year-old who thinks she's immortal, and keeps on drinking and smoking and not eating right. Are there birth defects in your family?"

Edwina shook her head. This information was in her chart, but she knew he wanted to hear it again from her. It was common for patients to remember things that they had forgotten, or were too frightened or embarrassed to say, the first or even the third time around.

"Or in your husband's? Toxic exposure, drug use, radiation exposure, anything like that?"

She shook her head again. "No, it's only my age that makes me nervous. I'm scheduled to get the amniocentesis results back in a couple of weeks, but until then . . ."

Looking surprised, the intern consulted her chart. "That's funny," he said, and paged back through it. "It says here your results are due back the day after tomorrow. Someone should have called you."

"The day after . . . but I thought it took eight weeks."

"Give or take. But if the lab's not too busy, and the cells culture up just right . . . All I can say is, there's a note here to call you for an appointment. I'm sorry, I guess it got missed."

This, she thought irritably, was the trouble with medical-center clinic care; the treatment was superior, but the office staff was often overworked, so that things could get lost in the shuffle. In her situation, and at her age, Chelsea's high-risk clinic was the best possible place for her, but she could already hear Harriet's I-told-you-so. Harriet believed democratic choices like clinics were fine, for people who could not afford aristocratic ones. She did not understand the difference between most clinics and this one, or pretended she didn't.

"We can schedule you right now for the appointment," the resident said, turning to the order sheet in the front of her chart. "Again, I'm pretty confident everything will be all right. But have you and your husband decided what you'll do, in case . . ."

"I thought we had," she said slowly. "Decided, I mean. But now that it's so much more real, so near . . ."

"The reason I'm asking," he went on gently, "is that I just had an OR cancellation for that afternoon. Usually it takes about a week to set things up, if you decide to terminate."

"I see. But instead, I could take that open spot. I could have the procedure the same day."

Like tearing a bandage off quickly, Edwina thought; it was the skill she had taken longest to learn, when she was a student nurse. Fast pain was better than slow pain, so everyone said.

The kindly resident was not much more than thirty, wearing no wedding band. "Perhaps you'd better discuss it with your husband again," he said. "I'll just set up this one appointment, and you can decide later about anything more. Call me if you have any questions."

He looked up. His eyes, she noticed, were crinkled around the corners with fatigue, the pale skin there resembling crumpled tissue paper.

"If I'm not on duty, anyone here at the clinic will be

glad to help you, or you can wait and talk with your regular doctor at the appointment. You'll want to do that anyway," he went on.

The kindness of strangers had always struck Edwina like a hammer blow, and never more than now. She felt her eyes prickle maddeningly with tears, and took a deep breath.

"Thank you. You've already been a great help. I think you'd better go ahead and book the OR. I'll call you if I . . . if my husband and I decide anything else."

She got up, feeling the nubbly institutional brown carpet under her bare feet, and held out her hand. "You've been very kind. I don't see a wedding ring on your finger. Why do I get such a sense that you know just exactly what I'm talking about?"

The resident laughed. "Um, well, since you've asked, I'm not probably ever going to be married, not the way you mean it, but my partner and I have adopted a little boy. Well," he amended, "not legally. But he's ours. His parents are dead, he's HIV-positive, and I have it on pretty good authority that no one's going to swoop down and claim him."

Suddenly, all was clear: the absence of a wedding band, and the presence of a tiny indentation in the kindly young resident's earlobe. When he was not on duty, he wore an earring in it.

"His name," the resident said, "is Geoffrey. The little boy's name, I mean. He's four now. And in essence, he's always going to be four, for as long as he lives. He's got other problems besides HIV." A little blade of sorrow carved a groove in his forehead; just as quickly, the cut healed itself.

"We adore him just the way he is," the resident said. Then he frowned, looking down at his pale, clean hands. "I'm sorry, it was unprofessional of me to say that. I didn't mean to try to influence your decision."

What he meant was that he and his partner were men, living together as any two loving people might, and when they had wanted a child, damaged goods was what they had been offered. Damaged goods like themselves, so some people thought, only they had made a romance of it, hadn't they? Little Geoffrey's good luck shone undimmed from the young doctor's tired eyes; he, of course, thought it was his own luck.

And perhaps he was right. "I know you didn't," Edwina said. A memory of herself and Ned wading naked in the wading pool swam into her mind, quick as a little fish, and went away again.

"I appreciate your telling me," she said.

It wasn't going to work, Eric Shultz knew; in a word, he was ratfucked.

He sat in his apartment, in a high-rise building only three blocks from the hospital. He paid the rent on the place from his stipend as a surgical resident, but his parents paid the rest—phone; lights; an allowance for food, clothing, and so on; vacations and little luxuries.

Which, Eric thought, was only fair: After all, he had done what they had wanted. His sister was a doctor, his brother was a lawyer. All that was left for him was Indian chief, which they certainly would not have enjoyed even if it had been possible for a nice Jewish boy from the Five Towns, and which, considering what he had been reading that morning, was not even particularly funny.

Still, in a way they did owe it to him; what *he* had wanted was to be a rock star. In the corner of his apartment now stood a Fender Rhodes piano, from whose *faux*-ivory keys he had learned to coax a total of six janglingly electronic chords, three major and three minor. Fortunately, you could get a lot of songs out of three major and three minor; among his college pals, Eric had been regarded as something of a musician.

He felt that by abandoning the fame and excitement he would have achieved through a musical career, he had put his parents in his debt, morally and financially, and his parents had no problem affording that debt. In forty years, Eric's father had parlayed a small corner grocery into something like a financial empire. As far as Eric was concerned, in fact, the only trouble with living on his father's money was the precise origin of that money.

Other people's fathers were professors, politicians, and power brokers, or at least chief executive officers. They wore suits, or blazers, or jackets with leather elbow patches. Eric's father was a butcher, and he wore a bloody apron, hands-on supervision being a key to customer confidence in the kosher meat trade. Every time Eric spent any of his father's money, he imagined it bleeding out of some religious chicken's neck.

Now from the wide plate-glass window in the dining alcove of the apartment, Eric could see the dusty-blue copper dome of the medical library, the twin metal-and-glass spires of the Howard Hughes Research Towers, and the low, yellow brick building that housed the married medical students' dormitory.

Eric dragged his longing gaze from this scene to the telephone, which sat before him on the cluttered dining table. He had been staring at it all day, willing it to ring, but now he knew it wasn't going to. He had played back the messages on his machine, messages from Alison, from Chelsea's chief of surgical staff, even from the hospital's legal counsel. Each series of messages followed the same pattern: urgency, concern, anger, and finally disgust. Alison had been especially dismissive.

"I wish I could have helped you," her voice on the machine had said. "But I guess you really don't want my help, so good-bye and good luck. And do me a favor: Don't keep in touch."

Her chilly tone made it clear how likely she thought he was to receive much good luck anytime soon. But behind her tone, he sensed her baffled hurt. She was his peer. Accepting her help would involve no loss of pride. She wanted to be his friend.

And that, he realized dimly, scared him; it scared him a

lot. All his life, brains and hard work had gotten him ahead; friends made things pleasant along the way, but when they were no longer useful or convenient, Eric had shucked them like a soiled scrub suit.

Why should anyone behave any differently to him? He didn't understand it. But he guessed he was going to have to find out, because his original plan wasn't going to do the trick. Chelsea Memorial wasn't going to take him back, not without some big-time help from someone. His morning's research had taught him that.

Over the past thirty years, there had been twenty-four cases of resident physicians caught abusing drugs on hospital premises. Three had fatally overdosed, the fools; one suffered brain damage and was now in a complete-care custodial facility up in western Massachusetts. *His* parents, fortunately, were lumber tycoons.

Of the remaining twenty, none had been accepted back into Chelsea's resident training program, and only two had gone on to practice medicine at all. One, scion of a blue-blooded Virginia family with high income and even higher political influence, had finally snagged a spot in a hellishly impoverished inner-city medical institution, probably because no one else with anything on the ball would even dream of going there; Eric imagined the brain-damaged guy in the custodial facility, shaking *his* head no at the prospect.

The other, a Native American himself, was spending the rest of his career doing well-baby care on an Arizona reservation, than which Eric would just as soon slit his throat. Eric knew about all this because he had slipped into the medical library earlier that morning, looking for information, and found that some fourth-year medical student with a taste for social history and an aversion to laboratory experiments had written a thesis about it. "Dismal Prognosis: Follow-up of Twenty-four Medical Resident Substance Abusers" was the title of the thesis.

Dismal is right, Eric thought, staring at the telephone. Somehow, he had to find a way to talk to Alison, not that

she was likely to want to talk to him after the way he'd
behaved. But maybe if he agreed to go into rehab—he
didn't need it, but the hospital would insist—*and* if he got
testimonials from the surgical staff, *and* if he abased himself sufficiently in front of the stuffed shirts the hospital
would summon up to cross-examine him—

Well, then, *maybe* he could get back on the residency
roster. It all depended on Alison. If she stuck up for him,
other people would, too; people respected her. And he
deserved to be stuck up for, dammit; he was too *good* to
be junk-piled for one mistake.

Thinking this, Eric dumped a heap of white powder
onto the bright surface of a tortoiseshell hand mirror he
kept exclusively for this purpose; once, it had belonged
to his grandmother. With a single-edged razor blade he
chopped the crunchy white granules into an even finer substance, drawing them out into a long, thin line. In a
minute, he would telephone Alison and leave a message on
her answering machine.

Rolling a dollar bill into a straw, Eric bent to administer the dose to himself. His grandmother's mirror, purchased by her father in Prague and carried by her through
Ellis Island and beyond, glimmered in the light from the
big plate-glass window.

In a minute.

At seven-thirty that evening, Edwina parked in front of a
large white house in a quiet New Haven neighborhood.
The house had a gambrel roof, a wide front porch, and a
front walk edged with whitewashed stones; the porch light
was on, but lamps burned warmly behind drawn curtains
in several of the house's windows, and as she waited for
the front-door chime to be answered, she heard music
playing somewhere inside.

The door was opened by a small, balding man wearing
horn-rimmed glasses and a maroon velvet dressing gown
over a white turtleneck and slacks.

"Yes?" he inquired pleasantly, squinting through the horn-rims. "Can I help you?" His voice was high and reedy, with a suggestion of something neither soft nor musical behind it.

"I'm terribly sorry to have stopped in without calling, but I have something of Mrs. Glick's to return to her, and I happened to be passing by. I'm Edwina Crusoe."

She held out her hand; the man shook it and held it briefly, gazing for a moment into her eyes and appearing to approve of what he saw there. Edwina recognized a man who was accustomed to making accurate assessments of strangers' characters; also, he had a good, strong handshake.

"Come in, please," he said, his manner suddenly serious and urgent. "I'm Rollie Glick. My wife isn't at home, and I'm very worried about her."

Inside, the house was all polished wood and white enameled moldings; thick, soft carpets; flowers and burnished brass. A pair of old ginger-jar lamps with fluted cream shades flanked an overstuffed chintz sofa; the armchairs looked deep enough to drown in, and a log fire crackled comfortably on the fieldstone hearth where a white cat lay toasting itself.

The music playing on the stereo was Gershwin; Glick snapped it off. "She's been terribly upset since the shootings," he said. "And it isn't like her to get upset. There's something on her mind, but she won't tell me what. She did say you were at the office the other day, though. Do *you* know what it's all about?"

Ranged around the room were photographs in silver frames: the Glick children in prom snapshots, graduation photographs, wedding portraits. Prominent among them all were pictures of the talented Emily: on the ice, in publicity shots, and just once in an enormous hospital bed, waving happily even though her heavily casted leg was hung up in traction.

"I'm afraid I don't know what it's about," Edwina said. "Where is Mrs. Glick now?"

He shrugged impatiently. "Practice. She's there several evenings every week after dinner, until about nine-thirty. It's the only thing that has stayed the same in our lives since the shootings. I've told her and told her what a mistake it is to get involved in other people's problems, but . . . What's wrong?"

To one side of the fireplace, a large bookcase was set into the wall. Trophies filled several of its dark wooden shelves; on the other shelves stood plaques, mounted medals, and ribbons.

"Nothing." Casually, Edwina got up to examine the awards, realizing suddenly that the practice Rollie Glick had mentioned was not choir practice, nor anything like it. Several of the ribbons were like ones McIntyre had won, although with an important difference; for McIntyre, marksmanship had never been an amateur pursuit.

"I mean," she said, "I'm sure she's upset. She admired Dr. Clarke very much, I understand. And then there's the matter of her job, if his office closes. By the way, Mr. Glick, what is it that you do?"

But Rollie Glick was staring at her. "Admired him? Is that what she told you? Oh, good heavens."

He downed his glass of sherry. "Miss Crusoe, it's Dr. Grace to whom my wife is devoted—the surgeon, you know. He healed our daughter; she'd never have walked again without him. But Marion was *furious* with Victor. Something happened at the office the day he was shot; I don't know what. Why she's saying otherwise, I can't . . . oh." The color drained suddenly from his face.

"This is a wonderful trophy collection," Edwina said. "Has your wife been shooting long? And how is it that she's become so proficient with so many weapons?"

"Dear God," Rollie Glick said, "that's it. Oh, heavens. I'm a weapons dealer, Miss Crusoe. I've been selling guns forever, to the shops and, where it's legal, by mail. Now, don't look at me that way, I've got all the necessary permits. But I'm afraid I've also got a basement full of guns, just about anything you can imagine, short of real terrorist stuff. I could never bring myself to that. I could have made a million at it, but . . ."

The cat on the hearth stretched extravagantly and turned over. In the silence, the log fire hissed and popped.

"The basement is locked, of course, and you have security."

"Absolutely. It's like a fortress. No one could get in there except me and . . . and my wife. She knows as much about it as I do; she has to, in case we ever had a fire or something."

"And do you happen to have any handguns down there? Heavy, large-caliber handguns?"

'Yes. There are always some of those. They're very popular items. And to answer your next question, yes, my wife has access to them. She also owns several of her own."

Worse and worse. "Do you want to hazard a guess as to why your wife was so angry with Clarke? Or," Edwina added cautioningly, "perhaps you don't. Perhaps you'd both better speak to a lawyer before either of you say anything more."

"She's not *that* good a shot," Glick murmured, as if only to himself. "She's determined, and she practices. She gets her share of wins. But she's apt to hit one time, and miss another."

He looked up, stricken, as it apparently occurred to him that in the shooting of Dr. Victor Clarke and his wife, that had been precisely what happened.

"Mr. Glick, do you think your wife shot the Clarkes? Was she that upset?"

Deliberately, she refrained from mentioning Bonnie West and Bob Whiteside, and the second attempt on Clarke. Mrs. Glick had the knowledge to get into the hospital unremarked upon, as well as the physical strength to kill Clarke's nurse with her hands, and at least a general familiarity with respirators, all courtesy of years in Dr. Clarke's employ. Possibly Bob Whiteside had seen something or known something about her that made him an obstacle, too.

Or possibly in her outrage, Mrs. Glick was coming to be like that long-ago rat-killing terrier; looking at Rollie Glick and at the pleasant, comfortable room, Edwina added that sad possibility to her increasingly long list of sad possibilities.

"Mr. Glick? Was she that upset? And . . ."

But Rollie Glick followed this part of the conversation just as accurately as he had the earlier parts. "You don't mean 'Was she.' You mean 'Did she.' Don't you?" He straightened under the weight of the maroon velvet dressing gown.

"Yes. I'm sorry, you're right. That is what I mean. Did she? Do you think she did?"

But at this final hurdle, Glick balked gallantly. "She couldn't have. I was here all that night, and she was with me. That must be what she's so worried about: being suspected. But, you see, she couldn't have. I can testify to it."

If she knows she was here, and he knows it, why is she so worried about being suspected? Edwina thought it clearly, but said nothing; he was committed to his story. Still, in the pleasant room filled with photographs of his children, Rollie Glick was lying.

SEVEN

"THE PRIEST IS visiting him now," the nurse told Edwina the following morning. "You'll have to come back."

With the deaths of Bob Whiteside and Bonnie West, the staffing situation on the surgical ward had gone from terrible to extremely critical; Chelsea Memorial had itself begun employing private duty nurses to fill out the schedule. One of these had been assigned to Victor Clarke, and no one, her tone implied, could interrupt a priest, or at least not while she had anything to say about it.

Edwina glanced into Clarke's room, glimpsed briefly the reassuring uniform of clerical collar and black shirt, and turned back to the nurse. "Somebody finally figured out he's here, then? It's about time. Has he had any other visitors?"

The nurse, an elderly, capable-looking woman with short white hair and more than a hint of an Irish brogue, shook her head. "Probably most people think he's still too sick," she said, tactfully putting the best possible construction on the matter.

"Dreadful, how the poor man suffers," she added. "He had a lovely card from his office, though, and one from his social club. Some of his patients have sent him notes, too."

"Indeed. May I see them?"

The nurse's face took on a flat Irish mixture of knowledge and honorable refusal to tell; she took her duty seriously, not that there was likely to be any confidential material in the doctor's get-well cards.

Still, it was worth a look. Behind the nurse, stationed in the surgical ward corridor, the officer guarding Dr. Clarke turned a page of the *New York Post*. "Mr. Hunt has asked me to take an interest," Edwina said, "and since I'm sure the police have examined the cards anyway . . ."

There was in fact no confidence left to breach, and mention of Ned did the final trick; his galumphing presence was familiar to almost everyone who had ever worked at Chelsea, regular staff or not. They knew him as the guy from administration who bothered to come around on the holidays, pushing a cart loaded with holiday goodies, and they appreciated him for it.

"I'll get the cards," Dr. Clarke's nurse said. "And I'm sure you can go in soon; the good father has a funeral to attend. Such a devoted man, not like some of the young priests today."

She bustled back into the room, where because of her size it took her a few moments to maneuver between the traction apparatus and the respirator, to reach the cards ranged thinly on the windowsill.

The cop in the chair outside the room rattled his newspaper, and winked at Edwina over the top of it. "She's a pip."

"I'm sure. Everything's been quiet, then?"

He nodded, as she noted the stack of reading material by the officer's chair; the only thing he seemed to have his eyes peeled for was the printed page. Still, the department had put the same uniforms on duty every day, so they would be sure to know the faces that belonged here. Probably he would notice anyone that didn't, and an affinity for the printed page could not very well be called a negative qualification, either.

"Poor guy," the young cop added, meaning Clarke. "Must be rough. At least he's got the God squad rootin' for him. I dunno if I'd like it, though, all shot up like that, if when I came to I saw a priest. Like somebody's tryin' to give me a hint."

"Here we are." The nurse emerged, placing a small stack of cards into Edwina's hands.

"Like maybe somebody's rolling out the welcome mat," the cop said. "Like maybe the Man Upstairs."

"I'll have a look at these in the solarium," said Edwina.

"If you take my advice, you'll be making sure it's upstairs your welcome is rolling from," the old Irish nurse scolded the young cop feelingly; he ducked behind his newspaper again.

In the solarium, Edwina found the television turned to a popular afternoon soap opera. Watching it were two nurses' aides and an orderly, whose avid interest in Betsy's secret marriage to Todd, Mandy's illicit affair with Biff, and Biff's fatal disease (which, of course, he contracted via an encounter with Betsy), seemed higher than their interest in their real-life patients' troubles, in the unlikely event they happened even to notice any of the patients' call lights.

Naturally, no patients were in the solarium, the soap-opera addicts having occupied all the good chairs. Briskly, Edwina snapped off the television, turned, and smiled at the outraged hospital workers.

"Scat," she said, whereupon they sloped off with all the affronted dignity they could muster, which was not very much. Edwina thought being paid to watch television made a good deal of sense; in fact, under no other circumstances *would* she watch television, as McIntyre discovered anew each year during the NFL playoffs.

It was not, however, an idea that applied well to persons already being paid to do something else. Briefly, Edwina considered tuning this TV set to the educational channel, and sticking some chewing gum behind the knob. A set showing only symphonies, documentaries, and nature programs was almost better than no TV set at all, especially in a hospital setting, since it acted as a natural repellent for persons vulnerable to the charms of soap operas. But she did not have any chewing gum with her, and besides, getting the knob off was a time-consuming project, so she turned her attention to Dr. Clarke's stack of sympathy cards.

Fifteen minutes later, she got up, disappointed. All of the envelopes bore local return addresses; no card bore any sort of threat, taunt, or other unpleasant message. The printed verses and brief, handwritten notes were divided about equally between get-well sentiments and bereavement condolences.

Distantly, Edwina remembered that the doctor's wife was to be cremated this afternoon; alone, Edwina supposed, except for the required witnesses. The idea was depressing. Who, she wondered, would be there to mourn her when she died?

Not McIntyre, she hoped, for the thought of losing him was so dreadful that she instinctively wished that pain on herself rather than to think of him bearing it. And not Harriet, of course. No, the proper send-off came from one's child, if one were lucky enough to have one, or from some younger person whom one had managed to befriend. Someone who would grieve, but not *too* much. Someone who could go on.

Edwina gazed at the envelopes in her lap; not one of them, even the handwritten ones, had held any truly personal message, malignant or otherwise. No real friends, Sandra Carr had said, and apparently the assessment was accurate.

"Am I interrupting?"

She started; the envelopes slid to the floor. McIntyre stood there, the very picture of tall, dark, and handsome, bending at once to retrieve the envelopes for her.

"I was thinking," she said as he handed them to her, "that I will allow you to outlive me only if you promise to get married again."

He smiled, slinging a friendly arm around her, smelling as always in cold weather of fresh air and bay rum. "I see. And have you chosen the lucky lady?"

"Don't make fun, I mean it. And no, I haven't chosen her. But she's got to be young and gorgeous, and very sexy. Someone," she added, laying her cheek against his shoulder, "to console you and breathe new life into your doddering old age."

"But Edwina," McIntyre laughed, smoothing her hair, "you've already done all that. I can't imagine needing it done again."

She pushed him away. "Right. You'll change your tune in a couple of months, when I'm the size of a rhinoceros." *If I am,* she added silently, and squelched the thought.

"Yes, dear, but you'll be my rhinoceros." He patted her shoulder in the humoring way that always made her want to swat him, meanwhile squinting at something on the floor by her chair.

"Hello, what's this? Taken up a new hobby, have you?"

"No. Martin, what *are* you doing down there?"

She *would* be the size of a rhinoceros, she realized, if all went well: large, ungainly, and immensely uncomfortable.

She hoped. Sending a wordless prayer somewhere (to what, for what, and on account of what she simply was not sure, but it came naturally, anyway), she put the thought of the coming test results from her mind and crouched beside McIntyre. There would be time to tell him all the latest news this evening, after he'd been fortified by a martini.

"What *is* that stuff, anyway?" she asked, peering down at the utilitarian brown carpeting that Chelsea Memorial had purchased in carloads at the time of the last remodeling; remembering the days when a nurse could see the sole of her shoe reflecting up from waxed linoleum, Edwina particularly resented this carpeting.

McIntyre leaned back, frowning as he examined the tan, slivery bits he had gathered up.

"Well," he said, "I'm not sure what the carpet is made of, but I'm pretty sure *this* stuff is wood shavings."

Just then a cry came from the corridor. "Help! I need help in here, right now! Oh, help!"

Even in desperation, the voice still carried its Irish brogue; striding toward Dr. Clarke's room, Edwina could hear the nurse babbling frightenedly.

"Oh, dear, perhaps I oughtn't to have taken this assignment. Oh, but I wanted to help, and I was sure it would be all right. Oh, dear."

Someone had pushed her down into the young cop's chair, where she sat fanning herself with a paper napkin. Inside the room, the overhead lights glared whitely down onto the patient's bed, which seemed (although this, of course, was not possible) to be entirely soaked with blood.

"Get another line into him," someone snapped, while someone else hung an IV with one hand and got a cuff pressure with the other. "Jesus Christ, how the hell could this have been apart for so long? Call the blood bank and get three units up, stat."

"I'd turned his alarms down," the nurse said distraughtly, "otherwise they'd be going off all the time when the young father and then the doctor were with him. I was going to turn them on again. But I must have brushed against his arm when I went in to get the cards, and knocked the tubing connection loose. Oh, dear Lord, please don't let me have killed him."

But it was beginning to look as if she had. From the hall, Edwina could see the cardiac monitor tracing and blood pressure readout; the doctor's heart rate was 190 and his pressure was 60 over 40. They were pumping in fluids and pressors as fast as they would go, but if what the nurse was saying was right, he'd been busily bleeding out for plenty long enough to cause his death.

Alison raced down the corridor, peeling off her latex gloves as she ran, wisps of her red hair flying out from under her green surgical cap. "Goddammit," she snarled, elbowing her way into the room, "what the *hell* happened here?"

McIntyre came up behind Edwina. "What did happen?"

She walked him a little way down the corridor, out of the press of traffic. "His nurse turned his alarms down because he gets so agitated when anyone's in there. Strictly speaking, you're not supposed to, but it's done all the time. Then it seems she must have accidentally knocked his arterial line apart, and of course she didn't know it because his arterial pressure alarm was disabled."

She lowered her voice. "*And* she forgot to turn his alarms back on again, although she hasn't said so yet; I get the feeling she's not used to such very sick patients. So when he'd bled out enough for his heart rate to rise and his blood pressure to drop, there wasn't any alarm to go off for that, either."

McIntyre whistled softly. "Boy, has this guy got bad luck, or what? How come the bleeding didn't stop?"

"It won't, not from an arterial line. Blood pressure keeps it running, so it doesn't clot. It'll just keep on pumping until there's no pressure left to keep it open. Which is about what happened here, it looks to me."

"Forty over palp," someone inside the room called out. Not a good sign.

"Oh, *dear*," wailed the old Irish nurse.

"Tell the blood bank I want fresh frozen, five units, and I want it *right now*. And get his other foot up, for God's sake, it's his brain needs the blood flow, not his toenails. How're we coming on that new line? Okay, open me an intracath and hand it up here, I'm gonna stick his jugular."

This last was Alison, her voice only slightly raised, her fury of moments earlier replaced by intense concentration. The fury was arriving from another direction.

"Uh-oh," Edwina said. The overhead page operator had sounded the code and now from down the corridor came an angry muttering, growing louder as William Grace approached. His bushy eyebrows bristled with outrage, his blue eyes seemed to blaze lightening bolts, and if thunderclouds could have gathered over his head, they would have.

He shoved past Edwina, knocked the code cart aside, and pushed a medical student out of the way, nearly spinning the youth off his feet. Planting himself before the chair of the weeping nurse, he seized her by the shirtfront, shaking her until her head bobbled. "You killed my patient! You killed my patient!"

In fact, he had no reason to think the nurse had done anything wrong; he was simply blaming the first nurse he saw—a common reaction for Bill Grace. She clawed helplessly at him, protesting in faint, breathy shrieks. The medical student grabbed Grace by the shoulders, and received an elbow in the abdomen for his trouble. Grace went on raging, spittle flying from his lips; McIntyre took a step toward him, but the young cop got there first.

"That's enough, sir. Take your hands off the lady. If you don't calm down right now, I'm placing you under arrest."

Startlingly, Grace's rage switched off at once. He unclenched his fingers from the nurse's uniform, straightened, and turned, gathering up his dignity.

"You're . . . quite right, of course," he said in subdued tones. "I was upset, but that's no excuse for what I did. I apologize," he added to the nurse, who wept quietly. One of the other nurses gently urged her to her feet, and began leading her away.

"I'm afraid that might not be enough, sir," the cop said. "Nurse, do you want to press charges against this man? He's not allowed to do that to you. I can arrest him if you want me to."

She looked over her shoulder, tears still streaming from her eyes, her blotchy face a miserable mixture of guilt, fear, and permanent disillusionment.

"Nuh-no," she managed, her breath coming in hitching gulps. "I n-never want to see him *again*. He . . . he can go to the devil!"

A small, embarrassed smile twitched Bill Grace's lips. "I guess I deserved that." Shoving his hands into his pockets, he stared at his shoes, still covered with paper OR shoe covers.

"Dr. Feinstein seems to have everything under control,"

he added. "Perhaps I'd better get back down to the operating room."

By now, any patients who could stagger or crawl had
come to their doorways to stare at the spectacle of a
doctor assaulting a nurse in the middle of a hospital corridor. Their disapproving eyes followed Grace as he strode
off, head high, looking neither to the right nor to the left.

"He's lucky they don't have any rotten tomatoes,"
McIntyre observed.

"What? Oh, you bet." Clarke's cardiac monitor now
showed a heart rate of 155, and a blood pressure of 90
over 60. The third unit of fresh frozen plasma was running
in, and units of whole blood had arrived. It looked as if he
might squeak through.

For now. Edwina turned to watch Grace enter the stairwell at the end of the corridor. He did not slam the door, a
fact she found obscurely troubling.

"Boy, that was weird," the young cop said. "Is he
always like that?"

"Yes," she said distractedly. "Or almost like that."

And that was it: almost. But not quite. For while
Edwina had seen Bill Grace perform many outrageous acts
and heard him say many outrageous things over the course
of his career, there was one thing she had never known
him to do before.

He *never* apologized.

"Darling," Harriet said that evening as she helped with
the dinner chores in Edwina's kitchen, "women in other
lands have healthy babies, well into their fifties. Even
when they're past sixty, some of them. It's a well-known
fact."

She cut another scallion into the salad bowl, nipping it
with quick, precise snips of an extremely sharp kitchen
knife.

Edwina considered the probable source of Harriet's
information; the *National Enquirer*, probably. Harriet

combined the keenest brain Edwina knew with a near-pathological fascination for human-interest stories, no matter now obviously manufactured. Harriet, it seemed, simply *wanted* to believe that somewhere there were no-headed boys with eyeballs in their belly buttons, animals whose eliminations predicted political events, and people having interesting experiences aboard unidentified flying objects.

Also, Harriet called civilized places "other countries," reserving the romantic term "lands" for areas of the world where the fields were still cultivated by hand, or the diet consisted chiefly of cows' blood.

"Now, dear," Harriet said, catching Edwina's look, "I only wish you'd try expecting the best *while* preparing for the worst. It's a much more balanced approach, and more pleasant for those around you."

She quartered a tomato with surprising savageness. "I was thirty-five when I had you, and you certainly arrived with all *your* parts present and intact. Thirty-five's not so different from forty."

Statistically, as a matter of fact, it was. But statistics meant nothing, set against the quaver in Harriet's voice. Edwina turned to her mother in surprised, guilty sorrow.

"I'm sorry. I didn't mean to upset you. It's just that I wanted to tell someone the news, and—"

She nodded toward the living room, where the sounds of pleasant cocktail-hour conversation mingled with the tinkling of ice in glasses. "It's not the time to talk to Martin about it."

But Harriet wasn't listening. Putting down her paring knife, she wiped her hands on the gingham apron she was wearing. Taking a tissue from the pocket, she dabbed at her eyes.

"No," she murmured softly to herself. "That's not true. And I think now might be . . ."

"Mother, what's not true? What are you talking about?"

"I wasn't thirty-five," said Harriet, picking up the

paring knife again and skewering a green pepper with it. "I was forty-two. Eighteen months your father's senior, you see. It was," she finished sadly, "the only thing he never knew about me. And I regret it a great deal. I'm ashamed of it."

"Mother! You mean you . . . you lied? But how did you do it? And that must mean you're really—"

"I am eighty-two years old." Harriet straightened, assuming a regal air, and lifted her martini glass. "Not bad for an old lady," she said, "if I do mention it, myself."

She sipped. "I tell you this now because I simply cannot go on watching *you* go on torturing yourself. Your age is a factor in your situation, of course, and you do have some control over what happens. But from the first instant you become a mother, my dear, you begin *losing* control. And you might as well get used to it."

She drank once more from the martini glass and set it down. "*If* you have a child, some day it will want to cross the street. It will want to ride a bicycle. Or, God forbid, a horse. And you will have to let it, and not seem a bit afraid, even when you are very afraid."

Edwina had a clear mental picture of Harriet, turning away from the riding stable at the estate in Litchfield and marching alone back up to the house. It had been six-year-old Edwina's first try at the jumps, and she had felt quite hurt at her mother's casual departing wave. Now, though, she understood what the gesture must have cost Harriet.

"I altered my birth certificate and lied on my citizenship papers," Harriet said, "when I emigrated from Canada. I swore my family to my secret, what family I had left after that terrible, *awful* war. I knew I wanted to marry your father, you see."

"And you were worried that he might think you were too old?" The idea was ridiculous on the face of it; even now, Harriet had enough energy for four twenty-year-olds.

"Yes, or that his family might. And what a foolish worry it was, considering the way things turned out. Like so many of my worries. Take a lesson from my experience, darling, won't you? Since otherwise I hardly see the point of having had it."

"Yes, Mother," Edwina replied faintly, swallowing a hundred questions.

"And if you ever breathe a word of what I've just told you," Harriet added, "naturally I'll be forced to kill you. Oh, not by any violent means, of course." She covered the salad, placed it in the refrigerator, and laughed. "I'll simply *advise* you to death, as my mother did me. I watched you that day, you know, when you took your first jumps. I saw you just now, remembering it."

Harriet dusted her smooth white hands together and removed her apron. "You were on Stryker, I think, that terrible black Arabian. Awful-tempered beast, but your father *would* put you to school on the worst horse in the stable; he said it would prepare you for daily life."

Edwina blinked, remembering Stryker, whose muscular beauty had concealed a heart of pure brimstone; the horse had been inclined to behave beautifully in public and to bite when there were no witnesses. E. R. was right, she thought, unsure whether she wanted to absorb any more revelations.

"On the horse? But you were . . ."

"At the upstairs window, with your father's binoculars in one hand and the other hand pressed over my mouth, to keep myself from squeaking in fright. You looked," Harriet said, "positively lovely. And I've always wanted to tell you so."

She took Edwina's arm. "As you do now. Motherhood agrees with you, and I shall have my fingers crossed for you, the day after tomorrow. Now, let's go in, darling, and visit with your guest."

Speechless, Edwina allowed herself to be led into the living room, where McIntyre and Alison Feinstein were nibbling cheese biscuits and chatting happily over drinks. Between Victor Clarke's near-exsanguination and her own ongoing troubles with the hospital administration, Alison had earned a pleasant evening, but now, with her red hair loosened and her makeup on, wearing a green velvet dress and pale green stockings, she looked so lovely that Edwina felt, briefly, a pang of jealousy. Then Martin glanced up and winked at her, and she called herself ten kinds of an idiot.

"Penny for your thoughts," he said, coming to her side as Harriet seated herself beside Alison. Harriet believed it was her solemn duty to socialize easily and expertly; also, she wanted to pump Alison about Michael Munson's medical condition.

Edwina hoped her mother wouldn't be too unhappy with the news she was about to hear; the neurologist, Alison had already confided privately to Edwina, was not very encouraging. Munson's foot numbness resulted from a series of tiny strokes; not only was the numbness unlikely to recede, but he could have a larger stroke at any time. Also, his infection wasn't responding; an IV had been started, so he could get big-time antibiotic treatment.

"We find out the day after tomorrow," Edwina told McIntyre, glad for the unexpected moment alone with him. "The amniocentesis results."

"Really." McIntyre took a larger-than-usual gulp of his drink. "So soon."

Edwina nodded. "In forty-eight hours, we'll know if we're actually having this baby or not."

"Well, then." He smiled at her. "If all goes well, it'll be here in time to be a dependent on our next tax declarations, won't it? Father's little dividend."

She put her arm around him. "Always the optimist."

"Until proven wrong. Sorry, darling, I hope you don't think I'm being callous. It's just ... I'm awfully happy, you know."

And I want you to go on being happy, Edwina thought.

Perhaps Harriet was right, and this constant, gnawing worry was a natural by-product of having children, in which case she supposed she *had* better get used to it. No wonder Harriet had taken up writing romance novels, inventing one freshly dreadful doom after another for her plucky heroines, each of whom escaped by the skin of her teeth; it had helped keep Harriet's mind from all the real dooms that might have befallen Edwina.

None of which, of course, had. "You keep right on being an optimist," Edwina said. "Just think of it as your household chore. Speaking of which, it's time for dinner."

McIntyre complied cheerfully; soon thereafter, they all sat down to eat: veal medallions with noodles Alfredo and green salad for Harriet, Alison and McIntyre, broiled fish with parsnips and anchovies for Edwina.

Mewing, Maxie begged for an anchovy. "You're not going to like it," Edwina warned, dangling the tidbit before him.

Batting at it, Maxie opined that he would indeed enjoy an anchovy, a statement he proved by devouring one with a great deal of satisfied smacking and purring. Harriet and McIntyre enjoyed their dinners, too, while discussing the furnishing of the nursery; happily they compared the relative merits of cradles versus bassinets and concluded that a good stereo system was essential.

Neither of them, Edwina realized, could bear to think the results of the amniocentesis would be anything but favorable. And for now, she decided to let them go on that way; the idea, after all, was to have a baby, not behave like one. Martin would have said she was being too hard on herself; still, surely it was better to be hard on herself than on him and Harriet.

Only Alison Feinstein looked as if something was eating her, instead of the other way around. Frowning, she poked at a veal medallion, consumed a tiny bit of it, and frowned again.

"Stroke volume," she said at Edwina's inquiring look.

"Forty-seven cc's per beat," Edwina replied automatically, and ate another forkful of parsnips. "Except in cases of valve malfunction, or . . . wait a minute, are you thinking about what I think you're thinking about?"

Alison nodded unhappily. "And I've been thinking it all

afternoon, only I didn't want to say anything because I didn't see how it could be true." She sighed. "But I just can't get around it. He couldn't have been lying there bleeding for anywhere near twenty minutes."

Once Alison had said it, it was obvious: "If he had, he'd have bled out all his blood volume. He wouldn't have survived. Well, he nearly didn't."

Alison made a face, and began eating her veal medallion with more appetite. " 'Nearly' isn't the point. That nurse said she went in for those cards twenty minutes or so before she found his A-line running open, that she must have knocked it apart when she brushed past the bed. But it couldn't have happened that way."

Across the table, Harriet and McIntyre finished planning the nursery and began on infant wardrobes, with heavy emphasis on disposables versus a diaper service. Edwina definitely intended to exercise her veto power on this topic, should the occasion arise, but for now the two of them were enjoying themselves.

"When did you see Clarke?" she asked Alison.

"Early-morning rounds. I was in the operating room the rest of the day."

"Wait a minute, the nurse said you were in there after the priest left. I thought you must have just looked in on him."

Alison shook her head. "Not me. Maybe one of the other services. Anyway, what's a priest doing in with Clarke? He's not Catholic, he's Jewish."

Edwina swallowed the anchovy she was chewing, drank some water, and dabbed her napkin to her lips. "I beg your pardon?"

"We took a silver Star of David on a silver chain off his neck just before he went to the OR, and put it in a valuables envelope. He wasn't wearing other jewelry, so I assumed it wasn't for decoration's sake. Wouldn't you?"

"Yes," Edwina said, distracted, "I would. I'd say a Star of David means Clarke probably wasn't an altar boy. But I'll bet somebody was."

Alison looked puzzled. Across the table, Harriet and

Martin ended diapers, and began on bath time; Martin waxed enthusiastic about rubber duckies, while Harriet preferred little tugboats. Together, they beamed at Edwina, whom they obviously felt to be the source of present mirth and a great deal of future hilarity.

"You," Edwina pointed out, "don't actually have to *have* this baby."

"Of course not, dear," Harriet replied. "I wouldn't dream of depriving my daughter of the absolute *pinnacle* of feminine experience."

"Indeed," said the daughter in question, knowing full well that Harriet thought the pinnacle of experience, feminine or otherwise, had to do with the producing of literary creations, not human ones. Besides, Harriet had possessed so many servants at the time of Edwina's birth that snapshots of the nursery resembled still photos of a Cecil B. DeMille epic.

On the other hand, none of those servants had actually *had* that baby, either; Harriet had performed the feat herself. Now Edwina gazed at her mother with exasperated fondness, feeling rather like a glass of lemon juice that has just had a heaping cupful of sugar stirred into it.

"Excuse me, please," she said, getting up and handing her plate of anchovies down to Maxie. The black cat pounced purringly upon them, delight radiating from his every hair and whisker.

"Edwina," asked McIntyre, "are you all right?"

"Oh, yes. Absolutely, I'm all right. I've just got to make a few telephone calls. And the first thing I'll do is make sure that our friend Dr. Clarke doesn't get the unwanted visits of any more clerical types."

Alison looked enlightened. "He was there, the nurse said. But, Edwina, you don't think *he* . . . ?"

"I don't see how he could have; the timing's no more right for him than for the nurse. If he'd pulled Clarke's A-line, Clarke would be dead. But I *do* want to know what he's up to, and I *do* think that if there's anyone who can go around a hospital unchallenged, even in the middle of a murder epidemic, it's a priest. I'm going to call Dick Talbot."

She wasn't at home, and she wasn't in the hospital. It had taken Eric a while to get around to it, but by early evening he had started looking for her, and after leaving a dozen messages on Alison Feinstein's machine, he had called Chelsea Memorial and been told she was signed out.

But he had to convince her to help him. If he could just get inside the hospital, and get a look at the on-call schedule, he could find out when she would be back. Maybe if she was due to come in soon, he could even wait for her—lock himself in one of the stalls in the john, or something, just to stay out of sight.

On the other hand, if he were caught inside the hospital, he would probably be arrested for trespassing, or worse. And if Bill Grace should spot him . . .

Eric didn't even want to think about that. In fact, there were a lot of things he didn't want to think about, starting with what would happen if Alison wouldn't help him, or if his plan didn't work out.

Pushing these thoughts from his mind, Eric Shultz pulled a clump of tissues from his pocket and blew his nose for perhaps the hundredth time that day, then turned sideways on the bench across from Chelsea Memorial. In the relative darkness of the late-night city street, he bent his head into the protection of his winter jacket, and sucked up half of the last little bit of cocaine he'd brought along.

It was wearing off a lot faster now; twenty-four hours of being high did tend to deplete the old adrenal glands. But what the hell; after this was over, he could get more. Everything would be okay again. The thing was, he had to talk to Alison. And he *knew* she had to come back here. The bottom line was, he had to get inside; only how the hell was he going to do that?

Through the big glass windows, he could see security

guards at their stations, checking ID. Probably, he thought, they were watching for his; why else would they be checking, when they never had before? Most of the time, hospital security was a joke.

Eric guessed he must really have ticked them off. If he tried to waltz right in there now, they'd come down on him like a load of bricks. All the more reason to get to Alison as soon as possible and get the ball back in his court. What he needed, he decided, was fake ID, or ID that belonged to somebody else.

That was it: with a stethoscope around his neck and a decent ID card, he would be golden. Hospital IDs didn't have photos on them, so no problem there, and he still looked fairly clean; he had showered and shaved that morning. And his stethoscope was stuffed in his jacket pocket, where it always was when he wasn't on duty; otherwise he forgot and left it home half the time.

Yes, an ID would work. But how to get one? Eric sniffled, pondered, and snorted a little more; then a brainstorm hit him. The medical library was still open; he could simply walk in and browse around, until he came across a jacket with an ID pinned to it. People left their jackets hanging all the time while they rooted in the periodicals stacks or used the copying machines.

Grinning, Eric hauled himself to his feet, and aimed himself toward the medical library. Students hurried past him, looking grim, nor bothering even to glance up at his face; if he wasn't a textbook, a cadaver, or a set of lecture notes, Eric could be Dr. Frankenstein for all they cared.

To his left was the wide, landscaped quadrangle in front of the medical school cafeteria, silent and empty with the half-bare branches of the young maple trees gleaming in the moonlight. Next loomed the tall, many-windowed Stedman Building, once called the Kirkess Institute and housing a locked ward for the violently insane, now home of medical school classrooms and labs; the students said the name had changed but the inmates were the same. Many of the lights in the Stedman Building remained on, and the iron bars still bolted to the outsides of the windows showed like tic-tac-toe patterns. Eric remembered being locked in the cubicle in the ER, and felt nauseated.

Courage, though; only a little farther. The enormous white pillars of the medical library's portico, with the bright doors of the lobby behind them, threw giant shadows onto the sidewalk. Eric passed a row of newspaper vending stands, a mailbox and a Federal Express box, and at the curb the locked, wheeled hot-dog vendor's cart, with a couple of big trash receptacles standing alongside.

Fifteen minutes later, he was exiting the medical library with a hospital ID badge in his hand. Whistling as well as he could through his cracked, dry lips, sniffling and thanking his lucky stars, Eric headed back toward the big glass doors of Chelsea Memorial Hospital, toward Alison and the rest of his whole career.

Yes, he thought, and took another little hit.

Michael Munson lay gazing at the square of moonlight that was the window of his hospital room. On his bedside table, a Westclox alarm clock ticked companionably, its hands glowing green in the room's alien shade.

Otherwise, the only sound was an occasional burbling blip from his own intravenous apparatus, sending unknown chemicals into his bloodstream, trying to kill the germs that were trying to kill him. Distantly, he wondered which side was going to win.

As he wondered this, he turned over in his hands the small block of hardwood that Zinnia had given him. It was no longer a shapeless, undone thing; little edges met with the tips of his fingers, edges that he had created with the small, sharp knives.

Munson examined the object with his fingertips. So many things were beyond his control now. He looked at the color of the moonlight, which was exactly the same color as it had been when he was a little boy, and felt the edges of the block of wood which, as Zinnia had believed, was like a great block of granite, made small so that he could control it.

Only, he could not control it. Wood was not granite, his fingers informed him with brutal accuracy. And it was not *like* granite; not at all.

If he could not work, then he wanted to die. And that, Chris Whitsun had come back this evening to inform him, he *could* control; he could, for instance, order the intravenous removed, or take it out himself and refuse to have it replaced. Now that his living will and codicil were signed, he could also control other things: the manner of his departure from this earth, for instance. There would be no tubes, and no machines; Chris's work had made very sure of that.

Munson closed his eyes to the streaming moonlight, and his ears to the clock. He was an old man, and he was tired.

Still, there was Zinnia.

Tomorrow he would pick up the wood and the knives again, and have another try.

Edwina stood in the kitchen, finishing the dishes. It was nearly midnight, the guests had long departed, and she was feeling a touch morose: Poor Ned. Poor Bob Whiteside's family, and Bonnie West's. Poor everyone, in fact, and she couldn't think of anything more to do about any of them.

She'd phoned Talbot, who now knew everything she knew about Peter Garroway and his appearances in priest garb. After hearing her out, Talbot had been even more eager to find Garroway and question him, and with that plan, of course, Edwina agreed.

But Talbot seemed to think that Garroway had become his main suspect, which made Edwina feel even more unhappy about it all; telling Talbot that Garroway couldn't have pulled Victor Clarke's arterial line had only made the homicide cop dig his heels in. On the other hand,

Mrs. Glick couldn't have pulled it, either; she'd been at work in Clarke's office at the time, and for that she had witnesses other than her husband. *Drat,* Edwina thought; *maybe they're all in it together.*

"Harriet's older than I thought," she said to McIntyre. "She sprang it on me while you were talking with Alison."

"Mmm? Full of surprises, our Harriet." McIntyre looked up from the law journal he was reading. "Does it bother you?"

Edwina wiped the final glass and put it away. "I didn't think it did, at first. But if she's older, it means she's going to die sooner."

McIntyre tipped his head in sympathy. His own parents had died when he was a teenager, in a car accident. They'd been on their way to an amusement park, of all things.

"No, dear," he corrected gently. "The appointed day is still the appointed day. And Harriet seems in good health now."

"I suppose." She closed the cabinet, and hung up the dish towel. "It's just that I can't imagine a world without her. I don't see how I'll bear it. How did you?"

McIntyre looked down at his journal. "Badly. You might get better but you never get well. Wish I could be more comforting on the topic. But Harriet's going to go on for a long time; she *is* well-preserved, even though she'd kill me for saying it."

Edwina wiped the kitchen counters thoroughly as she digested her husband's comments. Then she did all the cabinets, and all the appliances. When she looked up again, he was watching her.

"Does the phrase 'nesting instinct' mean anything to you?"

"Ye gods." She tossed the sponge at the sink and snapped the kitchen lights out, hoping she wouldn't suddenly acquire the unquenchable urge to start wallpapering anything.

"Martin, you don't suppose there's a chance Peter Garroway might have tried to kill his stepparents after all this

time? I mean, maybe he just loosened that arterial line
somehow, so it would come apart after he left."

She shook her head as she came into the dining room,
and sat across from McIntyre. "No, that doesn't make
sense either. He couldn't be sure it would. But Talbot says
he talked to Mitch Frankau, Dr. Clarke's accountant, today, and there really *wasn't* any financial motive. She
didn't have much life insurance, it turns out, and if he dies,
all his will do is pay off their mortgage, and for their cars
and so on; he's borrowed several times against the policy.
Clarke made a lot of money, but he spent it as fast as he
made it. Faster, even."

"Or his wife spent it for him," McIntyre commented.

"What a thing to say. Except that in this case I'm afraid
it's true; their house was crammed with stuff, and I can't
believe he bought it all. He wouldn't have had time to
practice medicine. And if it's not a money motive . . . but
it's been twenty years since Peter Garroway lived with the
Clarkes."

" 'Revenge,' " McIntyre quoted distractedly, "is a dish
best served cold.' "

"Martin, it would be more than cold; it would be
moldy. Garroway might have been angry over the way his
stepfather died, and felt Clarke was responsible. But no
one waits this long to get even. And something else: Even
if Garroway could have separated Clarke's A-line, the
doctor who came in afterward would have seen it that
way, and put it back together again."

"Talbot's trying to get hold of the nurse, find out who
the doctor was?"

"Mm-hm. But she's not answering her phone. The service
she works for says she quit on the spot. She was *very* upset."

McIntyre bent to his law journal again. "Well, if Garroway had no credible motive *and* couldn't have done it,
then no matter how mysteriously he's behaving, I'd say he
didn't do it."

"Talbot thinks he did."

McIntyre frowned skeptically. "Talbot doesn't have

anybody else looking as good for it, and he wants to nail this one. And Talbot doesn't have much respect for medical evidence, or for medical anything else; it's his only failing, but it's a sizable one."

"Mmm. But then, what *is* Peter Garroway up to?"

"I don't know, Edwina. Maybe you'd better just find him and ask him about it."

McIntyre turned another page of his journal in the brisk, deliberate way that meant he really needed to finish reading this, and could she possibly find something else to do?

"Yes, dear," Edwina murmured, and went into the living room to examine the gift Harriet had brought her. It was a craft kit consisting of pink and blue yarn, knitting needles, and an instruction booklet. From it, one could knit a pair of booties.

In a pig's eye, Edwina thought. Still, the instructions did look reasonably well done, and Harriet was going to ask her if she had at least tried the kit. She supposed she might as well prepare an honest answer, and a halfway diplomatic one, even though she had never been very fond of sweet, feminine arts like knitting.

"Oh, no, you don't," she told Maxie, who felt certain the yarn was intended for him and was indignant when he found out otherwise. Cats' brains, Edwina thought, were imprinted with certain key concepts at the time of their birth; "yarn" was one and "pester" was definitely another.

Eventually, however, she settled to work. The yarn turned out to be pleasantly soft and pliable, and the directions were indeed excellent; Edwina made her way through the process called casting on with little difficulty. Actually knitting, though, was another story. She had seen women doing it while watching television and carrying on conversations, and thought it must be an extremely simple process, accent scornfully on "simple."

But an hour and a great many ripped-out stitches later, she realized that the feminine arts took more skill and intelligence than she had understood. Also, McIntyre was right: She *should* just find Peter Garroway and ask him what she wanted to know.

One thing was certain: Garroway had to be ruled out. As long as Talbot thought he was the best suspect, the police would concentrate mainly on him. And that could give someone else the chance to succeed in an effort that had so far met with failure.

There was also Ned Hunt to consider; she had been selling him short. If he was a bit of a bumbler in some ways, well, what of it? He was a sensitive fellow, and her oldest friend, and he was asking for her help.

Besides, Edwina needed something to occupy herself; Harriet had been trying to supply this need with her gift. Edwina looked at the yarn and at the pink plastic needles. Harriet meant well, of course; Harriet always did. But finding Peter Garroway was sure to be more interesting than knitting. Also, she thought with a final scowl at the tangles of pink and blue yarn she had managed to create, it would be more possible.

"I've got to leave," Ellen Biedermeyer said. "I'm sorry, you know I wouldn't if I didn't have to. But . . ."

"But *what?*" Mrs. Chetwynd, the night-shift charge nurse on the surgical ward, was a grim, unforgiving old battle-axe who usually worked the day shift in administration. But without Bob Whiteside and Bonnie, and with the ward full, staff was so short they'd had to pull the aging administrator from her usual chores of tabulating sick days and sending out licensing-renewal reminders.

Mrs. Chetwynd folded her arms across her chest and tapped her white-shod foot. "This *is* the night shift," she reminded Ellen unnecessarily. "There's no one to replace you. And I can't get anyone from any of the other wards; they're already trying to get help from us."

"I know, Mrs. Chetwynd," Ellen replied; she'd only had eight hours off since her last on-duty, and felt like the living dead. *I'd like to reach up and knock that white cap off your head,* she thought, *only it's probably nailed on.* "But my little boy is at home alone—his father didn't come home from work on time. Chuck's only seven, and he's scared. And I don't have anyone I can call."

Mrs. Chetwynd glared down her long, thin nose. "You left a seven-year-old home alone?"

Right, Ellen thought, *but first I tied him up and locked him in a closet.* How could she explain that she had had no choice? Usually, when she worked nights, Chuck dozed in front of the TV for the half-hour between the time she left and the time his father came back. It made for a late bedtime, but no sitter would come for only half an hour, and if he stayed with anyone else, he'd have to wake up to be taken home anyway, not that there was anyone Ellen would want to leave him with. They'd been leaving Chuck alone for two weeks, since Ellen's husband got the evening-shift job whose income they needed so much; Ellen was ashamed and anxious about it, but until now it had always worked out all right.

"Really, I'd have expected better judgment from a nurse," old battle-axe Chetwynd sniffed.

Ellen gripped the side rails of Victor Clarke's hospital bed; otherwise, she might just smack that scowl off Chetwynd's face. "I have to go," she repeated.

"As you think best. Of course, I'll have to put it in my shift report." The nursing supervisor let her voice trail off significantly.

Chetwynd might not remember how to take care of patients; her last hands-on experience was probably during the Civil War. But she sure knew how to twist the knife. Nurses who went home in the middle of a night shift were not regarded as reliable enough for promotion, no matter how much seniority they had.

"Leave your nursing notes and clipboard on the windowsill," said Mrs. Chetwynd. "And don't forget to sign out." She turned and stalked from the dim-lit hospital room; the rubber soles of her nursing shoes sounded like a pair of squeegees, going away down the corridor.

Nearly weeping, Ellen surveyed the room a final time. Dr. Clarke was full of morphine and reasonably quiet, but every so often his eyes rolled wildly and he began bucking the respirator, setting off all his alarms, sometimes thrashing hard enough to disconnect himself. Right now, his vital signs and meds were up to date; he wouldn't really need anything for another hour. But if anything did happen to him, Ellen knew she would never forgive herself.

"Tough broad," the cop assigned to guarding the room said sympathetically, meaning Chetwynd.

Ellen fastened her nursing notes to the clipboard. "I don't know why my husband's not home yet. It's not like him. And my little boy . . ."

"Hey, maybe his car wouldn't start. Maybe he had a flat tire. Bet you any money he'll be there when you get there."

Ellen sniffled. "Thanks. You're probably right. If he is, I'll just come back in. Dr. Clarke really does need someone to watch him, and there just isn't anyone else to assign."

The cop shook his head. "Nah, don't come back. Hey, you've been here every night. Some days, too, right?"

Ellen nodded, gathering up her coat and purse. It was the fatigue that made her feel so weepy, as if the weight of the world were on her shoulders and she couldn't carry it.

"Hey, I know that trip," the cop said.

He was thirty or so, with a round, friendly face and hound-dog eyes. Everything about him looked rumpled; he'd been here every night, too, Ellen realized, as well as some days, and was probably as exhausted as she was. "Do you always work the night shift?"

"Nah. And believe me, I'm not used to it. But hey, gotta make it when you can get it, am I right?" He smiled tiredly. "Look, I'm going to be here, and I've been watching long enough to know what it looks like when things are going wrong."

Ellen pulled her car keys from her purse and took a final look around the room. "There will be someone in every hour, for meds and vital signs," she said, trying to convince herself. If her husband *didn't* come home, she would have to stay home anyway, and start looking for him.

If he did come home . . . Dear God, but she was tired. "You really think he's just had a flat, or something?"

"Sure. Tell you what, if your old man doesn't show up in an hour, you call me here. I can call downtown for you, make sure he's not in any difficulties. Ease your mind. Meanwhile, I'll sit here and keep a sharp eye on the doc."

The cop leaned back in his chair, closed his eyes briefly, and opened them again with an effort, yawning. "Hey, I'm not going anywhere, anyway."

Ellen sighed. "Are you sure you'll be able to . . ."

"That number there, it stays around ninety," he said, eager to show her that he would. "The other one, that's usually around one-twenty over seventy. And from what I've seen, those alarms on the breathing machine go off, if anything goes haywire in that department."

The weight on Ellen's shoulders lightened a little bit; she might get a bad report for this, but Dr. Clarke probably would be all right. That was the important thing; that, and getting home to take care of Chuck.

And when that husband of hers finally did show up, he'd better have a darned good excuse for himself, or after Ellen got through with him he was going to need more nursing care than Dr. Clarke did.

"Mr. Munson, it's three in the morning. What in the world are you doing out of bed?"

"Can't sleep. Going for a walk." Munson leaned on his cane with one hand and gripped his wheeled IV pole with the other.

The young girl in the white uniform eyed him doubtfully. "Well, the doctor did say you could walk a *little* bit, starting tomorrow. I guess it's tomorrow now. And I suppose it's hard for you to sleep. But don't leave the ward, will you? Can you find your way back to your room all right when you want to?"

"Won't leave. Know my way."

Munson leaned on his supports and stumped slowly away from her. Who the hell was she, anyway, and where the hell was this?

Damn Victor; he must have taken the small silver bell that was always beside Munson's bed, in case he wanted anything in the night. Victor was good, but he was lazy. He didn't want to get up out of his own warm bed. Victor went through life pretending it was a tropical paradise.

Munson had left his room looking for Victor; now he couldn't find his way back. He didn't want to say so to the little girl in the white dress, though. She was part of something; he didn't know what, but he knew it could cause him a lot of trouble. He would find his own way back, himself.

Tropical paradise, he thought, disgusted with Victor, and then he thought he saw the door to his own room, only there was a police officer sitting in front of it. The police officer was asleep, with a newspaper fallen across his lap.

Rage seized Munson: One of his wives must be up to something again. *Arrest him, he's done this; fine him, he's done that.* Like a chorus of shrieking harpies, when all he wanted was to be left alone to work.

Shrewdly, Munson eyed the sleeping policeman, whose chin rested slackly on his chest, his lower lip quivering with his softly snoring breaths. Munson could slip past him, he was sure.

Once he was inside, he could lock the door, shout to Victor to let the dog out, and call old Whit. After that, he could go back to work while Marie brought him bread and coffee on a tray. Wielding his cane, he slid the IV pole silently past the sleeping officer and into his room. And for an instant, he saw it:

The rice-paper shades over the tall narrow windows. The big oaken table where all his papers were spread, under the lamp of hammered copper with the red parchment shade. The rug, so clotted with the mongrel dog

Buster's hair that it appeared beige, and on the wall by his bed the Stevenson oil painting of Gabrielle, from *The Madwoman of Chaillot*: "Let them out. Let them out."

Stevenson had painted Gabrielle's face old on one side and young on the other; Munson looked at it and preferred the old, again. Then, terrifyingly, the painting vanished, leaving in its place a plain beige wall. Shocked, Munson let go of the IV pole he had been pushing. His hands were suddenly very cold; leaning against the bed rails, he shoved them into his bathrobe pockets, unmindful of the aching pain in his foot.

A blood pressure monitor and a lot of electronic devices hung from the wall. Jagged green lines and numbers danced on the devices' screens. Wires connected them to a figure in the bed, a figure that seemed to have come out of Hieronymous Bosch, or one of the suppressed Beardsley prints.

The figure's position and its condition were horrific, not to be borne. Munson drew his hands back out of his pockets, meaning to clutch the IV pole and his cane and get away from here. But the fingers of his right hand came out wrapped around a small, shiny woodcarving knife.

"Hey, what are you doing in here?"

Startled, Munson dropped the little knife; it fell into the bed, and before he could retrieve it, the policeman's hand seized his shoulder.

EIGHT

"ALISON, IT *ISN'T* dangerous. Well, not that dangerous, anyway. Dealing with people is a lot like dealing with horses; if you even think they might be mean, don't turn your back on them. It's the ones you don't suspect at all who'll get you."

Edwina stood at the apartment's dining room window and watched the sun rise over Long Island Sound while she talked to Alison on the telephone. The only possible time to call the surgeon was very early in the morning, after she'd had a night off; the rest of the time she was either in the OR, on rounds, in the intensive-care unit, or frantically trying to catch up on her charting and medication-renewal orders.

"Look, all I'm asking for is a beeper that's hooked into the hospital's paging system. But I need it soon, before Garroway shows up again. Otherwise the cops are going to grab him the minute he steps onto the ward, and I'll *never* get to talk with him."

"Why? Why not just let them catch him?"

"Look, you said yourself he couldn't have done it. There's something else going on."

"So what's your plan?" Alison sounded reluctant.

"My plan is just to ask him a few things. And whatever he's doing here, he's got to talk to the police. I'll convince him of that. After he does, the police won't be wasting

time looking for him, instead of for whoever's really behind all this." *I hope,* she added mentally. "I'll be standing
there in the middle of the hospital lobby with people all
around me, Alison. Even if I'm wrong about him, he's not
going to do anything in front of so many witnesses."

"Edwina," Alison said, "you either tell me what you're
really going to do, or I'm hanging up this phone right
now."

Damn and blast; Alison always could spot a lie at fifty
paces. From the other room, Edwina heard Martin McIntyre's morning routine begin: sports radio, followed by a
brief romp with Maxie, then the shower hissing on.

"Okay. I'm sorry. But if you breathe a word of this . . ."

"I'll decide about what I breathe or don't breathe, and
right this minute, I'm about to breathe fire. Eric Shultz left
a dozen messages on my answering machine last night,
and I'm trying to decide whether to call him back or just
go out and buy a gun and shoot *him.*"

Alison took a deep breath. "And I've got another meeting with the damned residents' disciplinary board today,
and I'm on the OR schedule in twenty minutes. So spill it,
Edwina, and make it snappy, or I'm out of here."

Edwina spilled. She would head Garroway off, and keep
him with her for as long as she could. If anyone tried anything on Dr. Clarke during that time, the secretary on the
surgical ward would beep Edwina's beeper. Meanwhile,
Edwina would get as much information as she could out of
Garroway, and persuade him to talk to the police.

Half an hour later, she was stationed in Chelsea's lobby
equipped with a hospital paging-system beeper, her largest
handbag, and a cup of hot water with lemon in it, caffeine
being among the drugs she did not wish to inflict on the
tender young buds of a developing nervous system.

If it *was* developing. *Stop that,* she told herself for the
hundredth time. Her own nervous system felt as if
someone had been dragging a metal file across it. This, she
supposed, could get her into a lot of trouble. In her experience, the police dealt harshly with people who allowed

bad guys to escape, especially when those people could easily have summoned enough officers to overthrow the government of a small nation.

On the other hand, she also knew what was going to happen the minute Garroway was taken into custody: no more cops on the surgical ward, no more checking ID at the door. Less security than usual, in fact, because the bad guy had been captured and everyone could take a deep breath and relax for a little while.

The trouble was, even aside from the timing of the arterial-line episode, Peter Garroway made a very strange bad guy: one who could stay out of sight for twenty years, then surface to commit three murders and have three tries at a fourth. He was also clever enough to elude capture, but not smart enough to see that the risks he was taking now were needless. Wherever Garroway had been for all that time, what he ought to do was go back there and keep his head down. If he wanted Clarke dead, he could wait until Clarke was discharged from the hospital, if he ever was, and *then* take another shot at him.

Instead, Garroway kept doing the one thing he really ought not to do: returning to the scene of the crime. It was as if he wanted to be caught, or as if it honestly hadn't occurred to him that anyone might be looking for him. Also, he was about the most silent man Edwina had ever heard of; Talbot's computer searches had come up with nothing. Garroway padded through life on little cat feet; she wanted to know how, not to mention why, and she wanted Garroway in her presence the next time someone tried to kill Clarke. That way, she'd know for sure that Garroway hadn't done it himself.

Opening her bag, Edwina removed her knitting and began to work on the pink-and-blue bootie. It was as hopeless a task as it had been the night before, but it made excellent camouflage and allowed her to think. Visiting hours did not begin until ten, but clergy were not held to this rule, nor to many rules at all; religious visitors were so common in the hospital that the guards had probably waved Garroway right on by their ID-checking station.

Only they wouldn't today, because they'd been alerted, which was why Edwina had chosen her waiting area with care. The lobby's big plate-glass windows allowed her a view of the sidewalk in both directions; if Garroway arrived, she would spot him before he came in and was noticed by the lobby guard.

Ten minutes later, he did arrive, dressed in his usual black with clerical collar; Edwina hurried out to meet him. He looked confused as she strode up to him, and then, when he recognized her, surprised and guilty.

"If you go in there, the police are going to arrest you," she told him quickly. "Come with me. I want to talk to you."

Garroway blinked, but fell into step beside her.

"Listen," he began, "I'm sorry about the other day. But I can explain."

"Good, because you've got a lot of explaining to do. And you've got a lot of time to do it in, because you're sticking with me until further notice."

Garroway stopped. "What are you talking about? And where are we going, anyway?"

"The coffee shop next to the Stedman Building. And what I'm talking about is the murder and attempted murder of your stepparents."

She watched his face carefully as she spoke, but it betrayed nothing. "I see," was all he said as they began walking again.

The street in front of the Stedman Building was jammed with medical students rushing to classes, clerks and lab technicians on their way to work, and patients headed to appointments in the clinics. The coffee shop was crowded, too, but when the counterman saw Garroway, he took a "reserved" card off the table in the back booth and waved them to it.

"Hi, Father," the counterman said. "The usual?"

"Hi, Eddie," Garroway replied. "Yes, and my friend here will have . . ."

"A glass of seltzer and some dry toast, please," said Edwina, who had forgotten that the coffee shop was going to smell like bacon and eggs at this hour of the morning. "Plenty of dry toast."

"Now," Garroway said when they were seated, "would you like to tell me a little more? Because I must confess, I'm confused."

" 'Confess'? That's a good one. How long did it take you to think up the priest costume? And where in the world have you been living for twenty years, anyway, in a dungeon? For that matter, where are you staying now? There's not a hotel in fifty miles the police haven't checked."

"Well," he said as the counterman delivered their orders (Garroway's usual turned out to be a bagel with cream cheese and a large black coffee), "actually, I didn't think up the priest costume myself."

He ate a bite of the bagel and washed it down with coffee. "And I haven't been renting a room, either. But I *have* been living in a dungeon for twenty years. Or the equivalent of a dungeon, some people would think."

Edwina ate some of her toast and drank some water. The counterman threw peppers and onions onto the grill to begin making a Western omelette; the smell of the frying onions drifted through the coffee shop, pungent as poison gas.

"You see," Garroway continued, "I wear a priest costume, as you call it, because I'm a priest."

"A priest," Edwina repeated. "As in Roman Catholic. You're ordained, and all."

He nodded. "I belong to an order that's based in Ohio. I drove here in their car. And the order has a house near here, so I've been staying there until I go home."

Edwina assimilated all this as calmly as she could. "Which will be when?" she managed.

"After I'm sure that Victor can hear and understand me, or after he dies. Whichever comes first." Garroway finished the first half of his bagel and began on the second. "I don't know why you look so astonished. Haven't you ever seen a priest before?"

Not one who's suspected of multiple murder, Edwina wanted to say, and drank more seltzer water instead.

"And I don't know why the police want to arrest me. All I did was . . . oh." Garroway's face changed suddenly. "You don't mean they think I was the one who . . . oh, no. And that means *you* must think I . . . You do, don't you? I can see by your expression, you do."

Edwina looked past Garroway at the woman in the next booth, whose gaze remained politely fixed on her newspaper. But her face had the frozen, unfocused expression of a person whose ears are as alert as satellite dishes.

"Keep your voice down," Edwina said. "And no, I don't. Too many things don't make sense. But you've got to admit there are plenty of reasons why I should. How else would you have known they were shot? No one notified you, but here you were. And why haven't you told the police and the hospital that you're the Clarkes' next of kin? What do you want to tell Victor, anyway, and what were you looking for, the other day at his house?"

"I'm not their next of kin; neither one ever adopted me officially. The answer to the rest of your questions is kind of a long story, though. The police really think I shot them?"

The seltzer water and dry toast weren't doing the trick. Edwina willed her stomach to settle, but succeeded only marginally.

"Because I didn't," Garroway went on. "I came here because Victor called me. Well," he amended, "partly because he called me. He was getting ready to finish a paper he'd been working on for a long time, and some of the information in it was . . . Well, he wanted to talk to me about it."

"Right," Edwina said skeptically. "And I'll bet you've got a great reason for why you haven't told the police *that*."

"Yes. I wanted to convince Victor not to publish that paper; I certainly wasn't about to start talking about it with anyone else, and I'm still not. As for what I was looking for the other day, let's just say I didn't find it. I'm sorry I lied to you, by the way. I didn't know who you might be, or if you'd try to stop me from taking the files, so I made you think I was supposed to be taking them. And I didn't tell anyone who I am because . . . because I'm not always sure of that myself, for one thing."

"You told the housecleaner you're their stepson."

"Yes. But only so she'd let me in the house." He looked up troubledly. "You see, I got bounced around a lot, as a kid. My mom married several times. After she died, my stepfather took care of me, and for a while I was pretty happy. He was a good guy. But then he got married again, and then he died."

"Because of Victor Clarke," Edwina said quietly.

Garroway's face hardened for an instant. "That's right. I see you know some of this story."

"Some of it. I know Clarke married Renata only six months later, and suddenly was able to settle all his debts, after which the two of them left town. What did they do, pack you off to a boarding school? You must have felt pretty resentful."

He nodded. "You bet. The thing is, how was I going to tell anyone here who I am? 'Hi, there, I'm Victor's sort-of stepson, but I haven't seen him in twenty years, because' . . . Well. Except for that one time, it just seemed simpler to be what I *know* I am: a visiting priest. And I guess I was ashamed of myself, too. Priests are supposed to be experts at forgiveness, aren't they? But instead, I'd . . ."

He stopped, eyeing her narrowly. "Are you sure you want to hear the rest of this, here? Because if you don't mind my saying so, you're looking a little green. Are you by any chance expecting? A baby, I mean?"

Edwina felt her jaw drop. "How do you know that?"

He finished his coffee, and picked up the check. "Well, members of religious orders do work, you know. Some of them even with the public. It depends," he added, "on just what order you belong to, but the bottom line is if you're needed to work, you work."

"How interesting," Edwina murmured, and hastily drank a little more seltzer, but it was *definitely* not proving effective as a stomach remedy.

"And our order," Garroway went on, "runs a charity hospital. When I'm not saying the seven hundred different prayers I swore an oath to say every day," he concluded wryly, "I work there, as a medical technician."

He pulled some money from his billfold. "We get a lot of maternity patients, which is why I know the look. So do you want to stay here, or go someplace where the air isn't quite so aromatic? Oh, and congratulations."

"Thank you," Edwina replied faintly, while rapidly thinking several things at once. First, she would have to do something about the way she felt, and do so as soon as possible; becoming violently ill right out in public was not on her agenda, but letting Garroway out of her presence would ruin her whole plan.

Second, if Garroway was telling the truth, he could have known how to turn down Clarke's oxygen and might even have thought to make the tampering seem unskilled, in case suspicion ever did come his way.

Third, the fact that he was a priest didn't mean he couldn't figure out how to fire a gun, or hire someone else to fire one for him—if he really *was* a priest at all; for all she knew, he was lying about the whole thing. For that matter, if he could pose as a priest *and* a medical office manager, he could pose as something else; maybe *he* was the mysterious doctor who'd been in Clarke's room just before Clarke's arterial line separated.

Finally, he hadn't yet said what he wanted to talk to Victor Clarke about. There was plenty he hadn't said, in fact. While she was considering all this, her beeper went off.

"Listen, Edwina, I'm really sorry, but I couldn't help

it," Alison said hurriedly when Edwina had dialed her from the pay phone at the back of the coffee shop.

"What? Couldn't help what?" From the phone, Edwina could see Garroway getting up and meandering to the cash register.

"That detective, Talbot, was up here a couple of minutes ago, asking everyone about the priest who's been seeing Clarke. And of course when he asked me, I said I didn't know anything about it."

Uh-oh. At the front of the coffee shop, Garroway paid the check. "Hurry, Alison, what happened?"

"Well, he just about nailed me to the wall. He's something, that Talbot; he just *knew*. I'm sorry, Edwina, but he got it out of me."

Garroway stood by the cash register chatting with the counterman, his head turned sideways toward the front window of the shop, as if he were casually watching the street.

Damn and blast. When it came to lies, Talbot was even worse than Alison; he knew you were telling one even *before* you got it out of your mouth. "Did anybody else hear this?"

"No. And I explained to him why it couldn't be—"

"What did he say?"

"He wants Garroway. And he's looking for you, right now."

Garroway turned and smiled, as if in apologetic farewell. "Oh, Lord. Alison, thanks, I've got to go."

She hung up, just as Peter Garroway quick-stepped out the front door of the coffee shop. Five seconds later she had caught up with him. "And just where the hell do you think you're going?"

Garroway looked surprised. "I'm sorry, was I walking too fast for you? I thought you'd be right behind me."

"I am, and don't forget it."

"Me, too," said Dick Talbot, stepping up between them. "I'm a police officer," he told Garroway, flashing his ID. "I want to ask you a few things."

Garroway's look changed to one of resignation. "All right, officer," he agreed, as he and Talbot began moving away.

"Wait," Edwina called. "You didn't tell me what you wanted to say to Victor."

Of all the questions she might have asked him, she realized, that was probably the silliest, but it had popped into her head and out of her mouth before she had time to consider it.

Garroway looked over his shoulder. He seemed calm, for a man who was probably about to be arrested for murder. In fact, he seemed serene, which meant he was either innocent or crazy.

"I'd been angry at Victor for twenty years," he replied. "Now I want him to know that I forgive him."

"For what?" Edwina demanded, but Talbot was guiding Garroway firmly away, and neither of them looked back.

For bungling his stepfather's medical care, of course, she answered herself ten minutes later. *For frightening the man so much with a cancer diagnosis that he committed suicide. That much makes sense.* Glumly, she let herself into the apartment. *And Talbot can keep him out of Clarke's room as well as I can.*

But what Talbot wouldn't keep was the secret of Garroway's being in custody, and once word got out, security at the hospital would disintegrate. Darn that Talbot, anyway.

The apartment had the still, middle-of-the-morning feeling that she usually enjoyed, but now the silence carried an expectant air, like a smooth pond waiting to have a pebble dropped into it. She turned on the radio and busied herself making herbal tea, but it was no use. Her plan hadn't been perfect; still, it might have worked. Now she felt utterly at loose ends.

Irritably, she pressed the button on the hospital beeper,

which she would have to remember to return; it emitted a chirp. At the sound, like the peep of a strangling bird, Maxie peeked into the kitchen. "Why does Dick Talbot have to be so stubborn, anyway?" she asked the cat.

Maxie yawned, then eyed the kitchen cabinets meaningfully, as if to say that even his legendary curiosity was nowhere near intense enough to concern itself with mere human motives, and did there happen to be any more smoked oysters in the cupboard?

Edwina opened a tin of oysters and ate one; as usual, her morning upset had vanished as suddenly as a puff of stage smoke, and now she was hungry. Conscious of Maxie's yearning gaze, she gave one to him, too, which surprised him so much that he batted the oyster doubtfully a few times before gobbling it up.

"Somebody might as well get what they want," she grumped, and took her tea and a few more of the oysters into the living room, to nibble and think. It was after ten o'clock, and at the hospital, the day shift was in full swing; she could see it in her mind's eye. The wards were busy with bath carts, X-ray transports, and gurneys on their way to the operating room or returning from the recovery room. Rounds were over and order fulfillment had begun: oxygen, physical therapy, social work, new medication delivery.

In short, the whole place was in its usual state of mid-morning chaos; now was the perfect time to try killing Victor Clarke, especially if Talbot had gone ahead and arrested Peter Garroway, which he'd certainly looked angry enough to do. And on top of everything else, having a suspect in custody would mean the removal of Clarke's police guards, the department's budget situation being what it was.

Damn and blast. From the mantel, the big oil portrait of E. R. Crusoe gazed down at her as if waiting to see what she would come up with next. The artist had painted him in his old uniform, that of an admiral in the British Royal Navy, but after the war E. R. had taken American citizenship. This act, so disapproved of by his former countrymen, had in fact been a patriotic sacrifice, for a Crusoe who turned his back on jolly old England was a Crusoe whom England's enemies might trust more readily. In short, E. R. had been a spy, as a result of which profession he had begun amassing his fortune, while England's prisons had amassed a large population of traitors, turncoats, and other scoundrels.

Once, E. R. had been crawling filthily through a tunnel toward an enemy group's hideout, where he intended to plant a listening device, when he unexpectedly met a member of the group crawling toward *him*. Faced with having the listening device discovered, he swallowed it, then persuaded the group that he was escaping to them, not trying to infiltrate them. Afterward, he required abdominal surgery to remove the listening device, which he at last planted successfully. Many years afterward, telling the story, E. R. had added a lesson:

"You see, Edwina," he'd said, "if you can't get something done one way, very often you can get it done another. So don't feel too unhappy if your first efforts at a thing fail; just make sure you don't get shot for it, so you can have another chance."

Another chance. But at what? The Glicks were sticking to their story of being at home together when the Clarkes were shot; Talbot, still unconvinced, had ordered all their guns examined, but none was the murder weapon. So although Edwina remained certain there was something odd and unlikely about Mrs. Glick—why had she lied about her feelings for Clarke, and why were the Glicks lying about her being home that night?—there was no use questioning her further at this point. Nothing actually connected her materially to the crimes. And with Garroway in Talbot's custody, there would be no chance of talking more with him anytime soon, either.

In short, all the loose ends Edwina might pull were being clipped; nothing was left for her to tug on, to get the whole tangled mess to unravel. Except . . .

Garroway had said he wanted to tell Clarke that he forgave him. But what if that wasn't true, or wasn't the only thing Garroway wanted to talk with Clarke about? He'd said he hadn't found what he was looking for at the Clarkes' house. What if part of the reason he'd kept coming back to the hospital was so he could ask Clarke where it was?

The house didn't have an electronic security system, Edwina remembered. And although Talbot was probably too angry with her to let her have a key, there was almost certainly a set of them among the things Victor Clarke had been carrying in his pockets the night he was shot. Those things, right now, were in a manila valuables envelope with Victor Clarke's name on it, in a safe in the hospital's security department.

One thing was sure: When she knew what Peter Garroway wanted, she would know a lot more about him. Maybe she would end up being glad that Talbot had seized him. And who knew what else another look around the Clarkes' house might turn up? It was better than sitting here.

But first, there was the matter of the keys. She reached for the last smoked oyster, but the look on Maxie's face was so imploring that she gave it to him instead. She was not really hungry anymore, anyway, nor had her stomach resumed sending any of the other unpleasant signals she had been receiving from it in the past few weeks.

In fact, as she headed back to Chelsea Memorial Hospital, she felt marvelous.

"The policeman guarding Dr. Clarke's room fell asleep. When he woke up, he found Mr. Munson in there. The nurses brought Mr. Munson back to his room, but he had become agitated. They had to give him a drug to quiet him."

Zinnia's voice, low and musical, was sad. "He was confused and frightened, I suppose, so he got angry. Also, I am afraid the doctors think he has had another small stroke."

"Indeed." Harriet's comment fell like a little drop of acid. "And I gather tying him into his bed was an effort to make him less angry? Less frightened and confused?"

"I didn't like it, either," Zinnia conceded. "As you can see, I have removed the restraints. But without them, until the sedation took effect, he could have harmed himself. I might have done just as the other nurses did, if I had been here."

But she wouldn't have, he knew. She wouldn't have had to; the sight of her face would have brought him back to reality, as it had this morning: Zinnia's beautiful face with its dark, arched eyebrows, severely planed cheekbones, and determined chin.

Munson felt cool, smooth fingers touching his wrist, where the restraints had chafed. He kept his eyes closed, breathing slowly, feigning sleep. He had let Zinnia bathe him and change his linens. But at the sight of the awful hospital breakfast, the runny egg and gray creamed cereal, he had turned his face away, and she had not pressed him.

She understood, he felt, that his heart was broken by what had happened last night. She was giving him time to try to get over it. But he did not think he would get over it.

When the policeman seized him, he had become unable to speak. He had lost all control over himself. Finally, they had tied him up and left him. Now it was the middle of the morning, and whatever had happened inside his brain was not happening any more; he was rational and able to speak. Only, he had nothing to say.

"He'll be discharged soon," Zinnia said to Harriet. The two women discussed him as if he were not there, which would have enraged him only a day ago. Now he didn't care.

"The antibiotics are working," Zinnia went on, "and his wound is healing better. We will take the intravenous out, soon. He will need pills of course, but . . ."

"Discharged?" Harriet sounded horrified. "To where? He can't go home as he is. There's no one to take care of him; he has no one at all."

Munson smiled sadly, inwardly, at this truth. His ex-wives despised him, his children feared him, and if he had friends, he did not know where they were, except of course for Harriet. She had remained his friend, stubbornly, for a long time.

Now he thought it was because he was among the few people she knew anymore who were as old as she was: himself, the formidable Melinda Hunt, and Harriet's man of all work, Watkins, who grew a bit more gnarled and knobbly each year, but refused to retire. One or two others, Munson supposed, with nothing much in common but that they had lived too long; now they all leaned together like a stand of ancient trees, waiting for the axe.

"I won't have him in a nursing home," Harriet went on, "even if he would agree to go. It's out of the question, he must stay here. Especially if he really is getting . . ."

Senile, Munson finished for her. A useless old bastard who can't walk, can't think, can't work; he shuddered with impotent rage, and felt a shameful tear slip hotly down his cheek.

"He is not senile," Zinnia was saying, "but these small attacks, well, the doctors hope his new medication will help prevent them. To know for sure will take some time, though, and he does not need to be here. And the hospital needs the beds, you see, for patients who do require real hospital care."

Zinnia paused. "I have several weeks' vacation from the hospital coming. I was thinking I might stay with Mr. Munson. He and I get along together quite well. And after the time was up, then we will see about what next."

Munson felt a terrible happiness pouring through his heart; Zinnia was offering to stay with him. If only that could be, he would refuse to die; he would reform, instead. He would learn to be a clean old man, cheerful and tolerant of his own infirmities: He swore it to whatever gods there were, if only that impossibly wished thing could happen, that Zinnia should stay with him.

"And why," Harriet asked Zinnia, "would you do a

thing like that? I suppose you think there's some benefit in it for you."

Munson stiffened. Harriet was upset; if what had happened last night could happen to him, then it could happen to her. She was as frightened as he was; in her own way, she was only trying to protect him.

But she was ruining everything. He opened his mouth to say so, and found that Zinnia had given him another dose of sedative, or perhaps the last one hadn't worn off yet. When he opened his eyes, the room spun sickeningly, and all the sound he could make was a feeble moan, no louder than the fretting of an infant.

"I won't allow him to be put in a nursing home, and I can't possibly let some *stranger* take such—"

"Mrs. Crusoe," Zinnia interrupted firmly. "I do not wish to be rude to a friend of Mr. Munson. But what you will allow is quite beside the point. Also, his placement is out of my hands."

Munson heard the intake of Harriet's breath. "Young woman," she began, forbiddingly.

"Mr. Munson will be discharged when the doctors decide, to whatever place they send him: his home or a skilled nursing facility. I think he would be best at home."

Munson felt a sudden, anguished longing: *own room own house own bed*. He could hear Zinnia moving around the room; in his mind's eye he saw her putting things to rights. She was as clean as a cat in all her habits, was his Zinnia.

"Oh," she said suddenly, "here are his carving things, but one of the knives is missing. I wonder where it has gotten to?"

"I'm sure," Harriet replied, and from the sound of it she was gathering her coat and bag, "you'll soon be an expert on the location of *all* his things. You are *quite* impertinent."

She cares for me; I need her. Go away, please, Harriet, Munson thought.

Zinnia set something on the windowsill with a small, sharp click. "Mrs. Crusoe," she said in a tone that he had never heard from her before, "my father is a very successful businessman. My mother is a concert pianist. I myself am thought to be a wealthy and quite socially desirable young woman. By," she added, "the sort of people who judge other people along those lines."

"Oh," Harriet said, taken aback.

Don't say it, Munson thought at Zinnia. *Just don't say it.*

But Zinnia did. "There is nothing I want or need from Mr. Munson," the young woman pronounced scathingly, "nor ever will. My purpose, and that of my profession, is to meet a need of *his.* But perhaps it would be better if you took care of Mr. Munson's needs yourself, since you are so well acquainted with them."

No, Munson thought, thoroughly sickened now, and not by any lingering sedative. He struggled to speak, and could not; fought to move, but his body would not obey. *I'm having another attack,* he realized.

"My dear," Harriet began, apologetically.

But Zinnia was having none of it. "Excuse me, please. I have other work to attend to." There was a rattle of papers, a rustle of uniform, a whisper of nursing shoes.

And Zinnia was gone.

Ned Hunt listened quietly while Edwina told him what she wanted him to do. He had grown quieter in general, in the past few days; his fingers neither drummed his desktop nor fiddled with his pen, his body did not shift uncomfortably, and his gaze no longer darted about his office as if searching for an escape route. But most striking of all was his reaction when she had finished.

"All right," he said simply, and reached for the phone. Moments later, he was speaking in firm, executive tones to the hospital's legal counsel, explaining exactly what he intended to have happen, and remarking that he expected to hear no argument.

The hospital's lawyer, however, did offer an argument. Ned listened to about ten seconds of it.

"Ben," Ned broke in. "Ben? I want those keys. I'm writing up a letter about them right now, and I'm taking full personal responsibility for them, so I expect to see them here in fifteen minutes."

He listened a little longer, then interrupted again. "Ben, do you remember the case against the hospital corporation last year just about this time? The one from the woman who was lying in a hospital bed, waiting to be examined, and a mouse ran right across her . . . yes. Yes, I know she dropped the lawsuit. But do you remember why she dropped it, Ben?"

Leaning back, Ned gazed dreamily at the ceiling, while the tinny sound of the lawyer's voice came faintly from the earpiece. When the sound stopped, Ned spoke again. "She dropped it because my mother paid her off, Ben. Paid her to forget the little mouse feet scampering on her tummy. That's what happened, Ben."

Squawking came out of the earpiece; Ned winced, but went on speaking. "Now, we wouldn't want that to get into the newspapers, would we, Benjamin? Someone might think you'd had a hand in arranging it. Which I happen to know you did, and if someone were to ask me whether or not you'd . . . Yes."

Ned sat up happily. "Yes, that'll be fine, Ben. Fifteen minutes. I knew you'd see it my way, once the whole thing got reasonably explained to you."

Ned hung up, then noticed Edwina staring at him. "My mother had some chest pain last night," he said as if in explanation, "and they took her up to the hospital in Litchfield. She's fine for the moment, but it was an anxious couple of hours. Turns out she's been having pain for a while, but she didn't want to tell anybody. I'm telling you this in confidence; she doesn't even want your mother to know."

"Oh, Ned, I'm sorry. It's her heart, I suppose?"

He nodded. "The doctor took me aside and told me she could have more of these attacks. She could go any minute. And suddenly I realized: She's not always going to be there to fight my battles for me, is she? Or what she thinks are my battles. I looked at her last night, and it was true."

"Now, Ned, that's not really—"

"Sure it is. All my life. And I can let it go on. I can be as useless as I want, or I can start making things happen the way I want them to happen, the way I think they ought to happen."

He smiled reminiscently. "That's really the way she raised me, you know. It's not her fault that I took advantage of all my privileges. So, starting today, I'm in charge, and that's that."

He pushed the button on his intercom. "Miss Rogers? Could you come in and take a letter, please?"

"She's having her break now," someone said carelessly back. "She says she'll be there in a minute."

Ned gazed thoughtfully at the intercom and spoke sweetly into it. "Tell her I want her here *now,* and to make it snappy."

Moments later a startled-looking secretary arrived, followed by an angry-looking lawyer. Both of them did just exactly as Ned told them to, just as soon as he told them to do it; then he told them to leave, and they did that also.

"Here," Ned said to Edwina, handing a black leather key case across his desk. "Go see what you can find out. I'm going to call Melinda and tell her what I've done. That ought to make her feel better. Hell, it must have been sad for her all these years, having a worm for a son."

Still, Edwina thought, in the first fine flush of Ned's enthusiasm for life as a fully functioning vertebrate he was going a little far. "Ned, I didn't want you to bully anyone out of these keys, just find some legal way to get them. Through channels, somehow, but properly. Couldn't you get in trouble for this?"

A grin of ferocious joy spread across Ned's face. "Get in trouble for this? Oh, boy, you bet I could get in trouble for this. I can't even count all the kinds of trouble I could get in for this."

He sobered. "But don't *worry* about it, Edwina, because

I'm not going to. Worry," he confided blissfully, "doesn't come in color, and I'm all done with black-and-white."

"All right." She gave in, backing toward the door; what in the world was going on with Ned? "I'll be finished with the keys before five o'clock. That way, you can have them returned to the security department before the end of the shift, and no one else has to be any the wiser."

Ned's expression broke into mirth again. "You keep those keys," he managed, "for as long as you want them. I'll answer any questions anyone has. Could I get in trouble . . . oh, ho ho, could I get in *trouble*?" Ned guffawed.

Cautiously, Edwina returned to his desk. Ned was beginning to sound a little off the deep end. "Ned. Tell me something. Are you all right? I mean, sure, you're concerned about Melinda, but . . ."

But she's going to go on for a long, long time, Edwina was about to say, only the look in Ned's eyes stopped her. He was not an infant in a wading pool anymore. Impulsively, she put her arms around him.

"D'you know what she told me?" Ned whispered. "Melinda, I mean, last night at the hospital. She said when you know you're going to die, when you *really* know, that's when you start living. She said it's like the difference between seeing in black-and-white and seeing in color."

"Oh, Ned." She hugged him hard. After a moment, he pulled gently away, scrubbing his eyes with his fists; for an instant he was that little boy again.

But only for an instant. "Be careful," he said, and the smile on his face was like sunshine breaking through rain. "But I mean it, Edwina; don't worry about me. From now on, trouble is my middle name."

Edwina left the office, closing the door behind her. All down the corridor and into the lobby, though, she could hear Ned laughing. It struck her that she had never heard him laugh that way, before, and by the time she got out to the street, she was laughing, too.

•   •   •

The air in the Clarkes' house was chilly and damp, smelling of fresh paint. Someone had redone the front door, inside and out, and repainted the trim. Otherwise, everything was just as Edwina had seen it last: overfurnished and uninhabited. A sad atmosphere of hollow expectancy hung everywhere, as if the objects in the house knew they wouldn't be used again, and were only waiting to be carted away. Even the bar of pink soap in the bathroom soap dish looked sorrowful.

Edwina shook herself mentally; no point getting gloomy about it. But the happiness she'd felt at Ned Hunt's revelations—he really was going to change for the better, she thought; there was something quite genuine about the difference in him—now seemed unrecapturable. It was as if the Clarkes' house were sucking away all her happiness, into its own hollow self.

Stop that. She shivered, and strode into the living room to twist the thermostat; no sense freezing to death. A low *whuff* from somewhere in the basement signaled the gas furnace going on; moments later, hot water began tinkling through the baseboard pipes. She opened all the drapes; sunshine flooded the rooms, sparkling in the pendants of the chandelier and winking on the silver candlesticks, turning the enormous, awful painting above the mantel into an explosion of orange-and-green garishness.

Now, she thought, Peter Garroway was looking for something, and—he says, at least—he didn't find it; let's pretend that's true. Judging by where he was looking and what he took, one may assume it was paper, probably with writing on it.

Hidden pieces of paper, Edwina had learned over years of snooping, generally held information that would help someone (for instance, a will or a treasure map) or harm someone (a compromising photograph or indiscreet letter, for example). The object of Garroway's search might have been the threatening note that Mrs. Glick had spoken of, but he had supposedly taken that out of Clarke's office earlier on the day Clarke was shot, so he wouldn't have come here later, looking for it. Blast, that was another thing she hadn't had time to ask Garroway about; *darn* that Talbot.

Sighing, Edwina set to work. The leather-bound books in the bookcases contained thousands of brittle pages; patiently she fanned each volume and replaced it. Drawers and cabinets held paper bags, scribbled lists, balls of twine, and rolls of sturdy strapping tape, but no mysterious documents. Linens in the linen closet, sheet music in the piano bench, the bottoms of jewelry boxes and the tops of tall dressers: All were examined, and all proved unrewarding.

Under carpets; inside sofa pillows; at the rear of the ice-making gadget in the freezer; in the vegetable crisper. As she searched, Edwina consoled herself with the thought that if there were something here, she would find it. But she didn't; at the end of four increasingly unhappy hours, all she had was a pair of grimy hands, a sore back, and a gnawing feeling in the pit of her stomach, the result of not having had any lunch.

Still, one mustn't give up, especially when one couldn't think of anything else to try. Edwina imagined her father inching his way down a dark, cobwebby tunnel toward a gang of thugs. Then she went back to the Clarkes' kitchen, to see if there was anything there to eat.

The cupboard yielded an unopened box of saltines and a tin of liver paste; as she took them down, a chirping sound came from her handbag on the kitchen counter. *That beeper,* she realized, and dug it from the bag. Two minutes later, she was listening to Dick Talbot's voice on the telephone.

"Thought you might want to know your guy's story checks out," Talbot rasped unapologetically. "He got to the priest house or whatever it is around three that afternoon; I got a dozen holy guys swear he wasn't out of their sight until they all went to bed around midnight."

He paused significantly. "Also, I got a trooper says he saw Garroway at a rest stop on the turnpike, couple hours earlier, way down in Port Chester. No way he was in Clarke's office that day, Edwina. Marion Glick's been yankin' our chain, which I figured she was, but now I got her on something. So watch it, okay? 'Cause she ain't at work, I checked, and she wasn't there yesterday, either. I mean it, Edwina, watch yourself. I don't like this lady."

"Me, neither. Thanks, Dick. And . . ." *I'm sorry,* she wanted to say, but Talbot cut her off.

"Yeah, yeah. You were right, okay? That's what counts." He hung up.

The crackers and liver paste looked suddenly unappealing; Edwina put them away, and went into the bathroom to wash the dust from her hands with the bar of pink soap. She would walk around the house once more, she decided, and then go home; with Garroway free, she could simply ask him what he'd wanted here. But as she lifted the soap, the soap dish jiggled. Not much; only enough to let her know that it was not securely cemented into the ceramic-tiled wall. Instead, it was attached by a sort of tongue-and-groove apparatus.

Curiously, Edwina removed the soap dish. Behind it gaped a small, ragged hole in the tile; in the hole was a small cardboard box. The box rattled as Edwina fished it out.

In it lay a key, the key to a safe. Harriet had one just like it. But where was the safe? Edwina had examined every surface in the house. Everywhere except . . .

"Behind the painting," Marion Glick said from the doorway. "The safe is behind that dreadful painting, in the living room. Let's go open it."

Edwina thought that was not a good idea at all, but she had little choice. Marion's hand looked remarkably steady, and there was a gun in it.

NINE

JOSEPHA BRYANT LEANED against the green-tiled wall in the corridor outside the operating room, fighting to keep from crying. Scrub-suited men and women hurried past, not stopping to ask what was wrong, but being ignored was just fine with Josepha, who already felt humiliated at losing her composure; the last thing she wanted was to talk about it. Anyway, everyone already knew Dr. Grace was an unpredictable, unreasonable, pathologically abusive—

"Josepha? Is there something I can do for you?"

Startled, Josepha looked up into the friendly face of the OR nursing supervisor, Mrs. Tallent. She was a small, wiry woman in her fifties, who had been a supervisor for twenty years, and who was not inclined to put up with nonsense.

"N-no. No, thanks, Mrs. Tallent." Angrily, Josepha wiped her eyes. Her lips were still trembling; she struggled to control it, and thought for a moment that she had succeeded, but then she broke down. "He is just so . . . so *rude*. I just couldn't . . . I mean, *no* one should have to listen to that!"

"I see," Mrs. Tallent said gravely, and Josepha felt ashamed. Surgeons screamed at nurses all the time; it was a part of the job, like getting dirty if you were a coal miner. Now Mrs. Tallent would think that Josepha couldn't take it. After all, it wasn't as if Grace had hit her, only that he'd shouted in her face.

"I'm sorry," Josepha said. "I shouldn't let him upset me; it's just the way he is. But I don't think he wants me back in there today, so I'll scrub for another case, if you like."

But Mrs. Tallent didn't feel that way about it. "I think you'd better tell me exactly what happened. You're not the first to complain about him, you know, and whatever it is, it's getting worse. Come on, we'll go have a cup of coffee."

Josepha let the older woman lead her toward the conference room, wondering if she really should tell all of what happened; she didn't want an ongoing battle with Grace. But Mrs. Tallent understood this, too.

"Never wrestle with a pig," she began when they were seated with their coffee; "you both get dirty, and the pig likes it."

Josepha laughed in spite of herself; it was exactly what she felt about William Grace. He seemed to enjoy flying into rages, taking murderous offense over little things, and holding grudges that would have been ridiculous had he not been so deadly serious about them.

"So," Mrs. Tallent said, "I'm going to do some of the wrestling for you, but you'll have to help me. I gather you must have crossed him in some way. Corrected something: his sterile technique, perhaps?" Her shrewd eyes watched Josepha carefully; suddenly, Josepha realized that Mrs. Tallent had her own reason for asking the question.

"Well," she began hesitantly, "it was a little worse than that. You see, he'd . . . Darn, this feels like tattling on him."

She looked up in appeal but Mrs. Tallent said nothing, only waited. Josepha took a deep breath. Mrs. Tallent was always fair with the schedule, understanding when people made mistakes they could not reasonably have avoided, and an absolute terror in defense of the OR staff nurses.

"He'd tied off a vessel," Josepha said at last. "But then he was just about to cut one next to it; one he hadn't tied off. So I pointed it out to him."

Mrs. Tallent pursed her lips. It was not a responsibility of Josepha's to be making such corrections. "Who was assisting?"

Reluctantly, Josepha named the junior resident who had been assisting Dr. Grace in the surgery. "I'm afraid he might not have been observing just at that moment," she added. Her small, oval face with its wide blue eyes, pink cheeks, and a mouth that needed no lipstick had proven distracting to more than one male on Chelsea's staff, no matter how unflirtatious Josepha tried to be.

Mrs. Tallent sighed. "And then what happened?"

"Well, he ... he just exploded. He pushed over the instrument tray, threw his scalpel on the floor, and shoved the resident out of his way. He kind of *scrambled* at me and shouted in my face. I mean, his face was an *inch* from my face, and he was shouting at the top of his lungs."

Josepha winced at the memory of the surgeon's sour breath. "I was backing away, and he kept coming after me, until I backed right out the door."

"What was he shouting?" Mrs. Tallent asked.

"Oh, something about how everyone was against him, and don't think he didn't know it. And that I'd only said what I said to try to ruin him. You know, the usual Bill Grace screaming fit." She looked up. "This isn't just about this, is it? I mean, you're not asking me these questions because of what happened in there, just now."

Mrs. Tallent shook her head. "No. And I'm afraid I can't tell you why I'm asking, only that it's rather serious. There have been too many of these incidents lately. This isn't the first that's involved an error, or a near error."

She got up. "I want you to go down to my office and use the typewriter. Write an incident report about what happened, date it, and sign it. Can you do that?"

The suggestion frightened Josepha. She didn't want to get involved in some big administrative mess, and especially not one with Dr. Grace in it. But Mrs. Tallent was looking very grave, like a grade school teacher who is waiting to see which student has the strength of character to tell the truth about something.

"Yes, ma'am," she said finally. There was something about Mrs. Tallent that made a person talk like that, instead of just saying "Okay" or, even worse, "Yeah." She turned to go, but Mrs. Tallent hadn't quite finished.

"Josepha, have you ever seen Dr. Grace doing anything you thought was . . ." Mrs. Tallent paused, then shook her head. "But never mind, I won't ask you now. Sufficient unto the day is the evil thereof, don't you agree?"

"Yes, ma'am," Josepha said, and fled.

When the girl had gone, Monica Tallent disposed of the coffee cups and straightened the conference-room table. It was too bad to put Josepha on the spot, but something had to be done; stories had been circulating about the surgeon for months, each more outrageous than the last. Monica had thought the situation was at least on the way to being taken care of; the surgical head nurse, Bob Whiteside, had agreed to write up a report.

Bob had seen things, he'd said, that he didn't care to talk about unofficially, but that were very troublesome. As a professional, he couldn't let them go on, and he'd wanted Monica's help.

Monica had understood; when you went to administration with charges against a surgeon, you needed all the help you could get. Bob also said he knew of a physician, not on Chelsea's staff, who was willing to get involved, although only if necessary; doctors hated going against other doctors. But now, with the terrible thing that had happened to Bob Whiteside . . .

Monica Tallent paused in her straightening of the conference room. What she was thinking was too awful an idea to entertain. From the corridor came the sounds of the surgical suite's routine going steadily on: gurneys wheeling from the ORs to the recovery room, the monotonous, reassuring beeping of cardiac monitors on the post-op patients, the banter of surgeons and staff and the rustling of their paper shoe covers as they hurried from room to room. Nothing like what Monica was imagining could happen here.

Still, she could not get rid of the idea. Slowly, Monica went to the door of the conference room, and closed it. After a moment, she locked it from the inside, and pulled down the shade covering the door's glass window. Her heart, she noticed, was beating rather fast; had she been attached to one of the cardiac monitors, someone would probably be checking on her.

Silly, Monica Tallent thought at herself. *You're too old to be dramatizing things this way.* Nevertheless, she went to the telephone mounted on the conference room wall; from it she called the surgical ward.

Yes, he secretary on the ward said helpfully, when Monica had identified herself and explained what she wanted; yes, the police information number was right here on a card in the cardex, and did Monica have a pen? Monica did; dutifully, she wrote down the number.

But, the secretary went on, hadn't Monica heard? A suspect had been taken into custody, and the secretary thought whoever it was had been arrested, because the guard had been taken off Dr. Clarke's room and everything was pretty much back to normal now. Wasn't that wonderful? Everyone was so relieved.

Yes, Monica replied; yes, that *was* a relief. *More than you know,* she added silently, and hung up.

Opening the shade, unlocking the conference room door, Monica Tallent went to see if Josepha had finished writing her incident report yet. On the way, she threw the scrap of paper bearing the police information number into a wastebasket.

"The doctor told me where the safe was, once," Marion Glick said. "But I didn't have a key to this house."

Edwina hefted the hideous painting from the wall. "How did you know I was here? Only Ned . . . oh. You've been following me?"

Marion nodded. "I knew you'd begin figuring things out from the monogram on the handkerchief."

Edwina made a sound of assent; anything else might betray the fact that she had no idea what Marion was talking about.

"Poor Rollie," Marion said. "It's been tough on him. But I raised his children *and* I got Emily out of a wheelchair with no help from him, so it's his turn to sacrifice. You understand."

"Of course," Edwina murmured, understanding only that a gun was being pointed at her head.

"When I realized I'd handed you that handkerchief instead of my own, I didn't know what to do," Marion went on. "I was afraid to call attention to it, but of course you'd already noticed; why else would you carry it away with you?"

"Why, indeed?" Edwina repeated, even more confused.

"And a man like Bill, with a reputation to protect— well, I can't let Dr. Clarke harm him, and our relationship simply cannot be exposed. Emily would never forgive me. Open the safe."

The monogram. Bill. And Emily. Edwina stepped toward the safe, and realized: Emily, who had been in a wheelchair. Her scars were surgical scars, and the handkerchief's scripted initials were not "MG" for Marion Glick. They were so richly ornamental that it was easy to misread them, as Edwina had, but the "M" was in fact a "W," as in "WG"—for William Grace, orthopedic surgeon.

Edwina opened the safe. Inside was a spiral-bound notebook. "I'm not sure I understand. You and William Grace were having an affair? You thought I might learn of it, and harm his reputation by talking about it?"

But that couldn't be right. Marion Glick was a middle-aged woman with a muscular build, a motherly face, and an unglamorous wardrobe. Edwina would have bet her trust fund that Marion wasn't Grace's type, if he even had a type.

Greedily, Marion eyed the notebook. "Dr. Clarke told

me he'd written things down, terrible things about Bill that aren't true. He was going to Chelsea's board of directors with them."

Curiouser and curiouser. "Why would he tell *you* that?"

For the first time, Marion Glick looked doubtful. Edwina thought of all those socks McIntyre washed for himself, and of a great many other mundane details she would not have traded for the world. Still, none of them were tucked into her handbag. She didn't carry bits of her lover's linen around with her, as did Marion. Edwina played a sudden hunch.

"You were very grateful to Dr. Grace, weren't you? For what he'd done for Emily."

Marion's gaze softened. "No one else would even take her case. They said she'd never walk again."

"But then," Edwina persisted, "you began thinking of him in another way. And Dr. Clarke knew how devoted you were to the surgeon who'd helped your daughter. That's why Clarke told you what he was going to do: to prepare you. He knew it was going to come as a shock to you. He knew you'd been obsessing over Grace, perhaps even imagining an affair with him. An affair," she finished gently, seeing that what she was saying was absolutely true, "that never existed, except in your mind?"

"That's not so!" Marion flung back. "I was at Bill's house when . . ." She stopped; she was supposed to have been at home.

"When you spoke of the doctor being such a fine man, you weren't talking about Clarke. You were thinking of Bill Grace. And the story about a threatening letter, and Garroway at the office," Edwina went on, "that was a lie, wasn't it?"

Marion nodded resentfully, beginning to break down. "*You* described this Garroway person. I just went along with what you'd said. There had been a salesman, and he left; they do, sometimes. But if you thought it was Garroway, and he'd been sending threatening letters . . ."

"Then I'd suspect it was Garroway who shot the Clarkes, and never think of suspecting you."

"No! I just . . . I just wanted you to go away, that's all."

Edwina tried to calculate whether she could fling the notebook at Marion fast enough to startle her and throw off her aim. Probably not; at this range, Marion could hardly miss.

"Even your own husband began suspecting you. That's why he was so worried. But the police didn't find the weapon among the guns in your house, because you didn't use one of those. You had another—the one you're holding now, possibly?"

Edwina took a step toward Marion. "Clarke must have learned from his patient referrals that Grace was up to something unethical. That was the connection between them; maybe a patient complained about Grace?"

The ugly reddening of Marion's face confirmed this guess. "Then, to check it out," Edwina went on, "Clarke might have asked around about Grace at Chelsea Memorial, all in strict confidence, of course. Finally, he would have confronted Grace." Edwina took another step. "His one mistake was telling you. You shot Clarke to keep him quiet, and shot his wife in case he had confided in her, then bided your time until you could get at this notebook. Isn't that what happened?"

"Are you out of your mind?" Marion demanded. "I told you, I wasn't even there. I was waiting for . . ." She hesitated, then went on. "Bill didn't know about the note book. I went to his house to tell him. But he never came, because Dr. Clarke was shot and he had to operate on him. I . . . I took the handkerchief from a bundle of clean laundry that the laundry service had left on the porch. I just wanted something of his," she finished wretchedly.

Edwina opened the notebook. "And that was the only way you could get it. It's why you want this. To persuade him of your devotion."

Marion looked up and saw what Edwina was doing. "No! You mustn't, you *can't* read that. *No!*"

Marion Glick's hand whipped up, her other hand flying around to steady the pistol in a two-handed grip. The hollow click of the firing mechanism echoed in the silent house.

Marion stared, disbelieving, at the weapon. "Rollie," she said defeatedly. "He really does suspect me. He went through my bag. He took the damned bullets out of the gun."

"Good," Edwina said. "Otherwise, you'd have killed me, the way you killed Renata Clarke."

"But I *told* you, I was at Bill's house! Where else would I have gotten that handkerchief?"

"Maybe you stole it on some other night. And even if you took it on the night you say you did, it doesn't take long to steal a handkerchief; you'd still have had plenty of time to shoot the Clarkes."

"I didn't shoot anyone," Marion Glick repeated.

Edwina glanced at the notebook again, then went to the phone and dialed the police while Marion Glick wept.

It hadn't worked at all the way Eric had hoped. He'd gotten into the hospital okay; the guard had recognized his face and barely glanced at the ID. It gave Eric a bad moment, being known on sight, until he realized the guards weren't interested in him; something else must be going on around here. But he hadn't been able to find Alison and talk with her. He'd been here for over eighteen hours, it was early afternoon, now, and all he'd managed to do was get some soda and junk food from the vending machines in the canteen without anyone seeing him.

He couldn't just page her and tell her where he was, not until he was sure she would be on his side. And he couldn't just walk up to her, for the same reason. For all he knew, she might be mad enough to call the cops. But, fueled with sugary soda pop, chips, and a sandwich of Jimmy Dean sausage on a biscuit (cold, unfortunately;

he hadn't dared stay in the canteen long enough to microwave it), he had managed to formulate a plan.

On the surgical ward where Alison spent a lot of time when she wasn't in the OR, there was a small, almost entirely unused dictating room. There, attending physicians could put their discharge summaries on tape, after which the tapes would be transcribed by clerks in the medical-records department. At one time, the room had gotten a lot of use; patients could not be officially discharged without a discharge summary. Lately, the attendings preferred the new dictating facilities in the medical-records department itself, so the ward's room held empty filing cabinets, some old chairs, and some cartons of bottled distilled water and saline.

The room had a window looking out onto the surgical ward; it had been put in when attendings complained that no one could find them when they were dictating, and they couldn't see when their services had assembled on the ward for morning rounds. But—as Eric happened to know from the times he'd slipped in there to do up a little coke—when the lights in the room were off but the ward's lights were on, the window was in effect a one-way mirror; people outside saw only their own reflections, while someone inside had a great view of the nursing desk, and of the corridors leading to and away from it.

As if that weren't convenient enough for Eric's purposes, the room also had a telephone. Sneaking up the back stairs at three-thirty in the morning, a time he figured that all the staff would be hanging out in the surgical ward's conference room, he'd hoped the dictation room wouldn't be locked.

It hadn't been. Eric had been waiting, watching the nursing desk, for nearly eight hours. He was tired after coming down from the coke, and the room was chilly; he pulled his jacket on. But sooner or later, Alison would show up. When she did, Eric would pick up the telephone and call her.

God, he was brilliant. He knocked himself out sometimes, just thinking about how brilliant he was.

At the nursing desk, telephones rang and call lights blinked incessantly; a secretary answered phones with one hand and made up new charts with the other. Up and down the corridor, a brief after-lunch torpor was giving way to similar activity, as nurses realized they had just two hours remaining in which to complete at least four hours' worth of work. No one paid any attention to Edwina as she made her way between medication carts, gurneys, and loaded laundry hampers to Victor Clarke's room.

A lab runner carrying a metal basket of blood tubes strode by, the glass tubes clinking in the basket. An elderly lady in a red smock pushed the hospital auxiliary's gift cart from one door to the next. A man practiced getting along on crutches, his left foot encased in plaster.

All normal; Edwina sighed, approaching Clarke's doorway. She would tell him what had happened: that Marion Glick had been arrested and that Peter Garroway would be released. Perhaps Clarke would be able to hear her and understand. If he could, telling him would be a kindness; when he'd been awake at all, the poor man must have been terrified, lying here waiting for Marion to have another try at him. No wonder it had taken so much medication to keep him quiet.

Entering the room, she scanned Clarke's monitors and his respirator, his IV bottles and tubings and arterial catheter, his traction apparatus, and Dr. Clarke himself. He seemed well sedated now, motionless except for the steady rise and fall of his chest in time with the cycling of the respirator.

"Dr. Clarke?" she said, approaching his bed.

Clarke's eyes snapped alertly open. He was not under the effects of any sedative, merely resting. Examining his respirator more closely, she found the settings all lowered; he had begun needing less oxygen, less pressure, less of everything to keep his lungs working. In short, his condition was much improved.

"Dr. Clarke, I came to tell you that you don't have to worry anymore. Can you hear me, sir? Blink once to say yes."

Clarke blinked once. He was lucid, Edwina realized; she would have to call Talbot right away. If they got an attorney and a witness in here, they could get a statement from Clarke.

"Peter Garroway has been released; in fact, he's probably on his way over here right now. And the person who shot you has been arrested. Marion Glick, of course, but you probably knew that. So you don't have to be . . . What's wrong?"

Clarke's forehead furrowed, his mouth working wildly around the obstruction of the breathing tube. Then, abruptly, he lay as if frozen, his eyes widening at something just behind Edwina.

She turned; Bill Grace stood there, wearing a short-sleeved green scrub suit, green cap, and paper shoe covers. He had a long white cotton lab coat on over the scrub suit. A loosened green surgical mask hung around his neck.

Uh-oh, quick, now. Her path to the doorway was still clear. She turned back to Clarke. "You saw the person who shot you? You know who it was?"

Clarke blinked once. *Yes.*

"It wasn't Marion Glick?"

Blink. Blink. *No.*

At the same time, Edwina spotted something glinting dully from the space between Clarke's mattress and bedframe. It was a small metal knife with an arrowhead-shaped blade, of the kind used by hobbyists for wood carving.

Swiftly, Grace moved up behind her, raising a scalpel to her throat. "Step a few inches to your right," he said. "I need to get at the monitor alarms and the respirator."

The blade pressed more sharply against her skin as she did as she was told. Grace shut off the cardiac monitor and blood-pressure alarms. He did the same to the respirator's pressure alarm. He disabled the power-interrupt alarm.

The little carving knife in the bed twinkled tantalizingly, inches from Edwina's fingers.

"Good. Now, another step to the right," Grace said.

Edwina obeyed. Her fingers nearly brushed the wood-carving implement. Only, not quite.

"I'm going to let go of you for a minute," said the surgeon, "so I can reach the plugs and pressure lines on the respirator. But if you do anything foolish, I'll put this scalpel through his heart."

Victor Clarke's eyes snapped open, and rolled in terror.

"You wouldn't want that on your conscience, would you?" Grace went on. "I think you wouldn't."

"Right," Edwina whispered. "I wouldn't."

Damn and blast her nurse's training, anyway; Grace would kill Clarke. She could see by the look in his eyes that he would. And you weren't allowed to leave patients in danger so as to save yourself; not if there was a chance of saving them, too.

Not if you really believed in taking care of sick people, instead of just mouthing the principle when it was convenient. And not if you ever meant to face yourself in a mirror, again.

Victor Clarke's chest rose and fell each time the respirator gave him a breath; his gaze darted wildly and his arms battled against their cloth restraints. Edwina calculated that without the respirator, he might live five minutes.

Or he might not; he was better, but not that much better. A Volutrol cylinder piggybacked to his IV dripped steadily; a second was set to switch on soon, to dispense medication that could not be mixed with whatever was in the first. The whole picture—monitors, respirator, complex medication routine—testified to just how fragile Dr. Clarke's condition still was.

Edwina's fingers itched to pluck the small carving knife from between the mattress and the bedframe. But Grace's gaze kept darting back to her, his own weapon constantly hovering over Clarke's throat now, as with his other hand he began unplugging the respirator's oxygen source.

"Dr. Grace, it's too late. Clarke wrote it down, and the police have what he wrote. You can't help yourself by hurting him."

But he ignored her. A warning light winked on the front panel of the respirator, but he'd disabled the sound alarms. Victor Clarke struggled to breathe, but his heart rate began dropping. And with the alarms all disabled, no one noticed.

Clarke's heart rate dropped to 90, and then to 75. His blood pressure sank: 100 over 80, then 80 over 50. Respirations fast and shallow; it wouldn't take long before he had cardiac arrhythmia. After that, and quickly, would come cardiac arrest.

Warning lights on the monitors were blinking; at the nursing station, EKG paper would be spewing from the electrocardiograph machine, recording a cardiac event. But the ward was busy, and the secretary probably wasn't even sitting at the nursing desk anymore; without the sound alarms, it could take a while before anyone noticed that Victor Clarke was dying.

Grace pushed the alarm silence button again and shut off the respirator's power switch. He pulled the plug and was instantly behind Edwina, the scalpel pressed once more to her throat.

"You don't understand," he said. "I'm not killing him because he can hurt me. There's a report going up from an OR nursing supervisor. She just told me. My life is over. I'm killing him because I hate him, the self-righteous son of a bitch."

Victor Clarke's heart rate dropped faster. Grace laughed softly. "Now," he said, "we wait."

Clarke's heart rate was 50, his pressure 70 over 45. His respirations were barely visible, and the first irregularities began appearing on the monitor screen.

The blade prickled the skin over Edwina's jugular. Now she knew why Grace had straightened out so quickly the previous day, when the cop had challenged him: He couldn't take any official scrutiny. Maybe he'd even been high at the time. And that was why his behavior had degenerated so much lately. His addiction was catching up with him—the addiction Victor Clarke had done his best to document in the spiral notebook.

Another colleague might not have understood the signs, or might not have done anything about them. But Victor Clarke's notebook made it clear why he had: The research paper he was writing was on drug-addicted physicians, a topic Clarke knew all about. He ought to. As his notes also made plain, he had been one all those years ago, when he carelessly informed a patient of a cancer diagnosis, and the patient had committed suicide as a result.

Clarke hadn't married Peter Garroway's stepmother out of greed; he'd done it out of guilt, and spent the rest of his life atoning. Somehow, Garroway had finally understood that. But Bill Grace was beyond understanding— and with his scalpel at her throat, Edwina could do nothing; one abrupt motion of his hand, and she would bleed to death before anyone could reach her, much less get her to the OR. That was what he meant to have happen anyway, probably; he intended to use her as a shield, to get out of the building. After that . . .

"Marion Glick didn't kill anyone," Edwina said; maybe if she could get Bill Grace interested in what she was saying, she could distract him. "And she wasn't trying to divert my suspicion from herself. She was trying to protect you. She realized what you must have done; maybe not consciously, but she knew, and she was trying to save you."

At the mention of Marion Glick's name, Grace made a sound of contempt; in that instant Edwina despised him completely. "You hired someone for the killings," she went on; "some horrid little coke-dealer buddy of yours, or one of his lowlife friends."

She took a deep breath, steadying herself. "I suppose Bob Whiteside had to go because he'd seen you doing something you couldn't have explained, doing it here in the hospital. And you killed Bonnie West yourself, because she was in your way."

Grace made a bitter, amused sound of agreement, but his hand stayed at her throat.

"But your *employee* botched half the job, and you thought you had to get rid of Victor before he recovered enough to expose you after all. You didn't know he'd written it down anywhere; Marion never got the chance to tell you."

The sudden crash of a wheelchair tipping over, out in the corridor, distracted Grace for an instant; that big woman, Edwina realized, who kept trying to climb out. Then the surgeon's hand was at her throat again.

Victor Clarke's heart-rate monitor readout registered zero. His blood pressure was absent, his respirations agonal shudders. It had all taken a little less than three minutes.

Grace's hand fell away. He seemed transfixed at the sight of Clarke's cardiac tracing, now a deadly straight line.

"That's it, then," said William Grace.

"Not quite, actually," Edwina replied, and plunged the blade of the wood-carving knife into his thigh.

Damn, where *was* Alison? Eric Shultz peered cautiously out the window of the darkened dictating room, then ducked and scuttled to the room's far corner, behind the filing cabinets. His brief peek toward the nursing station had shown him a scene of pandemonium: nurses running, the secretary dashing for the phone, alarms going off on one of the cardiac monitor readouts, and pure panic on everyone's face.

Hurling himself through it all was William Grace, running as if the hounds of hell were after him toward the room where Eric hid. Blood stained the surgeon's scrub trousers.

Eric crouched, feeling his heart pound, willing his ragged breath to be slow and silent. The door swung open, then slammed, and there was the click of the button lock engaging, but the room's light did not go on. The chair at the dictating station slid back and creaked loudly as Grace flung himself into it.

Then there came a tiny sound that Eric knew well: the faint, tinny *clink!* of the metal pull tab being removed from the top of a rubber-stoppered medication vial. With the pull tab removed, a hypodermic needle could be inserted through the stopper and the medication withdrawn into a syringe.

The chair creaked again. Grace sighed deeply and exhaled, while from outside came the sound of running feet, then hammering on the door. What the hell was going on? Slowly, Eric eased forward. Just a tiny bit more, and he would be able to see. . . .

The light from the cubicle's window showed William Grace at the desk, with his arm extended across it and his sleeve rolled up. In his right hand, he held a thin plastic syringe with a stingerlike hypodermic needle. The small syringes were used to administer TB tests, but Eric didn't think Bill Grace was giving himself a TB test. Frowning, Grace pushed the plunger of the syringe.

Suddenly, Eric knew what Grace must be doing: He was skinpopping cocaine. Eric had done that himself once or twice, but had soon given it up; the rush wasn't as sudden and he missed the taste of the drug, its abrasive bite as it burned its way up his nose. Anyway, a surgeon who stuck nonsterile material like street cocaine under his skin deserved a medal for stupidity.

Grace wasn't doing street cocaine, though. That medication vial contained the real stuff, pure and potent as lightning. He must have gotten it from the locked section of the OR medication room, accounting for the missing dose by faking an entry in the controlled-substances record book.

Grace wasn't supposed to have a key to that part of the medication room, but he must have gotten one somewhere. It was about the only way to steal pharmacy cocaine; Eric had considered trying it, too, but had decided it was too dangerous and lowlife.

The hammering on the door continued. People were pressing their faces to the window, peering in and shouting. *You scumbag,* Eric thought at Grace, *you slime toad, are you out of your mind?*

And then it hit him: Bill Grace wasn't doing anything much different from what Eric himself had done a hundred times. Grace was hooked, was all, and when you needed it, you needed it. Only something had gone wrong, and Grace had gotten caught.

Suddenly, Eric was so struck by this realization—*no different*—and so scared by it he felt as if he were falling helplessly down a black, bottomless hole, which was why he didn't notice that he was about to sneeze. At the last instant he managed to hold most of it back, but a tiny, strangled *peep!* escaped him.

And Grace was on him in a heartbeat.

"You little shit! You little shit! What the hell are you doing in here?" Grace bellowed, seizing Eric's collar in both hands and hauling him from behind the cabinets, propelling him toward the dictating desk.

Eric struggled, but Grace was powerful, and headed for the manic level on the dose he had taken. On the desk lay the glass vial, the syringe, and the metal pull top. Grace shoved him at them; Eric fell over the chair and collapsed atop them, his chest slamming the desk's edge. But as he fell, he managed to flail his arm and unlock the door's button lock.

The door swung open instantly; the light snapped on. Eric grimaced and tried to rise, but a sharp pain in his chest made him moan, instead. *I'll be damned; he broke my rib.* Twisting with a sharper jab of pain, he saw Alison Feinstein staring at him from the doorway. Her gaze took in the vial and syringe as well.

Eric's breath was coming in painful little gasps. *Man, get control of yourself.* Alison was looking at Grace now. Craning his neck with an effort, Eric looked, too. Grace's sleeve was still pushed up, and on the inside of his forearm was a welt: not very red, but raised and fresh. Eric's shirt-sleeves were long, double-buttoned at the cuffs, and he still had his jacket on over them.

He shoved himself up. He was still in a lot of pain, but it wasn't as bad and he was getting his breath back, so the broken rib probably hadn't poked a hole in his lung. Bill Grace wasn't in such good shape, though. His face had begun to twitch: first just his eyelid, then the whole right side. His right arm came up in an awkward hitching motion and his foot tapped as if he were getting ready to do some bizarre dance.

"Uh-oh," Alison said, rushing forward while Eric steadied himself. "Get the code cart over here," she yelled out the door, "and draw me up some phenobarb, stat!"

Half Eric's brain snapped instantly into doctor mode: Grace was getting ready to have a big-time seizure, pro-bably from the extra-pure cocaine. Hardly anybody was used to it. But then Eric looked at the vial again. It was empty. Grace hadn't been trying to get high; he knew the dose levels. He'd been trying to kill himself.

Eric reached out for the surgeon, to lower him to the floor before he fell and injured himself, while Grace kept jigging away, slamming into the wall and then into the filing cabinets, from which he rebounded in a series of forward-staggering lunges.

But the other half of Eric's brain froze in horror. It was awful, like watching some old B-movie monster self-destructing. Whatever his personality had been, Bill Grace had *been* somebody.

And now, whatever happened, he wouldn't be, anymore.

The code cart rumbled up to the dictation room. Alison reached out for the syringeful of phenobarbitol. Grace seemed to get some measure of control over himself, his eyes focusing with an effort.

"Okay," Eric said, holding out his hand. "It's okay, I know you don't feel very well. How about having yourself a seat in this chair? Hey," Eric soothed, surprising the living hell out of himself with the amount of sympathy he was able to summon up, "it's all right. Everyone gets a little sick once in a while."

The amazing thing was, he meant it.

But Grace wasn't processing sympathy very well. He wasn't processing anything, a fact Eric realized too late as Bill Grace lost consciousness and collapsed.

Instantly, a half-dozen people swarmed around the surgeon. "No pulse," somebody reported, "no breathing. Grab that Ambu-bag, and get a portable oxygen tank down here."

Alison glanced up at Eric, the look in her pale green eyes cool and clinically assessing. Eric felt about as welcome, and as trusted, as a malignant tumor. "Hey, anyone here know CPR?" she asked, and went on scissoring off Grace's scrub shirt.

Of course everyone here knew CPR. She was asking *him* to do it. Suddenly, Eric knew how the patients felt— the ones who went into surgery thinking they might have a malignancy, and woke up to discover they didn't. Something bad, maybe, but not *that* bad.

"I do," he answered shakily. "I know."

"Let's get to it, then," Alison said. "Might as well get in one more save, before you get packed off to the rehab clinic."

I don't want a rehab clinic, Eric thought as he bent over William Grace's inert form. But then another small vial rolled from the surgeon's pocket, and at the craving that seized him in the instant he glimpsed it, Eric knew he really did.

TEN

"TWO HEADS," REMARKED the technician as she passed by the ultrasound imaging room in Chelsea's high-risk prenatal clinic; she sounded quite unnaturally pleased by the idea.

Inside the room, Edwina lay on the padded examining table. Seven weeks earlier, on that same table, she had felt the cold swish of antiseptic and the pressure of the amniocentesis needle; today, only the smooth surface of the ultrasound imaging wand had moved across her abdomen.

Edwina had never learned to read ultrasound images, and in this particular room the screen was set to face the other direction anyway; she closed her eyes. Sitting on either side of her were Harriet and McIntyre, and at Harriet's side sat the nurse, Zinnia Martin, chatting amiably with the old lady.

Dear God, Edwina thought despairingly, what could that idiot of a technician possibly have been thinking, to say such a thing where the patient might overhear?

"Now," said the ultrasound specialist, a small fat man with a ruddy complexion and a jolly grin, "let's just have a bit more patience, shall we? The messenger is a tad late arriving with the amniocentesis results, but she will be here shortly, and then we'll discuss all the news."

How dare he say nothing, Edwina raged inwardly, considering what he must already know? But he was gone, bouncing busily from the room before she could demand answers from him.

"Martin," she said, and he squeezed her hand in reply.

"Let's just wait." His voice, beneath its surface calm, was grim and terrible; he must have heard the awful comment, too.

"Dear, are you sure you won't bring Michael to Litchfield?" Harriet asked Zinnia. "We have an enormous house up there, you know. Possibly you would be more comfortable."

In Harriet's hands were the materials for the pink-and-blue booties, which she was determinedly completing. Only the awkwardness of her fingers betrayed her pain: She was concerned about Edwina, and grieving over Michael Munson, who had not yet regained consciousness.

Nor would he, probably, unless he did it very soon; his attorney had brought to the staff's attention a legal document forbidding even so much as a feeding tube. Under the terms of Munson's living will, there was no choice but to discharge him from the hospital in a day or so, whatever his condition.

"Thank you, Mrs. Crusoe," Zinnia said, "but I am certain I shall be quite comfortable at Mr. Munson's house. I will bring my aunt and my cousin. I think we will be able to take care of everything."

Her fingers moved, ceaselessly and silently, over the piece of needlework in her lap. "I only wish Mr. Munson had known," she added. "It would have made him happy."

"I wish so, too, dear," said Harriet. "And I wish I hadn't quarreled with you. Forgive an old lady's foolish suspicions, won't you? It was uncivilized of me to speak to you as I did."

"That's all right, Mrs. Crusoe," Zinnia said, somber. "We won't quarrel anymore."

There was an extended silence. Edwina wondered again what was taking so long, although she knew: Everything in the hospital took more time than it ought to, even a messenger. Still, given the ultrasound results, what was the point? It was obvious from the technician's careless comment what was going to happen.

We weren't even planning to have a baby, she thought, and then: *But we can try again.* "Damn and blast," she whispered.

McIntyre smiled with an effort. "Don't worry. It will be all right, Edwina. No matter what."

She managed a smile in return; it would indeed be all right, just not as all right as it could have been.

Not nearly. "Ned called me," she said, trying to distract herself. Once he'd discovered that Edwina was without injury, McIntyre had spent the previous evening in a last-minute bout of studying, and this morning in a torts quiz, so he still needed a bit of bringing up to speed.

"Ned's very happy with his promotion," she went on, grimly refusing to let her lips tremble. "Giving them a run for their money in the boardroom, I gather, and he says Victor Clarke is doing better. I can hardly believe they managed to resuscitate Clarke. He must be under a lucky star."

"After all he's been through, he deserves to live," McIntyre agreed. "Peter Garroway must be pretty happy about it, too. It would have been rotten if Clarke died before the two of them made up their differences."

"Except that on Garroway's side, they already had. I talked to him this morning also; he called to thank me." She glanced up at the clock; only five minutes had passed.

"He *was* looking for Clarke's research paper," she went on. "In it Clarke admits he's an ex-addict, himself, and that was why Garroway came: to try to talk Clarke out of publishing the information. He thought Clarke was just punishing himself. But by the morning after he got here, the shootings were already all over the news."

Edwina shifted uncomfortably on the table. "Garroway knew if Clarke died and the paper turned up later, that was the only part of it that would get reported, and Clarke's reputation would be ruined forever. All along, he was trying to protect Clarke."

She sighed again. "But Clarke's work wasn't on paper. It was on a computer disk at his office." She paused as footsteps sounded in the corridor, but no one came in.

"Drat. What *is* the difference between 'knit' and 'purl,' again?" Harriet asked, fumbling anew with the sweet feminine art that had been her idea in the first place. *Serves you right, Mother,* Edwina thought, but without any real sharpness.

McIntyre squeezed her hand again, and she glanced anxiously at the doorway as footsteps returned. Given that the news she would hear would break her heart, she supposed she shouldn't be impatient for it. But then the whole dreadful episode would be over, except for the procedure itself. And for that, she would be under anesthesia.

Too bad the painkiller can't start now, Edwina thought, and went on waiting.

Michael Munson peered about his hospital room, uncertain whether he was alive or dead.

Alive, he decided. He'd had a dream, and now he was waking up. Grumpily, he reached for his cane, but it was not there, so he slammed his fist onto the call button.

Damned hospital. Damned doctors. Where was Zinnia?

"Mr. Munson?" The ward secretary's voice came through the intercom, sounding doubtful and even frightened. "Is that you?"

" 'Course it's me. Who would it be? Where's my nurse?"

For punctuation, he hurled a water glass; it smashed against the opposite wall most satisfyingly. Moments later, the room had filled up with people, all wearing white coats.

"Mr. Munson, you're awake!" one of the young doctors said, as if this were a major medical discovery.

Damned whippersnapper. "Help me up. Where's my wheelchair, and who are all these fools? What am I, a circus freak?"

"Guess the stuff worked after all," someone murmured.

". . . miracle," someone else commented.

Munson opened his mouth, intending to refute this, but then thought better of it. The dream *had* been strange.

Victor had been in it, but when Victor turned to go, he said that Michael Munson would have to stay. *Another time,* Victor had said kindly. *Another day, I will come for you. Not today.*

And Victor had said something else.

"Mr. Munson," the young doctor said, sounding serious now, "you had a blood clot in your brain. It must have dissolved on account of the new medication, or possibly all by itself, and that's why you woke up. But I have to warn you that at any time . . . ."

The young doctor spoke slowly and distinctly, as if to a little child. Ignoring him, Michael Munson began to laugh: *Another day.*

Laid out on his bedside table were the set of small knives and a new block of hardwood. One of the knives was missing; he would have to get another. And the old carving had not been very good, he remembered, but he had a new idea. What could be better in the world than a new idea? Eagerly, he reached for the tools.

Zinnia needed nothing from him, but he could give her a gift. Not great art, but something she would like just the same. He could give it to her as a surprise.

The idea filled him with pleasure, and with an odd kind of freedom. Not art; neither bribe nor payment. A gift: Why had he not thought of it before? Easily, the dream of Victor faded away as Michael Munson began to work.

The ultrasound specialist went on speaking, but Edwina could not hear. "Twins," she echoed. "Are they . . . are they all right?"

"Perfectly healthy," the ultrasound specialist assured. "Do you want to know if they're boys or girls? The genetics tests do give that information, you see. Or shall we keep it a surprise?"

"Well," McIntyre began, sounding happily uncertain.

"Yes!" Harriet demanded. "Grandsons or grand-daughters?"

"I shall make crib quilts, of every bright color together," Zinnia chimed in. "Full of good things for boys or girls, and I shall begin at once."

Full of good things, of every bright color together.

"Surprise," Edwina whispered.

ABOUT THE AUTHOR

MARY KITTREDGE, a former respiratory therapist for a major city hospital, is the author of six novels featuring Edwina Crusoe, including *Kill or Cure* and *Fatal Diagnosis*. A native of Milwaukee, she lives in Eastport, Maine.